PLACE OF BIRTH

gnotes

Nieu Bethesda, 2023, August.

For Robyn, Sarah and Dylan

Also by Graham Lang
Clouds like Black Dogs

PLACE OF BIRTH

A novel

Graham Lang

JONATHAN BALL PUBLISHERS
JOHANNESBURG & CAPE TOWN

Published in 2006 by
JONATHAN BALL PUBLISHERS (PTY) LTD
PO Box 33977
Jeppestown
2043

ISBN 1 86842 252 6

*Although this story takes place in a recognisable historical context and
includes extracts from public speeches and statements by real people,
all of this novel's central characters are products of the author's imagination and are not
intended to resemble any living person. Creative liberties have
been taken with real places such as Bulawayo and Shangani; none of the
events ascribed to these places in this novel originate from fact.*

Cover design by Flame Design, Cape Town
Design, typesetting and reproduction of text by
Alinea Studio, Cape Town
Printed and bound by
Paarl Print, Oosterland Street, Paarl, Cape
Set in 13 on 15 pt CgCloister

ACKNOWLEDGEMENTS

The author wishes to thank all those who provided advice and encouragement during the writing of this book, in particular, Dr Kim Cheng Boey, Valda Strauss, Francine Blum, Peter Lang, Nabeel and Farida Lang, and Marika Osmotherly. Special thanks are also due to Jonathan Ball and Barry Streek for their counsel and faith in fiction.

'This country is our country and this land is our land ...
They think because they are white they have a divine right to
our resources. Not here. The white man is not indigenous
to Africa. Africa is for Africans, Zimbabwe is
for Zimbabweans.'
Robert Mugabe, 2001

'... in this world everything is pardoned in advance and
therefore everything cynically permitted.'
Milan Kundera

*T*here is no easy way to put it but this is what happened. They were having their evening drinks out on the veranda as usual. No one else was at home except Joseph and Anna who were in the kitchen getting supper ready. It was a quiet evening, Joseph told me. Even the birds had stopped their noise along the river. Joseph and Anna put the food on the table and Joseph went out to tell them it was ready. Dad got up to unlock the gate for them to go. Joseph went back to the kitchen to fetch his coat. Anna was still cleaning up. Then they heard the first shots that killed Dad at the gate. They heard Nan scream and the dogs going crazy. Then there were more shots. Nan got hit in the stomach and the lung. She came staggering into the house. Joseph said she tried to say something but she just gasped for air and then she collapsed.

Joseph had the presence of mind to activate Agric Alert – that probably saved him and Anna. They carried Nan out the back and hid under some old sheets of corrugated iron behind the sheds while the terrorists shot the dogs and hunted around in the house for her. Joseph said they could hear the dogs yelping as they died. They could hear them laughing and fooling around on the piano before they smashed it. Nan died as they waited. The bastards could probably hear the talk on the radio and knew the police would be on to them soon so they eventually gapped it out the house. Joseph and Anna watched them go down the drive. At the gate one of them stopped and spat on Dad's body where he lay. Then they disappeared. No one has caught them yet. Sorry to write this. It's a shit business, I know. But I thought you would want to know what happened. Just as well you're in Australia and not here to wake up to reality.

1

PART I

BETWEEN PLACES

We descend. The hazy expanse of Zimbabwe rises. Abstract brown swathes acquire the raw detail of bush and rock, blurred horizons become solid. As we cross the Matobo hills on the approach to Bulawayo, the plane shudders through pockets of turbulence. I close my eyes, trying to gather my thoughts. I try to think of what lies ahead.

I am returning to my place of birth for the first time in twenty-six years. In all this time away I have existed between identities. Between being Australian and what amounts to a ghost nationality. A small detail in my passport sums it up. Zimbabwe is given as my country of birth. I don't know why this inaccuracy troubles me. I should find arguments about origin trivial, if not futile. Places change – names change, especially in Africa. But the fact remains: I was not born in Zimbabwe. I know nothing of what it means to be Zimbabwean. The real country of my birth, Rhodesia, no longer exists. This simple fact has, in one way or another, been the source of existential angst for many like me. One of our more insufferable traits is that we Rhodesians assume the world cares. No one cares.

It exhausts me, this limbo. Always between places ...

*

Robert Mugabe stares at me as I emerge from customs into the arrivals hall. He watches from his portrait on the wall near the currency exchange counter, his eyes following me, this stranger

5

in his land. For a moment I meet his stare, intrigued by its blankness. The violent Father. There are no other familiar faces. My brother promised to pick me up but there's no sign of him. I sit on a bench with my luggage and wait. Then amid jovial laughter Gus emerges from the bar upstairs. He takes leave of some acquaintances, sees me on the bench below and comes down the stairs.

'Hey, Vaughn! Howzit, you Austrylian wanker!' he greets me in what he imagines to be an Australian accent. We shake hands – no hugs with our generation, thank God. We size each other up; Gus big as a bull, in his farmer's khakis and velskoens, me very much the puny, bespectacled academic. Somehow brothers. The last time we crossed paths, at Angela's place in England, he still had the thick beard he'd grown during his army days. Now his clean-shaven face is that of an aging cherub. Red and round, split by a lopsided grin. He gives my new *Hard Yakka* strides and shirt, Australian gear for the working man, an amused glance. I note his smell of beer and spreading paunch. 'It seems the stories of starvation in Zimbabwe apply only to some,' I say.

He laughs. 'How about a quick beer? What's it been? Twenty years?'

I shake my head dutifully. 'A bit early for me, Gus. Let's go. Christ, it took an hour to clear customs.'

'Don't complain, boet. You got the express lane.'

I make for the foreign exchange counter but Gus stops me. 'Forget about that now. You'd need a wheelbarrow anyway.'

We go out to the car park in the hot noon glare. It's late October and the temperature is in the mid-thirties. Suicide month, they used to call it.

'Where're Jenny and the kids?' I ask.

'At home. Probably in the pool – only place to be on a day like this.'

Home is a house in the suburb of Burnside near the Hillside Dams that Gus began renting a year ago. Since his wife Jenny moved off the farm Gus has been living a nomadic existence. Weekdays on the farm, weekends in Bulawayo. We climb into an ancient Toyota Cressida and drive the fifteen-kilometre stretch through grey acacia scrub to Bulawayo. I soon notice his car is pretty upmarket compared with the other heaps we pass.

Gus stops in the city at a farm supply co-op to pick up some cattle-dip mixture, which he complains is in drastically short supply and costs the earth. As he goes about his business I wander around, glad to stretch my legs after the long flight. To her returning son, Bulawayo presents two faces, old and new. At first glance, nothing seems to have changed. The same bland modern architecture that proliferated in the fifties, during Rhodesia's heyday. The wide streets lined by jacaranda and flamboyant trees, just beginning to bloom. Some shops from the old days are still doing business: Meikles, Haddon & Sly, Solomon's Supermarket, among others. Bulawayo smells like it always used to at this time of year – like an unwashed body, ripe and stale. But beneath the familiar lies the face of change. The different street names. Colonial stalwarts replaced by heroes of the war for liberation. The absence of Rhodes's statue in the city centre. The old founder, the vision-ary, on his stone pedestal, hands clasped behind his back, star-ing wistfully north across Africa towards Mother England. Gone.

And neglect. I'm not prepared for the drab, dirt-stained

walls and razor wire, the cracked and littered pavements, the hordes of sullen, ragged people hanging around listlessly.

Gus just laughs as we continue on our way to Burnside. 'No development, boet,' he says. 'Just decay. Mugabe's been starving Matabeleland ever since he took power. Part of his plan to screw the Ndebeles.'

'Have you heard from Angela?' I ask.

'Nah, but I reckon she'll just pitch up out of the blue, like she always does.'

'You did tell her about the graves?'

'I told her we have some grave business to attend to.'

'You're hilarious, Gus. What did she think about digging up the family?'

'You know Ange. Takes everything in her stride. By the way, you haven't picked up much of an Aussie accent. You sound pretty nondescript, actually.'

'I *feel* pretty nondescript, to tell the truth.'

Gus's place is typical of Bulawayo's outer suburbs. A big house with a big yard, surrounded by a big wall. We pull up at the gate; a gardener appears and lets us in. As Gus parks under a tree, a sleepy-looking cross-mastiff comes strolling up from behind the house, grinning amiably. Gus chuckles, 'In your own time, old fella. That's Monty, our slightly less-than-zealous watchdog.'

Jenny and their two teenage girls, Jessica and Lauren, come walking up from the pool, wrapped in towels, the girls' hair plastered over their tanned shoulders. It's been at least ten years since I last saw them so I kiss the girls and make a bit of a fuss, as uncles are supposed to. They are blond and pretty, having inherited their mother's genes. Jenny and I kiss and shake hands rather formally. She has an ethereal, blue-eyed gaze – the disconcertingly vacant look of someone unusually intelligent or not quite on the same planet. I suspect the latter – she did, after all, marry Gus.

We go inside where I'm introduced to the maid, Gladys, a buxom, happy soul. 'Sakubona, Nkosi,' Gladys greets me and laughs shyly. When I ask her to call me by my first name, Gus sighs exasperatedly – no doubt, when it comes to the protocol that separates masters and servants, he doesn't like to rock the boat. They show me around the house. Practically every room has at least one of Angela's paintings on the wall – charging elephants, stalking lions and cheetahs, beautifully done but not quite art in my book, though I would never say that to Angela. Nothing of mine, of course. Gus always considered my brand of art to be a sign of delayed intellectual development. I'm allocated a spare room where they leave me to sleep off the jet lag. I unpack my things and lie on the bed with my head swimming, thinking how odd it is that Gus and I married nurses. One of the few things we have in common.

*

I wake in the evening to the calling of turtledoves – that most peaceful and evocative of African sounds. *Come nearer, come nearer* – for the traveller, birds are among the surest proclaimers of place. Still feeling jet lagged I get into some swimming trunks and go down to the pool. Gus and the gardener are there near the thatched summerhouse next to the pool. Gus is giving instructions in fluent SiNdebele for the gardener to start a fire for a braai. Watchdog Monty keeps one eye on proceedings from the shade of a nearby jacaranda tree. I take my glasses off and swim a few lengths, then rest on the side, feeling faint from exertion. I lament my appalling physical condition. As a schoolboy I'd been a good swimmer and once nearly made the Rhodesian Schools team in backstroke. Now Gus disrobes to reveal a bright yellow and blue floral Speedo and a vivid farmer's tan. The Selous Scouts' eagle tattooed on his shoulder and the thick ridges of scar tissue on his right thigh are a sobering reminder of the different worlds we have inhabited. He plunges in and does a terrific medley, no doubt to remind me that he *did* make Rhodesian Schools, despite swimming being his third sporting preference after rugby and cricket. Then he stops and treads water at the deep end. 'Thought we'd have a quiet braai tonight,' he says, hardly panting. 'Before the serious stuff begins tomorrow.'

I gesture at his tattoo. 'I thought you would've got rid of that by now.'

'Too much hassle, man.'

Later we sit around the fire in deckchairs while Gus goes about doing the meat on the braai. The smell of the meat has propelled the indolent Monty into action. An old pal, he sidles up to Gus, smiling ingratiatingly. A couple of cold beers have finally dispelled the remaining jet lag, and I become quite sociable after a shot of some duty-free whisky I bought at Sydney airport. We chat about mundane things, like the girls' school and sporting achievements. They attend BCG – Bulawayo Christian Girls High, a private school – and are apparently promising swimmers and hockey players. From what she says I gather that Jenny's social engagements around Bulawayo are waning, since so many of her friends are leaving the country.

I give them an abbreviated, sanitised version of my life in Australia. Finally we eat. The old standard fare of steaks, chops, salads and sadza.

'Well, at least the national diet hasn't changed,' I note.

Jenny smiles. 'Don't kid yourself. The average Zimbabwean doesn't eat like this. Not even the whites. We're lucky to still have the farm.'

'Ja, we rely on the farm for practically everything,' Gus says. 'Most of the time you can't even get bread in the shops.'

'And when you do, you pay through the nose for it,' Jenny says.

'You know how much you pay for a roll of toilet paper?' Gus asks, always one to make an earthy point. 'Twenty thousand bucks! It's actually cheaper to wipe your arse with hundred-dollar notes!'

Jessica and Lauren look at each other and giggle.

'Oh Angus, man! Not in front of the girls!' Jenny scolds.

'Just showing the old professor how bloody ridiculous it is.'

Jenny shakes her head. 'It is ridiculous. You people overseas have no idea. I tell you, it's a miracle how people survive here. This country's been totally bankrupted – *ruined!* If it wasn't for the farm, who knows what we'd do.'

'Leave like all the other whites,' I say.

'It's not that simple, Vaughn. It's a hell of a thing to just walk away.'

'Vaughn found it easy enough, Jen,' Gus taunts. 'Hey, boet? You didn't have much of a hassle gapping it. One minute you were here, the next – psheew! – you'd gone AWOL to Australia! Not much soul-searching then, from what I remember.'

'At least you've got the option,' I say, ignoring him.

11

Jenny sighs. 'We hope it won't come to that. We're hoping things will come right.'

Gus laughs. 'You know that won't happen until that bastard Mugabe is gone.'

'Please, Angus. Don't talk in front of the girls, man. We don't want them repeating things at school.'

'Ja, well, until that bloody clown joins the big circus in the sky things will just get worse. You know it, Jenny.'

Jessica and Lauren giggle behind their hands, no doubt used to their father's outbursts. Gus throws Monty a chop bone which he catches with an agile snap of the jaws. 'Go on, bugger off, you parasite!' Gus chuckles, waving Monty away. He takes a deep swig of Lion Lager and begins the task of dissecting my private life. 'So how's the marriage tally going, boet?' he asks. 'Any more irresponsible adventures of a conjugal sort?'

'Angus, don't be rude!' Jenny exclaims.

'One was quite enough for me, Gus. Just happy to be a free man.'

'You mean Beth took you to the cleaners.'

'No, I mean I'm not cut out for it. Not like responsible husbands such as yourself. And for the record, Beth let me off very lightly.'

Gus grins, his eyes glinting in the firelight. 'And what's happening with my nephew? With Jess and Lauren's cousin who we never hear from? Last I heard he was a bit of a surfer dude.'

'You mean Michael.'

'There aren't any other nephews, are there?'

I decide to put an end to this jocular line of interrogation. 'Michael stays with his mother in Brisbane. Since we split up he doesn't want anything to do with me.'

There is a long silence. Jessica and Lauren look embarrassed.
'Sorry to hear that,' Gus grunts eventually.

'We just never hear anything from you, Vaughn,' Jenny says
plaintively. She slaps at a mosquito on her arm.

I struggle to sleep that night, so consumed am I with guilt.
I yearn for Beth and Michael. Yes, always between places.
Neither here nor there.

*

There is some baggage I didn't declare. I thought my messy
history could be avoided, that I could speak of the present without opening the past to inspection. That is simply impossible.
There must be more detail, more openness on my part. But
that's easier said than done. Navel-gazing has never been my
forte. The ways of the Rhodesian male do not dissipate easily.
So let me compromise with a version of the past – a simple set
of facts.

My family, the Bourkes, were regarded as 'old Rhodesians'
because we were among the first settlers in Matabeleland. We
have owned and occupied a farm called Hopelands near the
railway siding settlement of Shangani since 1897, just after the
Chimurenga Rebellion. I was born a fourth-generation Rhodesian, the youngest of three children: Angela, Angus and me,
Vaughn. My father had always envisaged Gus and me taking
over the farm, since it was too big for one man to manage. But
I had different plans and left Rhodesia in 1974 to study in
South Africa, one of the last to be allowed to go to university
before national service. My father was not exactly enchanted by
my choice of study. Art was not something a bloke wasted his

time with in Rhodesia, especially if you were of farming stock. To my father art was a hobby for women with time on their hands – it was therefore okay for Angela to pursue her love of wildlife painting – but in the real world it had, as he succinctly put it, about as much use as tits on a bull. In such down-to-earth terms he made his views clear on the matter, but I had a strong-willed mother who believed in my talents, so there was not much argument. Thankfully, Dad was able to be philosophical about such things. He'd married a cultured city woman blessed with a creative bent; he should expect this to surface in the children, even the males. Prior to Angela and me, the Bourkes had never produced an artist of any sort. My father looked on it as something I just needed to get out of my system. Like acne.

Like many of my young countrymen I took the option of study partly to evade military service and the escalating civil war in Rhodesia. In my final year at university in Pietermaritz-burg I applied to migrate to Australia, unbeknown to my family. In 1978, as soon as I'd completed my Fine Art degree, and much to my parents' surprise and dismay, I climbed on a plane bound for Sydney. Gus, whom I'd never got on with, exercised his usual callous wit by calling me 'Sir Chickenheart'. This reaction was born of his perception of me deserting kith and kin while he was in the army, keeping our little piece of Africa out of the hands of the black barbarians. I told them I would only go back to Rhodesia when the illegal Smith regime had been ousted from power – in those days I fancied myself as something of an activist, though in truth my activism was strictly of the armchair variety. Only Angela supported my move – she would always support her siblings, whatever their political persuasion. At the time I was sorry about the pain I caused but

14

felt quite sanctimonious about my decision – was I not on the side of liberation and justice, on the side of the people? After my parents were killed by guerrillas – tragically, less than a year before the ceasefire – my proletarian views collapsed in a pathetic heap, and I never went back. Guerrillas, comrades, cadres ... the euphemisms I continue to use, despite what they did. Though I haven't used the term 'freedom fighter' in quite a while.

I continued to study in Australia and eventually found myself safely ensconced in academe as a painting lecturer at the College of Fine Art at Hunter Valley University in Newcastle. I became moderately successful as a painter in the early eighties, making hay while the neo-expressionist sun shone, just prior to the deadly virus of installation art. I married a nurse called Bethany and we had a son, Michael. We lived in a terraced house in Cooks Hill in Newcastle, known for its trendy, bohemian pretensions. On the surface things were going well. In those early years I worked hard and was promoted to senior lecturer and then to associate professor in recognition of teaching excellence and a strong exhibition record.

From my distant ivory tower I watched Rhodesia change into Zimbabwe, promisingly at first and then disastrously, as Robert Mugabe's rule turned to tyranny. Gus had continued to run Hopelands and seemed to be coping reasonably well. Since he was determined to hold on to the farm, Angela and I conceded any right to it (it had been left to the three of us in my father's will). Angela had continued to live periodically on Hopelands, but during the dissident crisis in 1986 she left for Britain, where, as fate would have it, she found huge fame and fortune as a wildlife painter. Angela and I regularly correspond, these days mostly by e-mail. I've visited her a few times at her picturesque

15.

country house in Hampshire while on sabbatical, and she came to Australia once to see whether she might broaden her wildlife repertoire. I drove her all the way to Alice Springs and back, a tiresome journey that convinced both of us that we had been irreparably spoiled by the splendour of the African bush and its beasts.

On one occasion my visit to Angela in Hampshire coincided with a stay by Gus and his family. Jenny's father was a well-to-do London stockbroker and she and the girls made the trip to England quite often whereas Gus only went that once. It was not the best of reunions. The quaint environment of culture and history brought out an acerbic contempt in Gus for all things British. Like so many Rhodesian die-hards he blamed Britain for the new horrors of Zimbabwe. His constant negativism precipitated some unpleasant arguments and we parted on angry terms. Over the years I've remained in minimal contact with him, our correspondence limited mostly to an annual Christmas card and a birthday phone call, usually dependent on whether sufficient liquor had been consumed to induce brotherly sentimentality. It didn't help that Gus's calls usually began with his childish emulation of a chicken clucking. Letters have been few and far between. The only times Gus ever wrote anything seemed to be in bad times. I have kept those letters because they provide a rare glimpse of sensitivity usually hidden behind his brute exterior.

Ordinarily my attitude towards Zimbabwe's tragedy had been one of detachment. It got to the point where the reality of Zimbabwe so eclipsed the dream tumble-down lefties like me had in the seventies that I could not even bear to think about it. Revolutionary philosophy proposes the end justifies the

16

UK,
York

means; it depressed me to think that all the spilt blood of the war, including that of my parents, had been in vain. It was easier to dispel Zimbabwe from my mind than to acknowledge my ideological bankruptcy.

But I could not dispel the stirrings of angry emotions when the farm invasions began in 2000. My emotions were unsettling and confusing because they swept me into uncomfortable political territories. Despite my family's long association with the African soil, I'd always seen the issue of land rights as quite straightforward. The redistribution of Zimbabwe's white-owned farming land to black farmers was not only inevitable, but historically just. Was that not what the war had been about? Black Zimbabweans reclaiming the land stolen from them by the British? Given the post-liberation power shift, how could whites think that they could hold on to the bulk of the best land in perpetuity? But the crooked and murderous way the invasions were conducted was not what I had in mind. I could not remain aloof to the stories of murder, torture and rape. The victimisation of defenceless farmers and their workers, the destruction of crops and the senseless slaughter and mutilation of livestock shocked and appalled me. And my detachment unravelled completely when one of our Shangani neighbours, Tienus Gerber, was killed. The Gerbers were an Afrikaner *youth* family, well-respected in the district and among our closest friends. Besieged in his farmstead by dozens of 'war veterans' Tienus bled to death from wounds sustained during a lonely, desperate battle, while the police stood by and watched. His murder was reported around the world. I recoiled at the gory pictures of his body in *Newsweek*. It put a face to the killings. Someone I'd grown up with, gone to school with.

17

By the end of 2002 all of the farms around Hopelands had been taken over. Inevitably, Hopelands had its scare. While Gus was away attending a farmers' meeting in Gweru, a mob pitched up at the security gate to the house. As Gus related in one of his rare letters, they terrorised Jenny who was there alone with the family's two old servants, Joseph and Anna – the girls, fortunately, were away in boarding school. Jenny phoned the police at Shangani and was told they would not interfere in 'political matters'. She tried the police station at Fort Rixon and got the same message. The mob hung around the gate, chanting and singing. They toyi-toyied around the security fence, brandishing axes and pangas. Stones were thrown and a few windows broken. After two hours they dispersed. Jenny moved to Bulawayo soon after that.

Gus then demonstrated more intelligence than I had previously thought him capable of. He formed an unofficial partnership with a retired policeman, an Ndebele called Saxon Ncube. Ncube had been forced to retire because he was a member of the Movement for Democratic Change, the only viable opposition party in the country. Despite this, he still wielded enough influence in the district to keep the veterans at bay, for the time being at least. But clearly the future was uncertain. This was why Gus decided to exhume the bodies from our family graveyard on Hopelands and re-inter them at the small Anglican church in Shangani. A precautionary measure, Gus wrote.

And so I climbed aboard a Qantas jet and came back to my place of birth. To witness the reburial of my family. To say a final goodbye.

*

No, that will not do. Before this journey I pledged to be honest with myself, at least. I have not been entirely forthcoming. There are more complex reasons behind my decision to return. More baggage must be opened and inspected before I am allowed to proceed. I have a fear of exposing my flaws, but they will become self-evident anyway. I accept fallibility to be one of my more obvious traits, but acceptance, as I'm so often reminded, is no substitute for remedy.

There came a point a few years after my last university promotion and ten years after marrying Beth, where my life began a downward spiral. The art world in which I had lived so comfortably at first suddenly became a hostile place, where I was no longer welcome. It became a home for cynical philosophers who ridiculed art's traditions and mocked the notion of the artist as solitary hero imbued with God-given skills, wresting meaning out of life. It had no need of old skills and intuition. It no longer demanded the silences of introspection. A scourge of conceptualism held sway, where art seemed to consist only of bad photographs of fat women looking oppressed, boring arrangements of found objects (the endless reincarnations of Marcel Duchamp) and banal, repetitive videos. All you needed to call yourself an artist was an *idea*, nothing more. My brand of art, steeped as it was in the abilities of the eye and hand, became defunct, irrelevant. I stopped exhibiting.

Without the sustenance of relevance my painting shrivelled on its vine. And I withered too. Beth is a woman of extraordinary fibre, as nurses tend to be. Her ability to stomach the sights of injured and diseased bodies is something that still humbles me. Yet all her years of training and hard experience did not prepare her in the slightest for the job of nursing me.

19

How she coped for so long, I don't know. *Why* she coped, I don't know.

My professional life became meaningless. I found myself out of my depth in academe, despite a CV that could be beefed up with obsolete achievements to look quite impressive at first glance. In reality, I could hardly describe myself as an academic, given the complete surrender of university art schools, such as mine, to intellectual pretentiousness. The only thing academic about me, as Beth often joked, was my looks – gaunt and greying at the temples, a dreamlike air that others mistook for studious reflection ... yes, the intuitive artist can only survive in academe these days by appearances, by pretence.

But I chafed under the yoke of pretence and, inevitably, my teaching began to suffer. In the new scheme of things I had nothing to teach. My colleagues began to refer to me as 'dead wood'. Skulking behind an illusory calm intellect, I protected myself from the slings and arrows of my detractors with some Marxist existentialist jargon (a flimsy prophylactic, in hindsight) I'd picked up during my student days in South Africa. Sartre unplugged. Just when everyone else was into the wild new religion of post-structuralist theory whose subversive prophets ran amok in the eighties, undermining the foundations of everything I held dear.

I began to flounder. The contradictions weighed heavily. Everything I did was at odds with the dated claptrap I mouthed. I was the ultimate 'unauthentic' man, as Heidegger might have described my inability to be myself. It seemed nothing I did in Australia was through that most sacred of existentialist maxims – choice. With me things just happened. My life unfolded by accident. My marriage had not occurred through choice – Beth became pregnant. My professional life had become more the result of artistic redundancy and an inability to do anything else than actual choice. Yes, the people Sartre was thinking of when he spoke of man's 'choice to be' were intelligent, rational beings – not those standing helpless to the winds of life.

And my sense of purpose ebbed further when the Australian government embarked on a prolonged and savage campaign of funding cuts to universities, ostensibly to generate greater efficiency. What this produced, in fact, was massive staff reductions, falling standards and increased, ill-defined workloads, especially for those of us in the Humanities. Desperate for money, universities opened their doors to virtually anyone who felt like picking up a degree, providing they paid for the privilege. Foundation courses, enabling programmes ... no stone was left unturned when it came to prostituting the status of higher learning. Suddenly academics started wearing all sorts of funny hats that didn't fit, most notably that of entrepreneur. To sell our courses to a diminishing market we all graduated as doctors of spin.

Because of my past record I kept my job. But I felt a stranger in this new world. My behaviour became increasingly erratic. I became sarcastic and sometimes belligerent towards my colleagues, and ill-tempered with students, especially if they mouthed the trendy post-modern mantras of Derrida or Baudrillard. Students began complaining of their treatment and enrolment in my courses began to drop. Perceiving myself to be the last true liberal in the western world, I no doubt became insufferable. On a social level, I discovered that alcohol was useful in expelling my frustrations – letting off steam, so to speak. While it should be said that my consumption was always outside of work hours and never of the truly excessive or unruly sort, it did, however, unlock a suppressed philanderer. I had two stupid (and very brief) affairs with female colleagues that would prove disproportionately damaging in their consequence.

Intent on hammering nails into my coffin, I became a virtual pariah when I brought my faculty's research profile into disrepute. The dean of my faculty, in a philanthropic attempt to resurrect my artistic career, had been instrumental in procuring for me a fairly large research grant to 'investigate the political/creative spaces of Australia'. I was even allocated the faculty gallery, a prestigious exhibition venue in Newcastle, to present my 'findings'. With the grant money I bought enough paint and canvas to last several artists a lifetime but, to my dismay, found the desire to paint just would not come. After months of apathetic procrastination I came up with the smart-arse idea of exhibiting the gallery – the *empty* gallery. If the art world wanted concepts, I would give them one – nothingness. All I provided the bemused spectators who turned up for the opening was a small pamphlet explaining how this 'work' was an ironic manifestation of the contemporary sublime – Sartrean nihilism in its purest form. Now, if I were a professional smart-arse like those post-structuralists, I might have pulled it off. But I wasn't. There can be no creature more pathetic than the tired old traditionalist trying to mock the new. I will never forget the withering look of contempt on the face of my dean as she stormed past me out the gallery door. An art historian of some standing and a lover of all things French, she had worked for many years to elevate the profile of art in academe, and now this! If her look wasn't humiliating enough, her words flayed me alive.

'Ever heard of Ives Klein?' she snapped as she blew by like a sub-zero Siberian wind. 'Quite famous, actually. He did the same thing *forty years ago*! For God's sake, couldn't you at least be intelligently unoriginal?'

The spiral gained momentum. Soon I became the focus of dreary committees whose task it was to investigate not just my inappropriate use of research funds. My unethical behaviour towards students and colleagues, not to mention my affairs, also came under the microscope. My two former lovers colluded against me, providing my interrogators with vivid testimonies of improper conduct. The upshot was that no one could decide quite what to do with me. I was what they called 'borderline'. There were no precise grounds on which to impose any punishment. So I was ostracised instead.

Naturally, this all spilled over into my private life. Beth disapproved of my new drinking habits. She got to know of my affairs and we began to have terrible rows. I had made the fatal error of mistaking Beth's seemingly limitless tolerance for my character defects as docility. The one thing she would not abide was infidelity, even of the most superficial sort. Michael, never an outgoing boy, retreated into himself and became hostile towards me. Beth found marijuana hidden in his cupboard. He began to get into trouble. One day he was caught breaking into a car. The police let him off with a caution, after I spoke with them and paid for the damage – thank God for the endless latitude Australia shows its youth. Finally Beth left me, taking with her my troubled son.

For a year I hung from the flimsy rope of my fraying ego. I had created a limbo from which there seemed no escape. I could not live with anyone, yet could not live alone either. I resented my profession, yet sucked my sustenance from it like a sad leech. For the first time I began to feel out of place in Australia, yet had nowhere else to go. I reached a point where it was obvious a breakdown of sorts was imminent, so I took a year's long-service leave. I think the university was more relieved than I. This was meant to be a time where I could sort myself out and find a renewed sense of place and purpose.

But the knowledge that I had wasted my life weighed heavily and things only got worse. I started seeing a psychiatrist who diagnosed severe depression and prescribed daily medication. None of it worked. The only constant in my life seemed to be a sense of futility. So, when Gus contacted me about the graves, I almost wept with relief. I could not get on the plane fast enough.

*

Sunday. I decline the family's invitation to attend church with them. While they are out I try to phone Beth but cannot get through. Zimbabwe's telephone system is a shambles, it seems. Jenny rustles up some omelettes for breakfast when they return. There's a bit of a squabble between Jessica and Lauren about whose turn it is to wash the dishes, since it is Gladys's day off. Jenny sighs and does it herself. Gus rummages around in a wardrobe and finds me an old floppy sports hat with *Rhodesia is Super* still visible on it. He slaps a blue sweat-stained baseball cap on his balding dome and we leave for the farm. We pass long queues outside the petrol stations. Gus says people sometimes wait days to fill up, sleeping in their cars. He gets his petrol and diesel courtesy of his new partner, Ncube. 'The benefits of being in league with an ex-cop,' he says.

'I'm surprised you have anything to do with him,' I say. 'Fraternising with the enemy was never a negotiable concept with you, as I recall.'

Gus seems peeved by my remark. He takes a while to respond. 'People in this part of the world do what they must to survive. I'm surprised you've forgotten that. But then, of course, you never did have much of a handle on things here, did you, Chickenheart?'

'You should cut your bloody losses and leave, Gus.'

'What, and let those criminals take over our land?'

I shrug. 'It's going to happen anyway. Sooner or later.'

'Always quick with the reverse gear, hey boet?'

'I'm just a realist.'

'Ja? Funny how some realists suddenly experience powerful bowel movements in times of trouble.'

To signal he's had enough of this line of talk, Gus shoves a Creedence Clearwater Revival tape in the cassette. He takes the Harare road past Kumalo. It's another hot day as we drive through the flat, drab countryside, past the old PPC cement factory and McDonalds brickworks that have been there for as long as I can remember. I sit back and take in the passing sights behind my sunglasses, the rush of air through the opened windows mercifully drowning out the music. I breathe deeply, trying to dispel a lingering anger. Gus and I have always clashed; it exasperates me that we never see eye to eye. One day together and already we're at each other. He hasn't changed a bit. His boorish mannerisms, his infantile politics – that arrogant assumption that everyone in the world spends all their waking hours riveted to the plight of Zimbabweans. Even the jaunty way he drives, drumming his blunt fingers on the steering wheel, whistling tunelessly. Bloody Neanderthal. How is it that we sprang from the same womb?

A short while later we come across an overturned truck, partially obstructing the road. The driver, apparently unhurt, is sitting patiently alongside the road, with a pot of sadza cooking on a fire. Gus stops and asks him if he's okay. The man gives us a stoic thumbs up. Gus shakes his head as he negotiates his way around the wreck. He laughs. 'Dead straight road – how the fucking hell ...? What's the bet he'll still be there when we come back.'

A bit further, Gus pulls over to take a leak behind a tree. He returns to the car, zipping up his fly. 'Had a kidney stone op last year,' he tells me as we continue our journey. 'I swear to God, the pain was worse than when I got shot. The stone was so big they had to shove a bloody catheter up my cock to pull it out. Jenny, bless her nurse's soul, makes sure I drink gallons of water to prevent a recurrence. That's why I'm forever taking a piss.'

'Nice to be properly informed,' I say, wincing.

We come to Shangani, my tiny 'home town', consisting of no more than a police station, a post office, a petrol station-cum-store, the old farmers' club, the Anglican church and a few houses scattered like bleached bones among the marula trees on either side of the railway line. Dust-strewn, sun-leached, fly-blown. Seemingly unchanged. Once the social hub of my universe, where farming families gathered on weekends either at the church or the club, where isolated, monotonous lives intersected briefly, mostly happily, then went their separate ways. And where, according to my grandfather, the King of England himself once climbed off a train to stretch his legs and quickly climbed back on again.

Gus wastes no time, though, going down memory lane. He turns off onto the Fort Rixon road and heads south towards the farm. The vehicle kicks up clouds of pale brown dust as we barrel along the rutted dirt road, the Creedence tape blaring away – sadly, there's been no change to my brother's barbaric taste in music. It's hot and uncomfortable in the car. There is a shimmering haze over the neglected maize fields and scorched pastures of now ruined farms. The first rains have not come. The only winds they've been getting, Gus tells me, are hot dry westerlies from Botswana that just aggravate the drought. He says veld fires have plagued them all spring.

We pass several squatter camps on the farmlands adjacent to the road, mostly random shanty dwellings made of bush timber, old bits of corrugated iron and sheets of plastic. Zimbabwe and Zanu-PF flags hang limply on poles. Except for a few men dozing in the shade of trees and some women tilling the arid plots there is not much activity. Gus explains how at first Ncube had been able to keep the local war veterans' leader, a man called Elias Zondi, on his side. Unlike most of his fellow squatters Zondi was a legitimate veteran, a former Zipra cadre, like Ncube. He and Ncube struck up a rapport and for a while Hopelands seemed safe from invasion. But then, almost a year ago, Zondi disappeared (one rumour had it he was murdered, another claimed he had succumbed to AIDS) and another leader, Victor Mtunzi, took over. Mtunzi was a different kettle of fish, as they soon discovered. It was Mtunzi who oversaw the killing of Tienus Gerber. Not long after that Gus received a Section Five notice officially designating Hopelands for compulsory government acquisition, the usual prelude to seizure. Gus has pursued what legal channels he can, but he knows the legal system is powerless against a regime that thumbs its nose at the law. Regardless of how successfully the designation of a farm might be contested through the courts, the fact remains that such civilised niceties as court edicts are ignored by both government and veterans – farms are invaded nonetheless. As Gus sees it, his only real hope lies with Ncube who still has some clout with his old police connections.

While I make no outward display of it, the sight of these squatter camps makes me nervous. The *Newsweek* image of Tienus Gerber's body lying sprawled in a pool of blood springs to mind. But Gus seems unperturbed about our personal safety. That we are probably the only white faces for miles around is of no concern to him. I can only trust he has a finger on the pulse of things here.

Gus slows as we pass the camp on the Gerbers' farm. There is a bit more activity here. A contingent of about twenty men and women are helping police offload supplies from an armoured personnel carrier. I notice crates of beer seem a disproportionate mainstay for this particular community.

Gus gestures at the scene. 'Behold, our impartial police force! Bloody corrupt munts! The ones who don't get involved in political matters. Mtunzi's turned the Gerbers' house into his headquarters – his centre of operations, as he calls it. Those bastards invaded the place just before the last maize harvest, just in time to cash in. The Gerbers lost everything – a big maize crop, cattle, machinery, the lot. Just plain bloody theft. That's why Tienus stayed and fought. And you watch, everything the Gerbers made out of this land will be fucked in a few months.'

'What's happened to the old folks?' I ask.

'They moved into Bulawayo before Tienus got killed, thank God. Mevrou Gerber was too sick with emphysema and needed to be close to the hospital. She died a few years ago. The old man's still in Bulawayo. Bella's also still here. Works as a secretary for a law firm.'

'Bella? I can hardly remember her – she was always so much younger than us. The laat lammetjie her folks used to call her.'

'She's grown up a bit since then, boet.'

Gus puts his foot down and accelerates past the camp. He falls quiet, though his anger is palpable. He taps the steering wheel in time to *Proud Mary*. 'Poor Tienus,' he says eventually. 'Just him with an old single-bore shotgun, trying to hold off those bastards. All armed to the teeth with AKs and FNs. You should've seen the house afterwards – completely riddled with bullets. Bloody cowards. Hey, Vaughn? Can you imagine it, man?'

I shake my head. 'No, I can't. You'd think the police would at least have made some effort to save him. I can't believe they just stood there and watched.'

'They didn't just stand there and watch, professor. They were in on it! They bloody well trucked in those bastards and then blocked off all the roads so no help could get to him. They provided guns and ammo. At one stage Tienus phoned for an ambulance, and even that was turned back. I tell you, these munts are not human beings. Bloody animals! Just like in the war. Target the weak and defenceless, that's their style. What is it about kaffirs, hey?'

'I thought that term had lost its currency in Zimbabwe.'

'What other word is there for those bastards? Don't lecture me, professor. You don't have to deal with these people. All those years in university and you still haven't twigged there're some pretty fundamental differences between us and them.'

My hackles rise with an old anger. 'Christ, Gus, how can you still talk like that? Where does Ncube fit into your classifications? Is he also a kaffir? An animal?'

Gus sighs. 'Oh shit, here we go ...'

'No, don't shrug it off, Gus. I'm amazed you can still be so bloody prejudiced. The man who goes to church every Sunday! Not every black Zimbabwean is invading farms, murdering whites. It pisses me off when you generalise. Okay, what happened to Tienus was terrible. I'm not trying to say otherwise or excuse what happened. But you've got to face up to reality here. These invasions were going to happen, sooner or later. Look at the big picture, for Christ's sake. White farmers are just symbols. Symbols of the colonial past, of oppression. Wasn't the war always about land in the first place?'

Gus eyes me sideways. He has an expression on his face we used to call pit bull – stubborn, impervious to reason. 'You know, sometimes I'd swear you were born yesterday. What reality are you talking about, man? Get one thing straight, those kaffirs back there are just plain thugs and thieves. Terrorists, like Mugabe himself. Most of them weren't even born in the "past" you're referring to. Veterans! It's a bloody joke, man! Mtunzi himself was four years old when the war ended. Don't fucking glamorise these munts, Vaughn!'

'I'm not glamorising them. You just never could put yourself in their shoes, hey? Of course they're going to target white farmers! You're a bloody symbol, that's all. You represent everything that was supposed to change with liberation. And face it, you white farmers did bugger-all to redress the problem of land rights when you had the chance. There you are, owning all the best land in the country, and you expect to just carry on, as if nothing has changed. Still the landlords, hey? Still the nkosi. How bloody deluded can you get!'

Gus shakes his head. 'Still the same dopey bloody hippy. You ignore the fact that that we feed this sorry nation. You ignore the fact that we've paid for our farms in more ways than one. Of course we're going to be concerned about our livelihood, our futures – our lives! These are *our* farms! But it's not just about the whites, Chickenheart. It's also about the way these bastards treat their own people. The thousands they butchered in the war, and in the twenty years since. Remember the eighties, Chickenheart? While you were all handing out honorary doctorates and other crap to Mugabe overseas, his thugs were throwing people down old mine shafts here in Matabeleland. And when you justify them stealing our land, what about all the poor damn farm workers who've been killed and tortured? And the women who've been raped, who now have AIDS? What about them, hey? You bastards overseas haven't a bloody clue about the extent of what's happening here. The only language Mugabe has ever understood is terror.'

I feel a wave of futility and blow out my cheeks in frustration. 'Look, Gus,' I say. 'I'm not going to argue with you, okay? Mugabe wasn't the only one who butchered blacks in the past. Ian Smith's noble army did its fair share, as you might recall.'

'At least we had the brains to figure out what would happen if Mugabe got into power. We were trying to prevent this fuck-up happening. At least we stood for something.'

'Of course. You Rhodesian army heroes are the only ones

who ever stood for anything, hey? Stop living in the past, Gus! Face up to reality. Whites have no divine right to Africa. That's all I'm trying to say.'

Gus gives a contemptuous laugh. 'Face up to reality? Tell me, Vaughn, do you know what the Gerber farm is now, according to its fine, upstanding new owners? I'll tell you. It's a "re-education centre". Do you know what that means, professor? It means it's a place where they teach by imprisonment and torture Zanu-PF policy to any poor bastard in this area who they feel needs re-educating. Quite a few have died or have gone missing through this educational process. But what do you bloody holier-than-thou experts overseas feel about them, hey?'

'That just tells me you're completely insane hanging on here,' I say.

We fall into an angry silence. I stare at the passing countryside, so familiar yet suddenly so foreign, so impossible to understand. Our argument hangs like a foul fog in the air. I curse myself. That this unfathomable place should expose my own prejudices so! Gus is right about one thing. Foreigners *do* accord more value to white life in Africa. While the deaths of a few farmers like Tienus Gerber make headlines around the world, the suffering of thousands of Zimbabwean blacks – immeasurably greater – is barely mentioned. That Gus, of all people, should associate me with such prejudice is intolerable.

The final stretch of road between Shangani and Hopelands crosses the Shangani River at a bridge where the homestead is suddenly visible on a hill to the east. The farmers called this bridge 'Rex's Crossing', after my uncle's accident there. As a boy it had another significance for me, more subtle and strange.

Whenever I returned to the farm from boarding school, I always looked out for the house with a mysterious fear. I feared perhaps one day the house would be gone, as if my life had been a dream.

But now it's there, as always. Only I expect to see our cosy thatched roof, not the hard glint of corrugated iron, and I recall now my father writing to me in Australia explaining his decision to replace the thatch – it was too tempting a target for terrorist RPGs, he said. We cross the cattle grid onto Hopelands and drive up the long winding road around the hill to the house. Two dogs come bounding up to the security gate. Gus unlocks the gate; we drive through and park in front of the house. I get out and stretch my legs. The dogs subject me to a cursory sniffing over. Rhodesian Ridgebacks are not famous for their intelligence, and these two oafs are no exception to the rule. Their names, Gus informs me, are Frik and Tiny – after the two Springbok rugby forwards of yesteryear, no doubt. Frik, in particular, seems given to boorish posturing and unnecessary noise. For no particular reason he barks at the empty countryside for a full five minutes, before joining Tiny back at their guard post on the veranda. While Gus walks up to the reservoir on the hill above the house to turn on the water I gaze out over the landscape that formed my earliest memories, the sounds of the veld sweet to my ears.

Despite the farm's altitude of four-and-a-half thousand feet, there is little sense of height from the vantage point of the house, only distance. Far off, the river meanders sluggishly north towards the Zambezi. The skies above are filled with small empty clouds that recede to a spittle along the horizon, and the plains and hills extend beneath them in endless textures of rock and vegetation. Miles of bushveld savannah, msasa-gondi woodlands and open vleis, and hills that burst through the earth – great domed granite kopjes that split and peel beneath the sun. On one of these hills a cross stands against the sky. This ten-metre-high copper and steel structure was erected by my grand-father in 1944 as a sign of thanks when my father and Rex re-turned from the Second World War. He and a gang of workers lugged it all the way up the hill and cemented it into the rock. He gave the hill its name – Long Cross Hill. No one else in the family possessed quite the same religious zeal as my grandfather. After he died Rex had even argued in favour of taking the cross down. He saw it as a foreign intrusion on the landscape, but it stayed because my father said we could get our bearings from it – Dad, mind you, was being pragmatic, not religious. To me, the cross always seemed a tenuous mark of our existence since the family graveyard is situated nearby.

It's noon and the land shimmers beneath heat waves. The smell of dung wafts across from the sheep pens near the sheds. Insects sing. A herd of cattle in the distance appears to be floating. Everything seems suspended. Only the ants and blister beetles down at my feet toil in the sun.

I walk around the house, noting that Gus has kept the gar-dens spic and span despite the drought. The house, never an aesthetic wonder and now in serious need of a coat of paint, nonetheless looks as solid and permanent as ever. It was begun by my great-grandfather back in 1897 and added to in later years, resulting in a large sprawling place with a veranda around three sides. The veranda has a wide stone floor enclosed by a low wall. Bougainvilleas and trumpet creepers cling tenaciously to the pillars and rafters. Flowers are struggling to survive in the beds beneath the veranda walls. My mother's favourites – roses, chrysanthemums, Barberton daisies and nasturtiums, that used to provide a brave sparkle of colour against the dusty land. The vegetable garden and apricot and orange orchards around the back of the house all look a little weary from the drought, but they still bear the signs of fastidious care.

Gus comes back from the reservoir and we go inside. The house is big and dark and almost empty. Most of the furniture and ornaments have been removed for safekeeping to the house in Burnside, Gus explains. Because the rooms are bare the house's crudeness is more noticeable; the stone walls appear to lack symmetry, the msasa rafters seem raw and primitive. I remember how my mother tried to impose some feminine authority on the house, but never quite succeeded. She hung original paintings on the walls; she bought tasteful rugs and good pieces of furniture. Her collection of books – on art, the great composers, along with a broad range of literary classics – existed cheek by jowl with my father's assortment of farming manuals, *National Geographic* magazines and Wilbur Smith novels. Her black Steinway piano (and the sound of her playing) in the lounge was an intimate, though incongruous symbol of her presence. She campaigned long and hard to phase out my grandmother's kitsch copper ornaments and Rex's hunting trophies. She did her best but the indomitable house always emerged the rugged victor and she was forced to accept that nothing, save a tidy demolition, would have any real effect. Only the dining room with the family photographs on the wall remains as I remember it. Gus says he keeps it this way because this is the place where the family always came together.

Gus goes to the kitchen and comes back with a couple of cold beers and we sit at the dining table. He explains our programme for the afternoon, which I gather entails a general tour of the farm. As he talks I peruse the photographs on the wall. There are pictures of my great-grandparents, Vaughn and Catherine, and my grandparents, John and Janice. There are my parents, Duncan and Nancy (Nan, as we called her). There's Rex. And, of course, us – Angela, Gus and me. Four generations of a colonial family.

The photograph of Vaughn and Catherine is old and yellowed. They are standing beside a half-tent wagon, laden with all their worldly possessions: six months' provisions, a bedstead, a table and four chairs, an anvil, a couple of trunks and a wood stove. There is a crate of chickens tied underneath the wagon and in the background there are some trek oxen, two cows and Vaughn's horse. Vaughn looks fierce and stern beneath his bushy black beard, his eyes dark and serious. He stands erect and dignified next to Catherine. At his feet a bull terrier is chewing at his quirt. Catherine stands solemnly, modestly, her face tired yet hopeful. She gave the farm its name – Hopelands. Below her feet are the handwritten words: Arrival in the Colony, 1897.

There is one of my grandparents on their wedding day. They are standing on the platform of Bulawayo station, about to embark by train on their honeymoon to the Victoria Falls. John has that lopsided grin which Rex and Gus inherited, and there is much of my father in Granny Jan's practical, almost haughty air. She is holding a map and has a pair of binoculars around her neck.

Then there is Dad and Nan seated together on the veranda steps, the shadow of the photographer, Rex, covering their feet. You can see it's Rex by the wide-brimmed hat he used to wear.

Dad and Nan are squinting against the sun. Both are young and handsome, and have the casual smiles of those who are secure and exclusive in their love. They are physically alike in many respects: both have dark hair and blue eyes, both look lean and fit, and wear dimpled smiles. Except for Nan's glasses, they could be brother and sister. They hold each other close, together ...

Rex. A lopsided grin next to a dead kudu with massive spiralling horns. He has a beer in one hand, a hunting rifle in the other. Hat pushed back, blond hair astray, and a look of carefree innocence that almost exonerates him from the debauched deeds for which he became legend.

I never liked the one of us. Nan had it done in a studio in Bulawayo. The photographer obviously aspired to higher things than family portraits. We are not children, we are angels. Angela, the oldest, stands with her arms protectively around Gus and me, suggesting a maternal instinct of sorts. I am five years old and holding a baby's rubber giraffe. Gus looks impossibly clean and odourless. Angela and I have had our glasses removed (we both inherited my mother's poor eyesight, along with her creative bent). It's all too much – our groomed, touched-up heads positioned before the sweep of a red velvet curtain, Angela's ethereal gaze. Angela and I have dark hair, while Gus is fair. She and Gus have blue eyes; mine are brown. In terms of looks Angela takes after both parents, and Gus after Rex and John. As for me, it was often said that I most closely resembled my great-grandfather. Dark and drab. I was always reminded how apt it was that I inherited his name.

There is another photograph that conveys a more accurate memory. A small snapshot of the three of us being pushed around the garden in a wheelbarrow by Joseph. We are sitting with our feet dangling over the sides of the barrow. Angela, typically, has her arms outflung, her mouth open wide. I am frowning at the camera; Gus has his lopsided smirk, minus a few teeth. That is how I remember us: barefoot, happy, candles of snot hanging from Gus's nose.

*

We follow the path that winds down the hill at the back of the house to Joseph and Anna's kraal. It's a twenty-minute walk through some thick stands of mukwa and msusu trees and by the time we reach the kraal I'm sweating profusely, while Gus, beer gut and all, seems hardly to notice the heat. Irritably I wave at the flies buzzing around my head.

'Thought you'd be used to flies, coming from Australia,' Gus remarks.

The kraal consists of two thatched mud huts, decorated with traditional blue and white zigzag designs, a cement block store-room with a corrugated iron roof and a goat enclosure. Chickens roam freely; a donkey stands asleep, tethered to a tree. There is a half-acre vegetable patch (now with just a few surviving mielies and pumpkins) on the approaches to the kraal, fenced off with dry sapling branches to keep the animals out. A scrawny dog announces our arrival with a tirade of yapping.

The old couple emerge from their huts, white-haired and wizened, of an age not even they can determine. They squint against the harsh light, recognising Gus at once. And then they recognise me, despite my years of absence, and they hurry forward, crying, 'Ah! Ah! Ah! Nkosana Vaughn! Kunjani? Uvela ngaphi?'

I greet Joseph first, shaking his hand African style. Joseph's white beard is split by a sparsely-toothed smile. Then I greet Anna, shaking her hand formally. Suddenly, to my bewilderment, I start sobbing and hold her close in my arms. Joseph cackles, shaking his head. Gus throws up his hands and turns away, embarrassed. I can't help myself. Anna is a second mother to me. I was nursed by her, carried on her back (indeed, my earliest memory is the texture of her neck). She and Joseph taught me their language before I could speak English. And so it was with Angela and Gus. In this, we were no different from most white farm kids. We were all little Africans before we were weaned away to become masters and madams.

Anna cries too, like a mother.

Joseph beckons us to some rickety chairs in the shade of an msasa tree. Gus fidgets impatiently as I gather myself. I wipe away my tears and present them with some gifts – a sports jacket and cigars for Joseph, an embroidered tablecloth showing a map of Australia and a box of Arnott's biscuits for Anna. They receive these small gifts with both hands, as is customary. I point out on the map where I live in Australia. They both nod and exclaim, 'Aheh!' Gus laughs and says, 'Manga, wena! Since when have you two been reading maps? You have absolutely no idea what Baas Vaughn is talking about, hey?'

They laugh, relieved at not having to persist with polite deceptions.

And we talk. In their rich language we talk. I ask them how life is in their retirement and they reply solemnly that life is good, though I gather their four daughters who are married and left many years ago have not visited them recently because of the trouble on the farms. Anna wants to know where all my children are and seems peeved and mystified to hear I have only one child. I don't dwell on the details. Anna looks at me closely. 'Uyajabula na?' she asks.

I nod and reply, 'Ngiyajabula – I am happy, Mama.'

'How can you be happy away from your land of birth?' she asks.

'I am a free spirit, Mama,' I lie.

She skilfully changes the subject and insists on cooking supper for us. Gus tells her he has brought meat for a braai that will go bad if we don't use it. Shaking her old head, Anna says Gus will turn wild if left to his own devices, not an exaggerated assumption. 'Tomorrow night, then,' she says. 'We will make a roast. Proper food for Vaughn.'

Gus smiles. 'Okay, Mama.'

After an hour or so we make the trek back to the house. Climbing through a barbed-wire fence I manage to get the crotch of my *Hard Yakka* strides entangled which amuses Gus no end. Some things never change. Following Gus single-file along the path reminds me of when we were kids and used to wander down to Joseph and Anna's kraal on Sundays. Angela leading, then Gus, then me. Joseph always relished our visits because it gave him the chance to regale us with stories about the old days. We would sit and listen to him out under the msasa tree. He would drink beer from a calabash. His eyes got bloodshot and his voice became loud and ragged. He rolled cigarettes out of newspaper and sometimes smoked with the lighted end in his mouth, a source of great wonder to us. Anna laughed as his stories got wilder and more far-fetched.

Sometimes, if he felt up to it, Joseph would teach us the ways of the veld. Heedless of the thorns and the hot sand, he would lead the way through the bush, the thin muscles of his bare back flexing as his huge, cracked heels thudded against the beaten paths. He wore only a pair of tattered khaki shorts and carried a panga. As he walked he imitated the birdcalls and barked at the baboons in the kopjes. He taught us the Si-Ndebele names for everything. Indwangu for baboon, umvundla for rabbit. He pronounced the word 'uxhakhuxhaku' as though he was chewing on something delightful – uxhakhuxhaku is the name for the azanza tree (or, in our childhood lingo, the snot apple tree) and mimics the sound made while eating its fruit. I remember Joseph's horny yellow fingernails probing the earth for roots, flies settling undisturbed on the sheen of his brow. He taught us what was edible, or medicinal. I remember him distributing the yellow fruit of the marula tree. 'The flesh of this is very good,' he said. 'There is a nut inside the pip that is also good to eat. Here, try it.' He hacked at the tree trunk with his panga and extracted a piece of the inner bark. 'The juice inside this can stop the bee sting, the scorpion sting, or the nettle.' He squeezed the bark until a drop fell on his palm.

It became another of Angela's tests to see who could stomach the white ants, slugs and grasshoppers that Joseph procured for us to eat; naturally, Gus always rose to meet the challenge. Yes, Angela pitted Gus and me together and it was, I confess, a sorry, one-sided contest.

As we continue up to the house I say, 'Joseph and Anna are a complete enigma. How old do you reckon they are?'

Ahead of me Gus replies, 'I dunno. Joseph must be close to a hundred.'

41

'It's incredible. They don't seem to have aged all that much since I last saw them. If only they could bottle the secret.'

Gus pauses to urinate on a bush. 'There aren't many old Ndebeles like them around anymore, that's for sure,' he says.

'Pity about their daughters not visiting them. It's a sad state of affairs when people are too scared to visit their old folk.'

'Well, now they've got you to slobber and bawl all over them.'

'Pity I'm not a tough guy like you, Gus.'

'Ja, it's a pity about a lot of things, boet,' Gus says, zipping up his fly.

Back at the house we climb into the Land Cruiser my father bought back in the early seventies and, followed by the dogs who are overjoyed at the prospect of a break from guard duty, drive down to the weir across the river and up towards Long Cross Hill. It's a rough ride, the track having deteriorated over the years. As we drive Gus explains that getting permission to exhume the graves had been no simple legal matter. He had to submit an application for an order to exhume through Bulawayo City Council. Since exhumations were normally for police forensic purposes, there was some debate surrounding his application but it was eventually approved on compassionate grounds. No doubt to allay my fears, he tells me he also made some enquiries from undertakers about the possible state of our dearly departed. They told him that coffins and bodies in aerated granite sandveld conditions generally decompose very quickly and more than likely there would not be much left.

My spirits buoyed by such cheerful news, we pull up at the small family graveyard under the towering dome of Long Cross

Hill. Frik and Tiny hive off into the bush, barking for the sake of it. We get out and walk around the wrought-iron fence, there to keep the stock out. As with the house, Gus has ensured that the graves are well kept. There are seven in all lying in the shade of a towering blue gum tree, planted there fifty years ago by my grandfather. Three pairs demarcated neatly with round whitewashed river stones, and Rex's with its tall granite shard off to one side, apart from the others. The others have conventional marble headstones with inlaid lead lettering. Gus explains that only Rex's remains will be left behind, since he would have refused point blank to be buried in a church cemetery. I nod in agreement.

For the first time I realise the physical task at hand. It will be no mean feat exhuming these bones. Up until now, Gus has been vague as to how we will go about it. When I ask him, he replies, 'You and me. With pick and shovel.'

Not quite what I had in mind, to be honest. I had pictured at least a few of the farm workers labouring side by side. Singing as they shovelled in unison.

Gus reads my mind and laughs. 'Just you and me, boet. On our ownsome.'

'Christ, Gus, surely one or two of your workers are willing to make a few extra bob giving us a hand.'

'You know Ndebeles won't disturb the dead. That's why Rhodes is still buried in the Matopos, isn't it?'

'If no one's going to disturb them then why don't we just leave them in peace?'

'And how're we're going to visit these graves if those arsehole vets take over the farm? Think, professor. Use that academic head of yours, man!'

'But won't this be a sure sign to them that you're relinquishing the land?'

Gus pauses. 'Who knows what goes through those munts' heads, other than dagga smoke. All I do know is that this country's in a state of anarchy and things can happen, just like that.' He snaps his fingers. 'I don't see what other option we've got.'

'Shit, it's going to be one hell of a job. You mean to tell me you couldn't find anyone else to give us a hand? What happened to the concept of machinery? Haven't they heard of bloody excavators in this country?'

'I want us to do it. You and me. It's our job.'

'You're a glutton for punishment, Gus. Is having access to graves really that important? I mean, surely once the soul's gone ...'

Gus laughs, eyeing my rustic work attire sceptically. 'You'll rationalise your way out of anything, won't you? I'll do it myself, if you don't feel up to it.'

'I didn't say I wasn't up to it,' I say.

As Gus turns to go, I pause at the graves of my parents. The graves I have never seen. There is one headstone for the two of them. I suspect Gus composed the blunt epitah: *Together on Earth, Together in Heaven. Always remembered.* Closing my eyes, I pay belated respects. An image comes to mind of Joseph and Anna carrying Nan out the house and hiding under corrugated iron sheets behind the sheds. Surely Nan was bleeding heavily – how did they prevent a trail of blood? I shake my head, dispelling yet another question I don't want answered.

Gus whistles for the dogs. They come bounding back through the long grass. Frik's head is covered with blackjacks. We climb back in the Cruiser and drive down an overgrown track towards the cultivated fields along the river. Strewn with boulders and cut by dongas, the track is a test for any vehicle. Gus whistles away tunelessly as we inch our way along. He points at a small scattering of sheep in the distance. 'You'll never guess,' he says. 'I've been losing the odd sheep.'

'Stock theft?'

'Nah, a leopard.'

'You're kidding! I thought they were shot out long ago.'

'They're back. There's a big male who's staked out his territory here. Seen him a few times.'

'And you didn't grab your gun and blast him to kingdom come? What's come over you, Gus? You're not getting soft in your old age, are you?'

Gus smiles. 'I tell you something, boet, the first time I saw him I felt like I could've died right then and gone to heaven. He was just so bloody magnificent, man. It was like a sign things would come right one day.'

'Not Africa reclaiming itself?'

'The *right* Africa reclaiming itself.'

Finally, we reach the gondi and msasa strewn plain and make for the ploughed maize fields. The fields are deserted, it being Sunday, and as we drive along with the dogs running behind, Gus explains the deal he made with Ncube. Ncube has the use of most of the arable land along the river to grow maize and some legumes – about fifty acres under irrigation and two hundred under the plough. Gus gets a five percent commission on net cash crop proceeds plus ten percent milled produce for stockfeed. Aside from the land, Ncube gets the use of Gus's tractor and implements. The plan is that Ncube will, in a few years time, earn enough capital to buy his own farm, and in the meantime keep the veterans at bay. Gus points at the irrigated land where the maize stands about knee-high. 'Saxon knows his stuff. Unlike the bloody squatters who just wreck everything. He put in a bean crop there first and ploughed the haulms under to improve the humus and nitrogen content of the soil. Fertiliser's scarce these days. The river's down to a trickle but at least these irrigated mielies will survive.'

He gestures at the other rain-reliant fields, still lying fallow. 'There's still time to plant, if only this bloody drought would break. But he needs some decent rain first. If the weather would just play along, Saxon could make some money out of this.'

By the look of things, a pretty sweet deal for Ncube. But, as Gus says, it's a small price to pay to keep the farm.

'If you ask me, I don't know why he doesn't just boot you off the farm and take over the whole place,' I say. 'What could you do if he did? Everyone else is helping themselves, aren't they?'

'Not everyone, boet. Stealing farms is a privilege reserved only for those who kiss Mugabe's arse.'

'Is Ncube still an MDC member?'

Gus nods. 'Ja, Saxon's MDC. I am too, for that matter.'

I raise my hands and drop them, as though resting my case. That the Movement for Democratic Change, led by the fearless Morgan Tsvangirai, still exists in Zimbabwe is a source of wonder. In Robert Mugabe's eyes political opponents are not people to debate with across a parliament floor – they are mortal enemies. People to be ruthlessly harassed, intimidated and killed. Consequently, Tsvangirai and the MDC have borne the brunt of Zimbabwe's political violence in recent years.

Reading my thoughts, Gus says, 'The MDC is the only thing in this world with enough guts to stand up against Mugabe.

You bastards overseas have done nothing. You stand and watch while he murders and terrorises at will. And all these bloody countries around us, including South Africa, aid and abet his tyranny by turning a blind eye. Zimbabweans have no one to turn to except themselves. The only thing Mugabe fears is the MDC. That's what the farm invasions are all about – destroying the MDC's rural support base. The way I see it, boet, every Zimbabwean who is sick and tired of Mugabe and Zanu-PF – and, believe me, that means the bulk of the population – should feel duty-bound to join the MDC.'

'Sure, Gus, why don't you and Ncube just paint big targets on your foreheads instead? You really have a weird notion of self-preservation, don't you? Christ, its sheer bloody madness for both of you to be MDC when the farm – everything! – hangs in the balance. You're both insane!'

Gus chuckles. 'I wouldn't expect you to understand, Chicken-heart.'

We continue on along rutted tracks to the eastern boundary of the farm. We pass flocks of dusty, tired sheep nibbling at the bare ground. Gus shows me the herd of Herefords that must be dipped tomorrow. The thin beasts are gathered around a water trough fed by a windmill, the ground bare and sandy around them. The only healthy-looking animal we encounter is Gus's Hereford bull. Fenced off in a separate pasture, the bull, affectionately named Wellington, enjoys special rations of stock feed to keep him, as Gus says, 'on the job'.

There always used to be a few horses on the farm, mostly for the pleasure of my father and Angela who were excellent riders. Gus explains how, over the years, he continued to keep horses because Jessica and Lauren liked riding, and for when Angela came visiting. But with the drought he couldn't afford any unnecessary stock, and they were the first to go.

The land, generally, is in a pitiful state, blackened in parts by recent veld fires. The ground cover has almost been grazed down to the roots. Unless it rains soon, Gus says, he'll have to start getting rid of his stock. In my mind are the images of previous bad droughts. The river reduced to small ponds writhing with barbel, the emaciated cattle forlornly probing the mud with their tongues. God forbid. Eventually we stop at the gate along the eastern boundary that abuts the Nalatale Ruins Road, and wait for the dogs to catch up. Gus points out a broken fence where squatters from a neighbouring farm have stolen droppers and wire. He also points to where a row of gum trees planted by my grandfather (a eucalypt enthusiast) as a windbreak have been chopped down. In the distance we can see the squatter settlements on the denuded lands of our former neighbours. When the dogs appear Tiny has a slight limp, so Gus lets them up on the back of the Cruiser.

The sun starts to go down as we head back. We go past Rex's old hunting lodge down along the southern boundary, now just a ruin festooned with wild fig trees. It's almost dark by the time Gus stops at the workers' compound near the Fort Rixon Road. The compound consists of a dozen separate cement and corrugated iron dwellings and one long block of single rooms positioned around a communal kitchen. In the old days we had an average of forty workers on the farm's payroll. Gus explains that he currently has eleven men working for him. Ncube also has a team of workers staying at the compound, mainly women, but most of them go back to their homes in Gweru each weekend. Except for a flicker of light in one of the

48

dwellings, the compound seems deserted. Gus hoots and a man emerges from the lighted dwelling and comes over to the Cruiser. The dogs start growling and Gus shuts them up. The man greets Gus, 'Utshonile, Nkosi.'

'Sa'bona, Witness. Where are the others?'

The man, Witness, makes a drinking gesture with his thumb and names a shebeen on a nearby occupied farm.

'I hope they don't get too pissed, Witness. The cattle must be dipped tomorrow, first thing.'

'Yebo, Nkosi.'

Gus gets out and lifts a drum of Valvasen dip mixture off the back of the Cruiser. He hands the drum to Witness. 'You know how much to use, hey? Kuyadula. So don't waste it. Stir it in well, okay?'

'Yebo, Nkosi.'

As we drive off, Gus says, 'That's the new headman. They come and go these days. It's not a sought-after job, with the vets around.'

Back at the house, Gus decides to do the meat in the oven rather than go to the trouble of a braai. We are both tired and hungry. Gus has a couple of beers and I have a shot of whisky from the bottle I've brought along out on the veranda while the steaks are grilling. The night is cool and there is a massive spray of stars. A nightjar gives its long, gurgling call. Crickets sing. The dogs lie on the floor next to Gus, gazing at him with besotted eyes. Gus recalls those intimate times when my mother played the piano in the evenings, how the notes of Brahms and Chopin would seep off into the darkness, and how my father would sit there outside with a brandy in his hand, his eyes closed, listening. Gus gives a deep sigh.

'Sometimes when I'm here alone I can hear that music,' he says.

'Good to see some decent music actually rubbed off on you,' I reply. 'But I never figured you for a psychic, Gus.'

'I'm not. I can just hear it in my head, that's all.'

'A closet sentimentalist, then. Who was it who said the most barren of all mortals is the sentimentalist?'

Gus just looks at me with that lopsided grin. I shift in my chair, uncomfortable with his moment of weakness, and my ill-timed flippancy.

'Yes, that was a sweet time,' I say, placatingly. 'Sometimes it's too painful to think of it. Dad and Nan – bloody amazing that two people from such different walks of life could be so suited. God, to think Dad couldn't sing two notes in key!'

Gus nods. 'Ja, it was pretty special. Until Rex came along.'

There is a moment's silence before I reply. 'Yes, but even that didn't tear them apart. I don't think anything could.'

Gus just turns and stares out at the darkness.

I try to make light of it. 'Trust Rex! Now there's a bloke who knew how to enjoy life, hey? The original happy-go-lucky bachelor.'

'That's how we all liked to see him. The dreamer. The free spirit. I suppose that's how he liked to see himself. But he had his demons. Rex could never stand the present because it was filled with the reality of his loneliness. So he drank and womanised to escape the present. Dad once said it was the present that killed Rex – the emptiness of it.'

I glance at Gus, wondering what has prompted such uncharacteristic reflection. His eyes are in shadow, inscrutable. I revert to the safer ground of flippancy.

'I never figured you for a deconstructionist either, Gus.'

'What the hell is a deconstructionist?' he grunts.

'Someone who tears saints and heroes apart.'

'Rex was never a saint or a hero. Rex was Rex.'

When the steaks are ready we wolf them down with boiled potatoes, standing next to the stove in the kitchen. After some coffee we decide to get an early night. Gus rummages around for some bed linen and tells me to sleep in my old room down the passage. I shower and make my bed. As I untie the mosquito net above the bed, the phone rings. I can hear Gus answer. He shouts down the passage, 'It's Beth!'

I sprint to the phone.

'I've been trying to get through, but the lines are always busy,' Beth says. 'How are you, crazy man?'

'I'm fine, considering.'

'You do realise that digging up people's graves is unusual behaviour?'

'Everything's bloody unusual in this place.'

'You're crazy, Vaughn. Of all places in the world ... By the way, the university has been ringing me, wanting to know your whereabouts. Don't tell me you didn't bother telling them!'

'I'm on leave, Beth. It's none of their bloody business!'

'Anyway, when I told them I got the impression I'd just confirmed their worst suspicions – that they had a real nutcase on their payroll. They said to let you know they'll be taking out travel insurance for you, just in case. Pretty considerate, I'd say.'

'It's nice to know they're so concerned about my welfare. But don't you worry yourself over me, blessed one. I'm fine. How are you?'

'Oh, you know me, Vaughn. Nothing exciting like grave-digging expeditions happens in my life now that I'm rid of you!'

I laugh. 'That's good to hear. How's Mikey? I worry about him.'

'Mikey has choices only he can make. Don't beat yourself up too much about it. Having a kid in this day and age is like playing Russian Roulette. He knows you love him.'

'I can't help it, Beth. I keep thinking that maybe it could've been different. If we'd stayed together ...'

'I love you, Vaughn, but I'm realistic enough to know our marriage never had a snowball's chance in hell. Don't kid yourself now because of Mikey. Mikey was going off the rails long before we broke up. What he needs is an honest father. Someone who doesn't take all the blame.'

'You've always been too kind, Beth.'

'It's got nothing to do with kindness.'

'Are you sure everything's okay? I worry about you both, you know.'

She laughs. 'Everything's fine. Don't worry about us. Just do what you have to do in that godforsaken place and get back to civilisation in one piece, okay?'

Later, I lie in bed thinking of her. I remember how she loved hearing me talk about life on the farm, especially about how the women coped. Beth would have made a good farmer's wife, I'm sure. The trouble was I was never cut out to be a farmer. The thought of her, the thought of my loss, is almost too much to bear. I wonder at the injustice of life. That I could be blessed with such a generous woman, and end up not loving her enough.

*

More baggage. All families have their moments of separation. With us, it came suddenly and with great pain. When Gus brought it up out there on the veranda it took me completely by surprise. I had expected it to be dead and buried, never to be exhumed.

Like Gus and me, my father and Rex never got on. The farm should have been big enough for both of them, but it wasn't. They just could not see things eye to eye. When they were boys it was said they had to be parted with buckets of water, so ferocious were their battles. At school, Rex was lazy and disobedient, whereas Dad won academic colours and went on to study agriculture at Rhodes University. Rex smoked, my father didn't. Rex had a serious thirst for women and alcohol; my father remained faithful to one woman all his life and only drank too much when it was considered excusable – though, to be fair, excusable occasions were always rather frequent in Rhodesia.

They both went to war, serving in the same battalion in North Africa. Rex was wounded in the shoulder by shrapnel and returned home six months sooner than my father. When Dad got back it seemed they had finally grown to tolerate each other. The former rancour subsided and for some years there was a period of truce. They were brothers, of course, and somewhere deep inside them there lurked a guarded love. So they occasionally enjoyed a beer together at the club, and sometimes teamed up for darts or tennis, despite Rex being contemptuous of my father's muscular coordination.

This time of truce came to an end when my grandfather died. Their joint inheritance of the farm provided a real bone of contention. The arguments began again. My father was a good, scientific farmer, not given to any hare-brained schemes. Like my grandfather, he was well-respected in the district and had been recently elected Chairman of the Shangani Farmers Association, a rare honour for such a young man. He knew precisely the carrying capacity of a twelve thousand acre farm like ours. He was for prime Hereford and cross Tuli cattle (no more than one beast per fifteen acres) and Dorper sheep in the pastures and maize along the river, mostly for stockfeed. Tried and tested, practical and productive. No bullshit except that which fertilised the ground. Above all, my father was *qualified*. On the other hand, Rex's only academic certificates consisted of school report cards that implied that the tobacco industry would suffer a slump without his patronage. Dad often said that Rex's ideas amounted to pipe dreams or alcoholic halluci-nations. It was true; Rex had some unconventional ideas. One of them was to turn half the farm into a private game ranch. In recent years such ideas have become commonplace, but at the time everyone in the district thought he was mad. My father was not about to concede the labours of his forebears to such romantic notions, and the arguments were loud and bitter. But, as Rex pointed out, he was entitled to half the farm. He was prepared, he said, to take the hilly part of the property that was no good for farming anyway. He got as far as building a hunt-ing lodge near the southern boundary. He also purchased a lone rhino that flattened our fences in its quest for a mate, and a few buffalo that enjoyed the mixed-veld grazing as much my father's cattle did.

But this was all water under the bridge, as it might have seemed all too briefly to Rex when he got drunk one night at the Club and drove his fancy Chev Biscayne, the only such car in the district, off the bridge into the Shangani River. He was found the next morning in the crushed, half-submerged vehicle, nearly decapitated.

Rex's death was a hard thing to come to terms with because we all – my father included – loved him more than we realised. In fact, the whole district mourned, since it had lost one of its more colourful sons. People spoke affectionately of his many escapades. I'm sure, too, that quite a few women around these parts would have grieved privately, while displaying discreet indifference in front of their husbands.

He was buried in the family graveyard in a simple grave with a rough shard of granite as a headstone, according to his wishes. Reverend Davis, the local Anglican minister, said some kind words, despite the fact that Rex had been an avowed atheist. A big crowd of people from the district turned up. I remember how the birds that day seemed to sing in the trees with a special sweetness and everything seemed so bright and clear. After the service the visitors gave their condolences and left – Rex's old drinking cronies heading straight for the Club to give him a proper wake. Angela placed a branch of thorns on the grave among the already wilting flowers. He would have liked that, she said.

There was a heavy silence that evening as we sat at the dinner table. As we ate, our eyes kept straying to the photograph of Rex with his dead kudu on the wall. We were sad and frightened that death had overtaken us so unexpectedly. Then Dad tried to cheer us up by telling us about some of the things they got up to in Egypt during the war. Gus recounted how Rex had taught him to hunt, how they lay stoically in wait at waterholes on freezing winter mornings, cold and numb, swapping jokes.

Angela said she would miss Rex coming by in the evenings on his way to the Club – that was when he lived down at the lodge. We all remembered that. He would be driving either his Land Rover or the sleek wing-tailed Chev Biscayne. The Chev's back bumper had been dented by one of the gateposts at the Club, but aside from that it was in pretty good nick. His lady friends were very impressed by it, which was the main thing. There were some jokes going around then about the Chev's springs being shot, and not from the bad roads. It was cobalt blue in colour and Angela called it the Blue Bullet, a title Rex liked so much, he had it painted on the rear fender. Rex would help himself to a beer in the fridge and make himself at home on the veranda steps. Mostly he would still be in his work clothes and smelling of sweat, but sometimes he'd be dressed in longs and a sports jacket and be smelling of Old Spice; this would mean he had more refined interests for the evening than the usual beer-swilling company he was apt to keep. When Gus was little he'd always sit next to Rex, there on the steps. Sometimes Rex would pick him up and hold him above his head, laughing and teasing. I always envied Gus his special place with Rex.

Then my father did a strange thing. He started imitating Rex, the way he would precede a statement by clearing his throat. He assumed Rex's slightly arrogant, jaunty air, thrusting out his jaw and half closing his eyes as he spoke. He grinned lopsidedly. And for the first and only time in our lives, Dad looked liked Rex. He turned and winked at Nan, the way Rex did with the ladies. For a moment Nan sat transfixed. Then she burst into tears and ran from the room. Astonished, Dad got up and followed her. Angela, Gus and I sat at the table in miserable silence. I remember how bad it felt to know that nothing is perfect. After a while Dad came back. He stood there at his place at the table, looking down at his unfinished food. Then he looked at us, his eyes remote and tearful. He reached out and ruffled Gus's hair. Then he walked out into the night. We could hear Nan sobbing in the bedroom.

And that was the turning point, our moment of separation. Even though Dad loved Nan so much that he could never allow anything to come between them – not even Rex – things were never the same again. It was not long after this that Rhodesia's war started and Gus went away for nearly eight years to the army. Angela started her career as a wildlife painter which ultimately weaned her away from Hopelands. And, of course, I went down south to university and eventually to Australia.

We were all dispersed, dispatched ...

*

To add something more about Rex and the psyche of the Rhodesian male: Rex had also tried to teach me to hunt, but I lost interest after my first kill, an event that was meant to 'blood' me. Being blooded was a farm tradition started by my great-grandfather where all the Bourke boys would be anointed by the blood of their first kill. I was nine years old when my turn came. I'd been looking forward to it – at the time I wanted nothing more than to be admitted into the exclusive world of *real* men like Rex. Gus had already shot his first buck, a young kudu bull, and he wore the blood on his face for a whole day.

The debacle of the experience is forever etched in my memory. I shot an impala while it was drinking at a water hole, about eighty metres away. I fired in a kneeling position, resting my elbow on my knee, as Rex had taught me. But the rifle was too heavy and the sights wavered. I squeezed the trigger never-theless because I didn't want to disappoint Rex and Gus who were crouched behind me, watching. We heard the *thwack* of the bullet as it struck. The impala reared up, staggered a bit and fell. The sound of it bleating in agony made me lose my composure. I threw the rifle to the ground and ran over to where the gut-shot animal lay, horrified by what I had done. Stupidly, I tried to comfort it. Wild-eyed, bawling, it thrashed around on the ground trying to get to its feet. I started blub-bering. Behind me, I heard Gus laugh contemptuously and say, 'Ah, Vaughn! You big bloody sissy!' Then Rex came up and pulled me away from the impala. He gave me the rifle and told me to finish the job. Never leave an animal to suffer, he said. Put it out of its misery. He pointed to where I should shoot – at the heart. By this time the buck was just lying there looking at us, seemingly resigned to its fate. I finished the job, but ran away when Rex tried to smear blood on my face.

Afterwards, Rex was kind. These things happen, he said. Next time, get him first shot. There was no next time. I never went hunting again. Whereas Gus would clean and oil his guns with devotion each year, impatiently waiting for the hunting season, I always found an excuse to opt out. Rex treated my weakness, for that's all it amounted to, with a circumspect sen-sitivity. He never made an issue out of it, unlike Gus who teased me relentlessly. He said there was no shame in not being cut out for hunting. But there was shame in it. I had failed a crucial test. Farmers hunted; that's all there was to it. I knew my father wasn't partial to it, but even he, to satisfy the rituals demanded of Rhodesian men, went on the odd biltong shoot. Nothing alleviated the shame.

More to the point, my shame heightened the antagonism between Gus and me. I did what I could to repair the damage. Instead of playing rugby at school, I opted for target shooting. Targets were a different matter entirely. I became an excellent marksman, especially in pistol shooting. I won cups and certificates. Even Gus was no match for me when it came to targets. It was all to impress Rex, and to win back Gus's respect. With Gus it was never enough. For one thing, you did not trade rugby for target shooting.

*

We manage a fairly hearty breakfast of boerewors, fried eggs and coffee before sunrise – sustenance, as Gus puts it, for the 'big dig'. As we eat he turns on the radio to catch the BBC Africa news. He gives a derisory grunt when we hear that the Zimbabwe Council of Churches has met to discuss the crisis surrounding land seizures, but pricks up his ears when a statement issued by the Council is read out:

Land reform, universally agreed upon as a matter of utmost urgency, has been twisted into a fast-track to further the self-aggrandisement of the ruling elite. What should have improved the lot of every Zimbabwean is now viewed as irrevocably partisan, and is associated with disorder, violence and displacement. Collectively, all of this has left the average Zimbabwean on the verge of utter destitution and hopelessness. All of this points to a very obvious deficiency in the leadership and governance of our country. Those who have been entrusted with authority have abused it. The various arms of the state have become rotten with corruption, nepotism and self-interest. The law has become a farce, used only to further the interests of a selected few.

Gus licks his teeth under his lips and nods. 'Hmm ... didn't expect that. That Council is normally just a damp squib. Things must be getting pretty bad for them to speak that kind of lingo.'

After breakfast Gus shows me the 'contingency' coffins. Six of them, stacked in the tool shed. Simple rectangular boxes he made from Rhodesian teak salvaged from the floors of a derelict house in Shangani. They are beautifully constructed with dovetail joints, hand-planed and varnished. Each has a brass name-plate on the lid. He has lined the insides with canvas tacked neatly to the timber. A labour of love. Woodwork had been Gus's favourite subject at school. How proudly he used to bring his creations – bookshelves, a coffee table, that chair on the veranda with the broad armrests – back home in the holidays to present to my mother. It was his way of making up for the artistic gifts she so valued in Angela and me.

I don't know why he calls them contingency coffins since we are not, as he morbidly reminds me, expecting to find the originals intact. But I don't press the issue.

We load picks and shovels on the back of the Cruiser and set off into the sunrise. Me in my *Hard Yakka* gear, neat creases intact, Gus in his usual faded khakis and velskoens. I affect an air of nonchalance as we drive along, though I fear my capacity to manage what lies ahead.

First we stop at the dip. Everything is in full swing as we pull up near the holding pens. The early-morning calm of the country-side is rent as Witness and eight other men drive the bellowing cattle one by one into the dip with sticks and piercing whistles. The beasts plunge into the slimy trough, wild-eyed, and emerge dripping at the other end. I am reminded that cattle are not amply blessed with memory. Once a week they go through this routine; one would think they'd get used to it, yet each time they panic and resist anew.

Once the herd is through, Wellington makes a regal appearance at the edge of the dip. He bellows and snorts at the men jabbing at him with sticks. Finally, he makes the undignified plunge, clambers ponderously up the dip's ramp and is diverted into a separate holding pen.

As the sullen herd waits to be driven off into the pastures, I sit in the Cruiser while Gus talks with Witness and the men. One of them has a badly swollen eye. Another has his arm bandaged with a bloodied rag. Two are missing, apparently. Gus berates them: 'You fools! I told you not to go near that shebeen! No, but you have to think with your dicks, don't you? When will you learn, hey?'

The men look at the ground ruefully.

'And where are July and Goodwill?'

'Hambile,' one of the men says.

'Hambile? Where the fuck have they hambile?'

Witness mutters something I can't hear. Gus remonstrates further, then returns to the Cruiser, shaking his head. As we drive off, he fumes, 'Bloody munts! I told them to keep away from that fucking dive up the road. Trust them to get into a fight with some of Mtunzi's mob. Looks like two of them have gapped it now. Too scared to stick around in case the vets decide they could do with a stint of re-education. Sometimes I'd swear to Christ I'm dealing with bloody children here!'

Gus drives down along the river course to the cultivated fields. We pass a gang of women hoeing witch-weed out the furrows. Gus stops and asks for Ncube. A woman with a baby on her back points further down the river to a weir. We drive on and find Ncube fiddling with an old car engine that has been modified into an irrigation pump. His vehicle, a rusting yellow Opel panel van, stands nearby. Ncube, dressed in some bright orange overalls, pauses with a shifting spanner in his hand as we pull up.

'What's up, Saxon?' Gus says.

'Piston rings,' Ncube replies, eyeing me with a flat stare.

'Need any help?'

He shakes his head. 'Nearly finished.'

We wait in the Cruiser for him to finish. At first glance, Ncube seems an imposing man. Broad-faced with tribal scarring on his cheeks, greying hair and a sparse goatee beard. While not especially tall, he carries an authoritative bulk, especially around the midriff. As he works, his cell phone rings and he speaks for a few minutes, staring into the distance.

'Saxon and his bloody cell!' Gus scoffs. 'Big shot businessman!'

'Seems a sensible thing to have in this country,' I say.

'Ja? When you can get reception, maybe. But you wouldn't catch me dead with one of those things. Can't imagine anything worse than being contactable twenty-four hours a day.'

Finally Ncube finishes with the pump and comes ambling over. We climb out of the Cruiser and Gus introduces me as his cowardly brother who fled to Australia during the war – an introduction complete with a flapping of the arms and his stupid clucking. Ncube guffaws and shakes my hand in the peculiarly gentle way Africans do.

'Hau, inkukhu!' he says to me with a wink. 'It is good to know there is someone with brains in your family, Angus.'

'How're the mielies, Saxon?' Gus asks.

Ncube gestures at the fifty acres under irrigation. 'These are surviving. But if there's no rain before Christmas to fill the river I am in trouble. But I think it will come.'

'Jesus, I hope so. I'll be in the shit too if it doesn't.'

Ncube points at the other fallow fields. 'Rain is our master, umngani wami. Without it I can forget about breaking that land.'

Gus shrugs. 'That's the chance you take with farming. Sometimes you win, sometimes you lose.'

'I don't like to lose, umngani.'

Ncube turns to me with an innocent expression. 'Tell me, Vaughn. Why does your prime minister – Mr Howard, is it not? – speak poorly of Zimbabwe?'

I flounder around for a diplomatic answer. 'It's not Zimbabwe he doesn't like, it's your president, unfortunately.'

Ncube looks shocked. 'But how is it possible to not like our president?'

There is an uncomfortable silence. Then he gives a great guffaw and slaps me on the back.

Gus smiles at my discomfort. 'Come up for supper tonight, Saxon. Joseph and Anna are cooking a roast.'

Ncube's eyes light up at the prospect, but then he shakes his head. 'Joseph and Anna will chase me from the house, Angus. To them, I am still a kaffir.'

Gus laughs. 'Don't worry about Joseph and Anna. I've been educating them about the strange new ways of Zimbabwe. It's taking time, but I'm making progress.'

We take our leave and continue on to the graveyard. Gus drums the steering wheel and whistles. Every so often he chuckles to himself. It seems Ncube has brightened his day.

'He seems a nice enough bloke,' I say.

Gus nods. 'He's a character, all right. A cut above the rest. People with a sense of humour are scarce these days.'

'Seems to be doing a good job with the mielies.'

'He's doing more than we ever did with that land along the river. The way I look at it, if we get to keep the farm *and* get a bit of stockfeed out of it, we're winning.'

We park in the shadow of a rock overhang near the grave-yard. Gus hands me a pick and shovel and I follow him through the wrought-iron gate. We stand for a while in the shade of the big gum tree. The sounds of the countryside are clear and res-onant – the distant lowing of cattle, the muted shriek of insects, the long bubbling call of a dove from a bushwillow thicket nearby. I shuffle uncomfortably when Gus abruptly removes his cap and bows his head in silent prayer. I'd forgot-ten his tenuous religious streak. He crosses his heart when he finishes. Then he takes off his shirt and says, 'Well, boet, we better get started – they're not going to dig themselves out. I reckon we do Vaughn and Catherine first. I think they'll be the hardest.'

'Depends on how you look at it,' I reply.

Gus gives me a dry look. 'Don't get deep on me now, boet. I mean it'll be a job just finding them. You ready? You look a bit grave, man.'

'You're a comedian, Gus.'

'You do Catherine. I'll do your namesake, okay?'

And so we begin. First, we remove the whitewashed stones and pile them neatly behind the weathered headstones. Then, side by side, we start digging. I keep my shirt on, lest I attract remarks about my physique not helpful to my self-esteem. As I heft my pick, I try to remember when in the last twenty years I have done any manual labour – serious labour – but can't think of a single instance. On the domestic front, I managed to convince Beth that I was not cut out for housework or gardening. Of course, Beth knew exactly why I was not cut out for it – it hadn't done me any good growing up with servants, she said. But she is one of those noble souls who is never happy without working their fingers to the bone, so I magnanimously kept the peace by allowing her to do just about everything that involved physical toil. Occasionally, if she was feeling poorly, I mowed the lawn or did some repairs to the house or car, but generally, manual labour remained outside my sphere of influence. After we were divorced, I once stuck to a fitness regimen for all of three weeks – this involved a modest daily jog and some light weights. It came to an end when I strained my shoulder doing bench presses. I also put my back out the first time I tried an aerobics video. After that I convinced myself that physical exercise was not conducive to an artistic temperament. Artists could not create in a state of wellbeing was my theory. The irony that my creative well was already dry never dawned on me.

I manage to keep pace with Gus for about ten minutes, then stop, ostensibly to unbutton my shirt and to wipe the fog from my glasses. The sun seems like a weight on my shoulders. A squadron of flies drones around my head. I pour with sweat and my hands tremble as I fiddle with my buttons. I feel blisters budding on my palms already. This, I realise, is going to be a nightmare. Gus ignores me. He is sweating too but continues at a steady pace, thumping his pick into the ground and grunting as he levers up the soil. The ground is not hard but I manage only another twenty minutes and then am forced to sit down, feeling faint and nauseous. Once again, I lament my appalling physical condition. As my head lolls forward onto my chest I catch the rank onion stench of my armpit and recoil in disgust. Thankfully, Gus keeps on without looking at me.

'There's some water on the back of the Cruiser,' he says.

After a short rest I get up and help myself to a long drink from the plastic water container on the Cruiser. I do the breathing exercises demonstrated by the attractive female instructor in the aerobics video, the only part that stuck in my mind. Then, dragging my feet like a felon approaching a flogging, I return to Catherine's grave and recommence my digging. A blister on the heel of my palm chafes and bursts – the first of a multitude, I suspect. My stiff new shirt is like sandpaper against my skin. My nipples are stinging. I feel a growing resentment towards Gus. That he could have conceived of such an idiotic plan! What is it about some people that they must insist on a solid dose of suffering to go with everything in life?

By noon I am a spectator. I lie on my back, my head propped up by the gum tree, watching as Gus toils in the sun. I barely have enough strength to wave the flies from my face. My body seems to want to sink into the ground, to become part of this hallowed burial site. Without pausing in his digging Gus speculates aloud as to whether he should have made an extra coffin.

His rhythmic motions make me drowsy and eventually I nod off. Amid the cooing of doves I dream briefly of the Newcastle beach Beth, Michael and I used to visit on Sundays in happier times, before my life began its downward spiral. I see Beth and Michael bodysurfing gentle waves. Michael laughs ecstatically as he clings to her back.

I am woken by the sound of Gus throwing the implements on the back of the Cruiser. As he buttons up his shirt, he tells me he's decided to call it a day because he forgot to get the roast out of the freezer for tonight's dinner. Food has always played an influential role in Gus's daily itinerary. From my prone position I note he has made fair progress with my great-grandfather's grave, whereas I have only scratched the surface, so to speak, of Catherine's. Painfully, I get to my feet and limp back to the Cruiser.

Gus eyes me balefully. 'I've seen some pathetic sights in my time ...' he says.

*

Back at the house I am so stiff and sore I can do no more than sit on the veranda and watch as Gus gets the meat from the freezer and leaves it in a patch of sunlight on the veranda floor to thaw. I'm instructed to keep the dogs away from it. Then he goes down to the vegetable garden and returns with a pumpkin, a few potatoes and some green beans. Joseph and Anna arrive. They don aprons and immediately set about preparing the vegetables. Anna shakes her head at the sight of the leg of lamb lying on the floor near the slavering dogs. She retrieves it and puts it in the oven at a low heat.

There is a slight breeze and it's pleasantly cool on the veranda. I debate whether to get a book and at least look intelligently engaged or simply to throw pride to the wind and enjoy a short siesta, when, in a wild cacophony of barking and scraping paws, the dogs charge off down towards the security gate. Startled, I crane my neck to see a man standing there holding an empty plastic container.

I'm about to raise myself from the chair when Gus comes hurrying past and goes down to the gate. He silences the dogs and a short discussion ensues. Then he opens the gate and beckons the man inside. They walk up the drive towards the house. The man is short and thickset. He wears a pair of black-rimmed glasses, a slightly-too-large beige jacket, new stone-washed jeans and a pair of joggers. Joseph comes to the door. When he sees the man he exclaims, 'Aibo!' and scuttles back inside.

As they pass the veranda I can see the man's jowls sweating in the heat. He sees me and raises his hand in greeting, saying in cultured English, 'Enjoying the shade? Splendid view, isn't it?'

Returning his wave, I reply, 'Yes, certainly better than being out in the sun.'

The man nods. 'As they say, only mad dogs and Englishmen go out in the midday sun ...' He fakes a rueful expression. 'But then that makes me the mad dog, doesn't it?'

He laughs loudly.

Gus glances at me and raises an eyebrow. As they continue towards the sheds, Joseph and Anna appear timidly at the door.

'Kwenze njani?' I ask them. 'What's going on? Who is that man?'

'That is Mtunzi,' Joseph replies.

'What does he want here?'

'Angazi,' Joseph says, ushering Anna back inside. 'I don't know.'

I watch as Gus and Mtunzi disappear into one of the sheds. It astonishes me that despite his modern wardrobe and impeccable speech, the overwhelming impression I have of Mtunzi is drabness. There seems nothing special about him – no hint of menace, no deranged psychopathic glint in his eye. His sweating jowls suggest a life more attuned to that of an indolent government bureaucrat than violent henchman. And yet, as Joseph and Anna have amply demonstrated, he instils fear. It makes me wonder how such an unremarkable physical specimen could wreak such havoc in the world. But then you could say the same about his president. Havoc breeds in drab men.

Eventually Gus and Mtunzi emerge from the shed. The plastic container Mtunzi is carrying is full of petrol. They appear to be chatting amicably as they climb into the Cruiser and drive off down the road. Twenty minutes later, Gus returns.

'That was the illustrious Victor Mtunzi,' he says, stomping up the stairs.

'So I gather,' I reply. 'He had Joseph and Anna scuttling around like frightened mice.'

Gus shakes his head and laughs. 'The bastard ran out of petrol just down the road. These vets are incredible, man. No shame, I tell you. One minute they're threatening to kill you and take your land, the next they're begging favours!'

'I'm surprised you complied.'

'Just doing what I can to be neighbourly, boet. Not much choice in the matter, I'm afraid.'

'What's with the hoity-toity English? Mtunzi doesn't come across as your run-of-the-mill country African.'

'Country African? He's a bloody town munt. Born and bred in Bulawayo. They reckon he's got a degree in political science or something. I dunno how true that is, but the obvious point is he knows sweet fuck-all about agriculture. But then farming was never his business here, was it?' Gus sniffs the air. 'By Jesus, that roast smells good! Man, I could eat a bloody horse! Let's grab a shower and crack a cold beer – how's that for a plan?'

'Sounds pretty good to me.'

Gus gives me a wry look. 'Spoken like a man who's done a hard day's graft.'

We are settling into a beer on the veranda when, just as the sun starts to set behind the hills across the plain, Ncube's yellow van arrives in front of the house in a cloud of exhaust smoke and dust. The dogs start their infernal barking and circle the van. Gus yells at them and they slink off around the house. Ncube goes to the back of the van and hauls out a crate of Zambezi Lager. As he comes up the stairs, Gus rebukes him for having gone to the trouble, since there is plenty of beer in the fridge. 'Always better to be safe than sorry, umngani,' Ncube replies. He sets the crate down on the veranda floor while Gus goes off to fetch him a cold bottle. We can hear Joseph and Anna fussing around in the kitchen and Anna berating Gus for associating with someone of Ncube's ilk. Ncube cackles, 'Hau! That Anna! She still belongs to Queen Victoria!'

Gus returns with Ncube's beer and we sit back, enjoying the sunset and the evening sounds. The river lies like a strand of golden hair across the muted plain below. The weaver birds are roosting down along its banks, and the doves are calling. The land exudes a sweet fecund smell. I am moved by the familiarity of it. I recall the evening ritual where the family would gather out here. How my father would show off his knowledge of the bush by identifying each bird sound. How my mother sat next to him playing Solitaire on a small card table, quietly revelling in his love of the land.

My body aches, every joint, every muscle. Ordinarily I am a whisky drinker, but the cold beers are doing the trick after today's exertions. I can feel the alcohol doing its work, spreading through my veins, soothing, numbing. As the darkness deepens, the land, fringed with just a slither of light along the western horizon, assumes a brooding sublimity, reminding me of the dark-red paintings of Rothko, my favourite Abstract Expressionist. Those heroic, yet tragic depictions of the ineffable. Gus and Ncube are engaged in some banal hale-hearty banter about Ncube's personal affairs, which I gather are somewhat chaotic. It seems he is an inveterate womaniser; he has two wives and a gaggle of mistresses who by his account have transformed his hometown of Gweru into a theatre of war. Their manipulative offensives to undermine each other have so exasperated Ncube that he prefers to spend most of his time at large. Since his deal with Gus he has been renting an old house in Shangani near the post office, leaving his spouses and lovers to their own devices.

'I tell you, umngane wami, you are my saviour!' Ncube laughs. 'I can live in peace in Shangani, far away from the quarrels.'

'I'm your saviour and you are mine,' Gus replies. 'Maybe we should start a religion. I bet there's some easy money in that!'

71

Somehow the conversation, spoken mostly in SiNdebele, switches from messianic interventions to the problem of blood circulation and impotence. Gus informs us that he refrains from wearing underpants at least three days a week to 'keep things shipshape'. Ncube seems mightily impressed and loosens the crotch region of his orange overalls. From there we move to the problem of testicular cancer. Gus has read something about men carrying cell phones in their trouser pockets. Alarmed, Ncube retrieves his and puts it on the floor out of harm's way. From there we move to the subject of dogs. Ncube says a friend of his is selling some bull terrier pups and that he can get one cheap for Gus, if he's interested.

'No thanks, Saxon,' Gus replies. 'With things as they are I'm not taking on any new dogs right now. But talking of dogs, we had a visit from a mad one this afternoon. Mtunzi himself.'

Ncube raises his eyebrows. 'Mtunzi?'

'Dropped in this afternoon to scrounge some petrol – his bakkie ran out just down the road. No problem. Just ask the umLungu umlimi. Today I ask a favour, tomorrow I steal your land.'

Ncube shakes his head. 'Inyoka! Mtunzi crawls on the ground, like the snake! It's impossible for him to feel disgrace. In this he is no different from his friends in the government. All thieves in stolen suits. A disgrace to Africans, yet they are immune to shame. They steal until everything is finished. They steal even from their own comrades.'

'Own comrades?' I say. 'I thought this was all about Zanu-PF feathering its nest.'

'No honour among thieves, boet,' Gus says. 'I'll give you just one example. The government had more than a billion dollars stashed away in what was called the War Victims Compensation Fund. This fund was meant to help out the thousands of genuine veterans – the very people who had fought to put Zanu-PF in power. And Mugabe's thieves couldn't even keep their hands off that. Can you believe it, man, this money – and I'm talking about when the Zim Dollar was still worth something – just disappeared into the pockets of government cronies, henchmen and their families. Stolen, looted.'

Ncube grunts with disgust. 'And what does Mugabe do? He bankrupts the whole country by just printing out more money which he throws at the veterans as compensation. A golden handshake of $50 000 to every veteran plus a $2 000 monthly pension. Overnight the Zim Dollar crashes. Just after liberation our currency was stronger than the US Dollar. Now, twenty years later, it's worth nothing. Now you need a lorry full of Zim Dollars to buy one US Dollar. So what does our great leader do? He bangs the old war drums. He blames all the problems he has created on the whites, the Asians and the MDC. He blames Britain and America. He tells people like Mtunzi to seize the property of whites. First the farms. Then it will be the businesses – already they've started on the businesses. And then he will start on the urban poor, because they are the MDC's core supporters. Like Pol Pot he will destroy their homes, their livelihoods, and drive them into the country. You mark my words.'

Ncube holds out his big stubby hands in a helpless gesture.

'How does Mugabe get away with it?' I ask. 'I'm amazed he has any grassroots support at all.'

'He has no support,' Ncube says. 'If there was a proper free and fair election tomorrow, Mugabe and his government would be gone. No doubt about that. Mugabe's power comes from terror and intimidation. The first principle of his government is terror. Mugabe can only conceive of power as something attained by force. The second is theft. Once in power, you just take everything for yourself, as though it is your entitlement. I tell you, Vaughn, it's beyond belief what this government does!'

I turn to Gus. 'If the situation's so bleak, how the hell can you even contemplate staying on the land? It's ridiculous, Gus!'

Gus shrugs and takes a deep swig of beer. 'The fact is, there is a black man running this farm. Hey, Saxon? You're the nkosi here.'

Ncube smiles and raises his beer.

'Come on, Gus! How long do you think this little ruse is going to work? You don't seriously believe those veterans down the road are falling for it?'

'It's worked so far.'

'But for how long? The veterans may be thugs, but they're not stupid.'

Ncube raises a stubby finger. 'Ah, but I should correct you, Vaughn. Those vultures down the road are not veterans. Ask your brother. He is a veteran. I am a veteran. And you, Vaughn, you are a veteran?'

'That's not the point, Saxon ...'

'I told you he was a bloody hippy peacenik, Saxon!' Gus pipes in. 'Chicken lickin' KFC, remember? Colonel Saunders' choice.'

'Aheh!' Ncube cackles. 'Henny Penny!'

Both bray with inane laughter. If it were not for the difference in skin colour you would swear it was Gus and Ncube

74

who were the brothers. Sadly, I realise there is a paltry limit to this pair's ability to maintain an intelligent conversation. I wait patiently until the jokers have had their fun. Listening to these two you would never think Zimbabwe was in perilous straits.

'That's right,' I say. 'Fiddle while everything burns around you. But tell me, Saxon. Right now, can you honestly say the farm is safe from this man Mtunzi?'

Ncube shrugs. 'I cannot say. Mtunzi is a hard man. He likes violence. I have spoken to the local police commanders and for now I think it is safe. But everything can change. Tomorrow is a different day. Mtunzi is unpredictable.'

'It's a dumb question, professor,' Gus says. 'Nothing's safe in this bloody country. While this government's in power, nothing will ever be safe.'

'Which is precisely my point,' I say.

But Gus ignores me and turns to Ncube. 'You see what you bastards did bringing that fool Mugabe into power!'

Ncube laughs. 'I fought for Nkomo, umngane, not Mugabe.'

'Nkomo would've been worse!'

'No! Nkomo would've been like Abraham Lincoln!'

'Bullshit! He'd have been just like Mugabe. Waging war against his fellow countrymen!'

'Well, Lincoln waged war against his countrymen, didn't he? No, no, Angus. You're wrong about Nkomo. He would've cared for the downtrodden. He would've loved his neighbour and cherished the children.'

'Cherished the children – what crap! He was just another bloody terrorist, man, like Mugabe. Just like you, Saxon. You're lucky we never slotted you.'

This brings out a great guffaw from Ncube and the two
trade some more war insults, leaving me with serious doubts as
to whether I will be getting any sense out of either of them
tonight. We continue to drink. I grow bloated from the beer
and switch to my whisky. I feel the alcohol going straight to my
head. Somewhere a tiny voice urges caution. But a recklessness
has overcome me. I feel a sudden desire to let go. Since I
arrived I've felt completely out of my depth in this mad world
where men make jokes while everything falls apart around
them. Ncube takes out a pack of cigarettes and offers them
around. Never a smoker, Gus declines. I've given up for a year
and have every intention of shaking my head, but to my sad
amazement, I reach out and take one.

Soon I've become quite hearty myself, quick with witticisms
and subtle innuendo which, to be frank, fly above the heads of
my companions. I'm filled with wonder at the phenomenon of
male camaraderie, forgetting that it normally fills me with
revulsion. When I attempt to express this wonder in words, in
a monologue complete with the pedantic gesticulations of the
long-term academic, Gus fixes Ncube with a stare and raises
an eyebrow. Joseph interrupts to announce that dinner is
ready. We go through to the dining room. My body feels lithe
and supple – an hour ago I was so stiff I could hardly walk.
We sit down to the roast lamb and vegetables and a gooseberry
pie for pudding, done to perfection. Nostalgia is a mysterious
affliction. The familiar smell and taste of the meal bring tears
to my eyes and I struggle to swallow with the lump in my
throat – such are the warm memories it conjures up. Gus,
immune to such sensibilities, continues his superficial banter
with Ncube. They consume more beer; I stick with my whisky.

At one point Gus suggests opening a bottle of wine to go with the meal, but since there are no women at table to nitpick about being cultured, the motion is voted down. Ordinarily, I like a glass of wine with a meal, but now such niceties seem of little consequence. The mood becomes increasingly jovial. I am impressed by the relationship between Gus and Ncube. They speak with the familiarity of old friends. I ask them where they met.

This brings a brief silence to the table.

'We go a long way back,' Ncube says. 'Not so, Angus?'

'Ja, it's a long story,' Gus replies. 'Too complicated to explain now. Don't get serious on us now, professor.'

'I'm not being serious. It's just that your friendship is intriguing. Male camaraderie is something ... I don't know ... something really, really *special*. Men find it so hard to express love ...'

Gus gives Ncube the arched-eyebrow look. 'You haven't turned into a poofter in Australia, have you, boet?'

Ncube gives another great guffaw. 'Just don't ask me to marry you, Vaughn. I have enough troublesome wives to think about!'

Such is the woeful level of my companions' repartee. I resign myself to the dreary fact that nothing of a sensitive nature will be under discussion tonight. Gus and Ncube laugh and gabble on like boys. At one point Ncube's phone goes off and he conducts another more serious exchange (something to do with the price of goats) while staring up at the msasa rafters. Gus, having regressed to a child, jabs him in the ribs, trying to make him laugh. Then Joseph and Anna come through and take their leave. I rise like a gushing tide and give Anna an affectionate hug, thanking them profusely. Gus rolls his eyes in despair. Old Joseph laughs. Anna wags her finger at Ncube, who is pocketing his phone – having forgotten its carcinogenic potential, no doubt.

'You see! You have corrupted this boy already!' she admonishes him.

'That fifty-year-old boy needs no help getting corrupted,' Gus says.

'Forty-eight,' I correct him.

Ncube, a picture of innocence, gives a plaintive laugh. 'Ai, Mama! I am just a lamb in the company of lions!'

'Hah! A hyena, more like it,' Anna snarls. 'Angus, you must watch this man!'

The old people depart. We can hear them jabbering away all the way to the security gate. Gus says, 'Well, who's for coffee?'

I roar with laughter, before realising he is being serious. Whereupon I reproach him for being a piker, as Australians might describe a man of timid disposition. So we trundle back to the veranda for what Gus optimistically calls a 'nightcap'. He goes down to his car and puts on some music, a Percy Sledge tape, and turns it up loud. *When a Man loves a Woman* ploughs like a ruptured oil tanker through the African night. My whisky runs out and I switch back to beer. My earlier euphoria is at the mercy of an outgoing tide. I drink more in a frantic race to save it, but it slips further and further from my grasp. Once we finish Gus's stocks we delve into Ncube's crate of Zambezi Lager. When that is finished we drink the bottle of wine Gus had debated opening at table. I fail to notice that the nightcap has become a huge sombrero, and that I am wearing it. There comes a point where I need to close one eye to avoid seeing double. Gus has changed the music to John Denver. To the childish ditty about Grandma's feather bed, I attempt an Irish jig, similar to those practised by the *Riverdance* troupes, arms held stiffly at the sides. Ncube guffaws and claps his hands. He has to stretch to catch me as I stumble and sprawl headlong. Gus shakes his head and laughs, more than a little surprised by my state. But he gets quite stroppy when I piss over the veranda wall into his beloved flower garden below – a bit rich, one would think, considering his own urinary extravagances. However he makes amends by finding an old bottle of sherry somewhere, once the wine is finished. Next, I engage Gus in an arm-wrestling match on the floor, apparently at my own instigation. When he slams my arm back in a split second he looks at Ncube in total amazement, as though his opponent were at best a sickly child. We try again, with the same result. Ncube wipes tears from his eyes as we resume our seats. And then, as though a hypnotist snapped his fingers, Gus passes out. One minute we're shooting the breeze, the next Rip Van Winkle is snoring in his chair. Disappointingly, Ncube takes this as a cue to call it a night. A dismal melancholy overwhelms me. I scoff at the drinking capacity of the two of them, the great soldiers of yesteryear. I give Ncube a solemn lecture on the dangers of drunk-driving and suggest he sleeps over, but he declines, saying it's no trouble to drive to his place in Shangani.

'Watch out for breathalysers, Saxon,' I slur.

He gives me a puzzled look. 'Breathalysers? Don't worry, umngane. There are no breathalysers in Shangani.'

Then he says a strange thing, as he gets up to go.

'Better to leave him outside to sleep. Outside he sleeps quietly.'

He goes inside and returns with a blanket and pillow. He

covers Gus with the blanket and puts the pillow under his head. He pats his unconscious form affectionately. Then he gives me what is left of his pack of cigarettes and leaves. I smoke and drink alone and don't remember going to bed.

*

A deluge of drunken dreams, all but one of Australia. In this dream – the exception – I am waiting at Shangani Station, a suitcase at my feet. It's dusk and the platform is deserted. I grow fearful. The surrounding bush is filled with shining eyes. Animals grunt and roar. A train approaches through the gloom – an old Rhodesian Railways steam locomotive pulling a single carriage. The carriage is bedecked with Zanu-PF flags and slogans and emits a bright blue glow and the sound of disco music. I wave frantically; the train slows and squeals to a stop beside me. The carriage door opens. As I heave my suitcase aboard I see Robert Mugabe and Ncube seated at a table in the centre of the carriage, arm wrestling. Ncube appears to be winning. Mugabe's hand sizzles as it is forced back onto a lighted candle. He rants and raves but cannot gain the upper hand. Behind them a party is in full swing. An entourage of fat bodyguards are bopping to the music, their white shirts brilliant in the ultraviolet light.

I hesitate and the carriage door closes. The train departs and I am left behind, minus my suitcase. Alone with the beasts that grunt and roar ...

*

I wake to the phone ringing. It takes me a while to register where I am. Somehow I have managed to sleep on my back on the floor with my legs up on the bed. An extinct cigarette butt still lies wedged between my burned fingers. One of the dogs, Frik, is lying next to me, methodically licking his testicles. Vaguely it dawns on me that I am in agony.

Down the passage I hear Gus answer the phone and talk to Jenny. I gather Angela has arrived in Harare and will be catching a connecting flight to Bulawayo later this morning.

Gus appears in the doorway, looking infuriatingly well. He feigns a kick at Frik and chases him outside. 'Go on! Voetsek, you mangy bastard! Christ, Vaughn, why'd you let him inside, man? That bloody Frik. Give him half a chance and he thinks he's lord of the manor.'

I just shield my eyes from the light and groan.

'Man, you look like shit,' Gus says. 'What happened to you last night?'

'I don't know. Probably something psychosomatic.'

'Psychosomatic? Your parachute didn't open, more like it. Quite a show you put on for us, twinkle toes. Let's get moving, professor. Angela's here.'

'I heard.'

'Keen on a bit of breakfast? Fried egg or something?'

'For Christ sake, Gus. Don't kick a man when he's down.'

I speak with the sad bravado of a loser. Last night's life and soul. Gus laughs and walks off, whistling merrily. I get unsteadily to my feet and drag myself off for a shower, sick and disgusted. I stand head bowed in the shower as though on a scaffold, wincing as last night's memories shuffle into view, one by one, like shabby conspirators bent on apportioning blame.

81

My drunken impropriety mortifies me. In particular, nasty little flashes of that Irish jig keep jabbing at my conscience. What is it about this dreadful place that has turned me into a buffoon? Like all reluctant clowns I fear ridicule more than anything else. Surely any deference Gus or Ncube may have had for my professional standing has been laid waste by last night's spectacle. Yes, the clown paint will not be coming off my face in a hurry, I fear.

I patch up the blisters and burns on my hands with band aids and cotton wool. I place two large round band aids over my chafed nipples before dressing again in yesterday's work attire that now smells quite disagreeable. Gus is in the kitchen. He has already cooked himself breakfast, washed the dishes and cleaned up last night's debris. With Gus I have always felt manifestly inadequate in virtually every male pursuit, but it is a new experience to also lag behind in the world of domesticity. A cup of coffee and a piece of toast do little to improve my outlook on life.

I'm not looking forward to what will be a long, complicated day, wary as I am of the malevolent devils who govern the netherworld of the hangover and pride themselves on unexpected torments. After Gus has fed the dogs, we climb into the Cressida and set off back to Bulawayo. Angela's plane gets in around ten-thirty, so there is plenty of time. Gus rummages around among his tapes and finds a collection of Kris Kristofferson ballads. We are immersed in maudlin songs of wasted lives, lost love and hangovers.

We drive without talking. Morbidly, I gaze at the passing countryside through my sunglasses, as Kris drones on about freedom being nothing left to lose – a depressingly apt observation, considering. I settle back in the seat and close my eyes, hoping a few minutes' sleep might soothe my nagging headache. But, sadly, there is no rest for the wicked. Not long after we cross the bridge, I hear Gus curse. Ahead of us three men are standing in the road, waving the car down. Gus slows down. I ask who the men are.

'Bloody vets,' Gus mutters. 'Let me do the talking, okay?'

Gus pulls up alongside the men. 'Sakubona, amadoda,' he greets them cheerfully. 'How are you today? Uya ngaphi?'

The three stare at us before one of them sporting a soiled white T-shirt emblazoned with *The Second Chimurenga* and carrying a battered woman's handbag steps forward and asks for a lift to the Gerbers' farm. He seems friendly enough, so Gus nods and gives a backward gesture with his thumb. They climb in the back of the Cressida and we drive on. From the reek of alcohol that eclipses my own, I surmise they spent the night at the infamous shebeen sowing their wild oats, which I imagine is probably as agricultural as these farmers will ever get. Only the man in the T-shirt seems inclined to speak. His friendly demeanour appears to have had a short life span.

'Stop the music,' he says, obviously in sympathy with his two comrades, one of whom is holding his head. Coincidentally, Kris is groaning about having no way to hold *his* head that didn't hurt. For a second I think, yes, there *are* universals (be they unsavoury) that unite all men.

Gus stops the tape. He catches the man's eyes in the rear-view mirror. 'You don't like Kris Kristofferson? You don't know what you're missing, my friend. What music do you like? Maybe I can brighten your day.'

The man just stares back with bloodshot eyes.

'What's your name, indoda?' Gus asks.

'I am Terror Yengwa.'

'Terror Yengwa, hey? That's a big name. I'm Angus Bourke. Your friendly neighbour.'

'I know who you are, Bourke. You are the umLungu who hides behind Ncube.'

'No one's hiding behind anyone,' Gus says. 'Ncube's my boss. I work for him. And you, Mr Yengwa? Where do you come from? I haven't seen you around these parts before.'

Ignoring the question, Yengwa glances at me. 'Who are you?'

'He's my brother, Vaughn Bourke,' Gus replies.

'Does your brother not have a tongue?'

I look back at Yengwa, slightly unnerved by his belligerent stare and mocking tone. 'I am visiting,' I say.

'Visiting? From where?'

'Australia.'

'You must go back to Australia.'

'I intend to.'

'And take your brother with you. He has no place here.'

'It's a free country,' Gus says with a smile. 'Our wonderful president has said so, hasn't he? We are all brothers under the skin.'

'It's a free country for Zimbabweans. Not foreigners like you.'

'That's strange. Last time I looked at my passport it said I was Zimbabwean.'

'You belong in Britain.'

'Thank you for correcting my mistake. I can see there is a place for you in the passport office.'

Yengwa gives Gus a bleak stare, unimpressed with his sar-
casm. We are silent for a while, then Yengwa turns to me again.
'Australia? I know Australia. You are like Britain. You make
trouble for Zimbabwe, not so?'

'I'm just a tourist. I don't know anything about politics.'

'Tourist? Tourists must pay for the privilege to stay in
Zimbabwe. Do you have forex?'

'What?'

'He means foreign exchange,' Gus says. 'He's angling for a
bonsella. Tell him you've got plenty – back in Australia.'

Feeling decidedly paranoid, I pat my pockets to indicate they
are empty. Yengwa regards me sceptically and points to the
slight bulge in my shirt pocket. I take out my passport and
show it to him. He reaches over and takes it. He flips through
it, studies my photograph with an officious air, then puts it in
the incongruous crocodile skin handbag beside him.

'Hey, what are you doing?' I ask, embarrassed by the nervous ring to my voice. 'I must have my passport.'

Yengwa gazes nonchalantly out of the window.

'You say I must go back to Australia. How am I supposed to
go back without my passport?'

Yengwa smiles. 'Don't worry, Mr Bourke, I will keep it safe
for you.'

Now his comrades are watching with interest. They laugh
when Yengwa resumes his nonchalant gaze out of the window.

'You have no right to take my passport,' I say. 'Give it back
to me.'

'Oh, you are giving orders now? I must remind you, Mr
Bourke, this is not Australia. You must treat the citizens of
Zimbabwe with respect.'

'I'm not giving orders. I'm just asking for my passport back.'

My voice has a silly, frantic ring to it. Yengwa laughs. His comrades laugh.

Gus heaves a loud sigh and suddenly brakes hard. The Cressida skids to a halt. The three men in the back lurch forward against the front seats. Dust envelops the car. Gus turns and faces Yengwa. For a few interminable seconds they stare at each other. Then Gus reaches over, hand outstretched. Yengwa hesitates, then retrieves my passport from the handbag and gives it to him. 'You should not take what doesn't belong to you,' Gus says.

The men just sit there, looking at Gus. You could cut the air with a knife.

'You abuse my hospitality, amadoda,' Gus says. 'Now I must ask you to get out. Because you have no manners, you can walk.'

Another excruciating staring match ensues. Yengwa gathers himself and smiles. 'Your turn will come, Bourke,' he says. 'Ncube is not as important as you think.'

Yengwa and his comrades climb out. Yengwa bows mockingly and says, 'Thenk you, my boss! Thenk you, master!' They wave and laugh as we drive on. Gus hands me my passport. We are silent for a while. I feel embarrassed, humiliated. My hangover, which seemed to have evaporated during the encounter, returns now with a Chernobyl-like vengeance. Gus drums his fingers on the steering wheel. 'Well, we didn't win any friends or influence people in that little exchange, I'm afraid,' he says. 'Fucking oxygen thieves!'

'What if they'd been armed, Gus?'

'You can't go through life saying "What if?"'

'But say they were.'

'No need to wet your pants, Chickenheart. Those bloody cowards only get gung-ho when the odds are at least twenty to one in their favour. But, if they did decide to get otherwise ...' Gus reaches down under his seat and pulls out a revolver. A 9mm Browning. He flicks the safety catch off and on. He looks at me and smiles, then puts it back under the seat again.

'Oh Jesus Christ, Gus! This is bullshit, man! Sometimes I wonder if there's anything resembling a brain in your head. You're going to end up dead or in jail. Get out of this damn country! There's no future here!'

'Those bastards are the future if no one stands up to them.'

'This country's not worth it, Gus! Get some sense into your head, man!'

Gus smiles and turns on the Kristofferson tape again.

At Shangani I ask Gus to stop at the general store. Casting shame to the winds, I borrow some money from Gus to buy a bottle of beer. Partaking in the hair of the dog is a cowardly custom I seldom stooped to in Australia, yet today there simply seems no alternative. I sip the beer with long teeth as we drive back to Bulawayo. Gus shakes his head but says nothing. He has cause to shake his head again when we pass the overturned truck, still there on the main road, along with its forlorn driver. 'What did I tell you?' he says.

Ncube appears through the fog of memory. 'Saxon said a strange thing last night. He said you sleep quietly outside.'

Gus seems surprised to hear this. Then he laughs.

'He's talking about the war. I went through a spell where I used to get nightmares. Really bad, man. It started while I was in barracks at the Selous Scout Fort in Bindura. Apparently I started making a hell of a racket in my sleep. It was a problem because they didn't know if it was safe to send me out on ops. You couldn't have a bloke yelling in his sleep out in the middle of injun territory. But then I found that once I was out in the bush the bad dreams didn't come. I don't know why. It was just a temporary thing during the war. I'm not like that any more.'

'How come Saxon knows this?'

Gus doesn't answer. He knows he has let something slip and seems uncertain of what to say.

'Come on, Gus. This is bloody weird, man.'

'Okay. But keep this to yourself. Not a word to anyone, not even Angela.'

'As God is my witness.'

Gus fixes his stare on the road ahead. 'I knew Saxon in the war. He started and ended the war as a Zipra gook. But he was on our side for a while.'

'What? In the Scouts?'

Gus nods. 'He was captured by our forces and basically given an offer he couldn't refuse. The gallows or work for us in the Scouts. We had lots of former terrorists working for us – half the bloody unit were what we called tame terrs. The reason the Scouts were so effective at counter-insurgency war-fare was because we had insurgents working for us – blokes like Saxon.'

'So you forced POWs to fight against their own. Pretty dirty stuff, Gus.'

'Ja, it was a dirty business, boet. But that whole damn war was dirty – on both sides. So don't get high and mighty with me, okay? It was the only way to fight those bastards. No rules.'

'There was such a thing as the Geneva Convention, you know.'

Gus gives a bitter laugh. 'I don't expect bedwetters like you to understand, Chickenheart. You want to hear about Saxon? Well, don't bloody interrupt then.' He pauses to clear his throat. 'Anyway, Saxon ended up in the Scouts doing pseudo ops up in the northern TTLs, along the Zambezi. Tangent Operational area. Trying to intercept Zipra terrorist gangs coming across from Zambia. That's where I first met him. I was in a team of five men – two whites and three tame terrs, including Saxon. For nearly a year we did ops together out there in the bush. We ate, slept and fought together. We lived like munts – the other whitey and I even blackened our skins to look like munts. Our job was to pose as gooks, to figure out Zipra's movements and set them up for the RLI Fireforces. Fucking dangerous business, man. I tell you, we went through some bloody heavy stuff.

'It all went well until the other white guy got killed in a contact. An arsehole called Kelty took his place. Kelty hated terrs, tame or not. He hated munts, full stop. The mood in the team turned bad. Kelty gave Saxon and the other two a hard time. Ordered them around like they were his personal servants, always insulting them. Too thick to realise it was a bloody dangerous thing to do, out there in the bush. I tried to talk some sense into him but he had a higher rank and didn't listen. He didn't only give Saxon and the other two a hard time. Sometimes we'd have to interrogate the locals in the area. It was lousy work but it was the only way to find out enemy movements. The local munts were the terrs' life-blood – gave them food and shelter, warned them about security forces in the area.

Interrogating was the part I hated most. But Kelty got a kick out of it. He behaved like a fucking animal, man. Always used unnecessary force. I knew Saxon and his two sidekicks hated his guts. One day he killed a mujiba, a kid who worked for the terrs. Just shot him – bang! – because he didn't answer a question. Like a dog – like he was nothing. This was after beating the living shit out of him beforehand. On our next op I woke one morning to find Saxon and the other two tame terrs gone and Kelty dead with his throat cut.'

Gus glances at me. He laughs at my incredulous expression.

'Ja, pretty heavy stuff, hey? According to Saxon, the other two were going to do me too, but he talked them out of it. The three of them split up and tried to gap it back to Zambia. Only Saxon made it – the other two got slotted in a contact near Vic Falls.'

'I'm surprised Saxon and his mates never "slotted" you before.'

'We basically had them by the balls. If they didn't work for us they'd get hung. Or, if they did manage to escape, their lives wouldn't have been worth shit either, once their former brothers-in-arms found out they'd been working for us. And, make no mistake, we weren't about to be too protective about the identity of any gook who managed to gap it, let alone kill one of our soldiers. But that's where Saxon proved so bloody slippery. He'd fooled us from the very beginning. When he was captured he gave us a false name – Edgar Tshabalala. That's the only name we knew him by. Tshabalala, as it turned out, was some gook friend of Saxon's who got killed in one of our air raids in Zambia – someone we had no record of. And so he was able to slip back into the Zipra ranks without being

90

exposed as a former Selous Scout. He became one of their best field commanders – this was towards the end of the war. Zipra was something else, man. Unlike Mugabe's rabble in Zanla, who ran whenever we confronted them, those Zipra gooks under commanders like Saxon gave as good as they got.'

'So what happened after the war, Gus? How did you meet up again?'

'To cut a long story short, after the war Saxon was appointed police chief for the Gweru District. I ran into him one day at a roadblock. I nearly shat myself because all the Scouts' records had been destroyed at the end of the war to prevent reprisals. Here I was eye to eye with a man who knew everything about me, even the kind of noise I make when I sleep. I also knew a lot about him that he wouldn't exactly like being bandied around – even today, the powers that be have a particular hatred for those of their own who served in the Scouts. But Saxon greeted me like a long-lost brother. We ended up in a bar in Gweru getting pissed together! So there it is, boet. The story of Saxon. A story only three people know. Saxon, me, and now you.'

I gaze silently at the ugly cement factory as we approach Bulawayo. Bulawayo – the place of killing. Only in this place ... only here could a story as bizarre as Gus's be believable. Yet his violent rite of passage to belong here is something completely foreign to me, beyond my comprehension. Earlier I spoke of the existential angst of living between identities. Implicit in that angst was an assertion of right, of entitlement to identity. Perhaps I have overreached myself, exceeded my moral fibre. Do I have what this place demands of people to assert the right to belong?

Confronted by this question, I scurry back into my limbo.

PART II

REMNANTS

Angela's plane has been delayed an hour, so we kill time upstairs on the airport balcony overlooking the runway. Yet another shabby Rhodesian relic with a name-change, Joshua Mqabuko Nkomo International Airport nevertheless exudes a bygone charm. I remember as a boy waiting on this same open balcony for my father to return from occasional business trips to Salisbury or South Africa – that was when fetching someone from an airport was a family outing of note. Gus visits the bar and returns with two beers. We sit watching some small private planes come and go. By now I'm in an abject state of damage control. I nurse the beer, grateful for its medicinal properties which, I calculate, will delay the full force of my hangover for an hour or so – that I should be in this condition to meet Angela fills me with disgust.

Her plane lands and we watch her disembark. As she strides across the tarmac she sees us and waves. As always, slim and attractive, though ever so slightly imperious in her safari-style khaki long trousers and jacket with a thousand pockets. Her trendy spectacles with their blue-and-silver rims seem the height of fashion, here in dreary Zimbabwe. Only her greying hair, now short and manly, belies her age. Of the three of us she appears to have aged the least; indeed, it makes me ruefully reflect that I, the youngest, am looking the worse for wear.

We go down to meet her. I'm so stiff I descend the stairs as though wearing callipers. Giving us each an affectionate kiss and hug, Angela immediately assumes her position as the family

elder. With a look of quizzical amusement she inspects us at
arm's length. Gus passes without comment. I must look a
sight, however. Hung over and unshaven, my hands covered in
plasters, reeking of stale booze and yesterday's sweat. Angela
wrinkles up her nose. 'What on earth have you been doing to
this poor boy?' she asks Gus.

Gus holds his hands out helplessly. 'Believe it or not, Ange,
that boy is master of his own destiny.'

Angela gives her high-pitched giggle, nostrils flaring. She
instructs Gus and me to be careful as we lug her massive trunk
to the car. On the way to Bulawayo she asks where she can draw
some money, since the exchange counter at the airport was
closed. Gus explains that cash is a scarce commodity these
days. The country has run out of banknotes – even the locals
are using travel cheques. 'Don't worry about money,' he says.
'I'll look after you.'

'I like to be independent,' Angela says. 'I hate cadging off
others.'

'Who knows? I might have to cadge off you one of these
days.'

'Seriously, Gus. Talk to your bank manager or something.
Even if it's just a bit to spoil Jessica and Lauren with.'

Gus nods. 'Okay, Ange. I'll organise some cash for both of
you.' He glances at me. 'Might as well – the professor's booze
bill is starting to mount up.'

Angela chats away in the car, exclaiming melodramatically at
the state of Bulawayo. As we pass the general hospital, now a
grimy hovel with broken windows and dirty sheets airing on the
balcony, she sighs and says, 'And to think I had my appendix
out in that dump. Where will it all end? Where will it end?'

Gus and I let her prattle on. We've always been hopelessly under her spell.

Jenny has some cold meat and salads ready for us at the house in Burnside. She greets Angela like an old friend and explains that the girls are still at school. We eat and chat for a while, then Angela begins to yawn and asks to take a nap. While she catches up on lost sleep and Gus and Jenny go over some accounts I slink down to the pool, accompanied by my lingering hangover. I swim a few geriatric laps and then lie on the slasto paving on my back, groaning from exertion. Authentic Man himself. It's just as well that I survive by pretence – did Heidegger or Sartre ever consider the hideous spectre of the self-actualised buffoon?

Close by, the gardener, whose name I've learned is Phineas, is digging in a flower bed. Every so often he gives me a sidelong glance, intrigued, no doubt, by my life of apparent leisure, but I'm too far gone to feel embarrassed. I close my eyes and drift off into an arbitrary reverie.

I see Angela as a girl on the back of my father's red Dodge truck as he drives around the farm. Standing up against the cab, like Boadicea riding a chariot. She is wearing one of the short cotton dresses that my mother cut from a roll of floral material bought at a sale at Meikles in Bulawayo. Her face lifted to the wind, eyes closed, lost to a special world. I see Gus too. Lost to a more basic world of sensations. Lying on his back on the floor of the truck, he makes gargling sounds as he is jolted around, his dirty face ecstatic – such are his primitive joys ...

My mind's eye shifts. Now Angela is leading us down past the sheds to the fowl run. She strides ahead imperiously, tall and skinny, her dark hair tied back with a red ribbon. 'Come on, you two!' she calls. 'Hurry up or we'll miss it!' At the fowl

run we watch as Joseph catches a chicken. Amid a frantic flapping of wings he snatches one by the feet and carries it to a
wooden block nearby where he casually chops off its head with
a cleaver. For our amusement he lets the chicken run around
spurting blood out its neck. Angela watches our reactions. I am
sickened. Gus laughs. He picks up the severed head and pushes
the eyelids open, intrigued by the way the chicken's yellow eyes
stare at him, as though still alive ...

'Hey there! Hope I'm not looking at a corpse.'

My limbs jerk involuntarily, startled by this voice. I sit up to
see a dark-haired woman standing at the pool fence, smiling at
me. A bit severe in her navy blue business suit, but attractive
nonetheless. To my annoyance she is eyeing my lily-white
physique (band aid nipple caps and all) up and down, an amused
look on her face. My male vanity, still flickering despite no
valid reason to exist, makes me flex what remains of my arm
muscles as I hug my knees to my chest. She laughs. 'Sorry to
disturb you, Vaughn. You looked dead to the world. Don't you
remember me?'

'I'm afraid not.'

'I wouldn't have recognised you either. I'm Bella. Isabella
Gerber, remember?'

'Good Lord, Bella!' I exclaim, getting to my feet. I quickly
put a shirt on and wrap a towel around my midriff and go over
to the fence. I wince as she shakes my blistered hand and give
her a clumsy peck on the cheek. 'Last time I saw you ...'

Actually, I have no idea when I last saw her.

'Was in seventy-five, I think, when I was about ten years
old.'

'Really? That long ago?'

'You were in university, and not about to remember a kid still in junior school.'

She eyes the plasters on my hands. 'What on earth have you been doing to yourself?'

I laugh weakly. 'Ah, you know. Digging up the past.'

There is an uncomfortable silence. I look into Bella's green eyes, wondering whether to offer my condolences about Tienus and her mother, but decide that can wait.

'You're looking ... great,' I stammer.

Indeed, she is. Bella is blessed with all the right curves, smooth olive skin and a face like Frida Kahlo's, without the single eyebrow. She smiles and is at least honest enough not to return the compliment.

I gesture at the chairs in the summerhouse. 'Won't you sit down for a while? Would you like a cold drink or something?'

She shakes her head. 'I must get back to work. I thought I'd just pop in to see Angela. I'll have to catch her later, when she wakes up. I didn't realise you were back too. You should drop by and say hello to my Dad. He'll be glad to see you, Vaughn.'

'Tell him I will.'

'You must tell me about Australia some time. Okay?'

Then she waves and leaves. I watch her walk back to the house, impressed at the tight cut of her business suit around her bottom. The desolate lust of a seedy clown, I know, I know ...

Later in the afternoon some storm clouds build up in the north. The thunder in the distance seems to lift Gus's spirits. Just as we are having our evening drinks in the lounge there is a short downpour. Hardly enough to wet the ground but the lightning is enough to deliver a power cut to Bulawayo, which puts paid to Jenny's plans for a roast dinner. Which gives Gus an excuse to fire up another braai.

We all repair down to the summerhouse. The evening is still in the wake of the downpour, the smell of the damp earth rich and overpowering. Gus hangs two hurricane lamps from the rafters and gets the fire started. Jessica and Lauren are racing each other in the pool. I nurse a whisky, glad that my hangover is finally lifting. Jenny regales Angela about the trials and tribulations of life in Zimbabwe.

'You people overseas have no idea. No *idea*! After all the whites have done for this country. Honestly, Angela, when you think of what we've contributed you'd think there'd be at least some appreciation. But no. Not one iota. They're killing the goose that lays the golden egg, and too damn stupid to realise it.'

This introspection I now find suffocating. The whole family demonstrates absolutely no interest in the world outside, just a relentless preoccupation with the injustices of Zimbabwe, principally as it affects them. The incredulity in Jenny's voice baffles and irritates me. Angela listens politely, nodding sympathetically now and then. Then Jenny interrupts her monologue to fetch some towels for the girls who have finished swimming. Angela asks me how my art is going and I reply it is not. Angela frowns, 'You shouldn't waste your talent, Vaughn.'

'What use is "talent" these days?' I reply, making that insufferable little gesture so frequently used by academics to indicate inverted commas. 'They don't even use the word any more.'

'Don't be so defeatist. Talent is bloody talent.'

'It's not defeatist. It's being realistic. Tradition is obsolete,

100

Angela. At one stage they were even talking about scrapping drawing in our art school. It seems everything *except* painting and drawing is art these days.'

'You shouldn't worry about what other people are doing.'

'You don't understand. You have no idea what's being done in the name of art these days.'

'My, but you're full of assumptions, aren't you, little brother? You talk as though I've no ability to comprehend anything outside my little world of wildlife art.'

'Sorry, Ange. I didn't mean it like that.'

'Just as well he's packed it in,' Gus pipes up from his fire. 'That stuff he was doing was a load of crap anyway.'

'Oh Angus, man!' Jenny exclaims, returning to her chair. 'Don't be so rude. I wish you had artistic talent.'

Gus scoffs. 'Artistic talent? Vaughn? I've seen better paintings by two-year-olds. Believe me, Jen, Vaughn could never do *real* art. Like Angela.'

Angela laughs. 'Oh nonsense, Gus! Vaughn isn't an art school professor for nothing. He's got paintings in national galleries in Australia, you know.'

'Australia? Say no more. What else could you expect from a nation that sees the world through the bottom of a beer glass? The Aussies have perfected only one form of art – getting pissed. As Vaughn so ably demonstrated last night. Jesus, what a bloody spectacle! Hey, twinkle toes? Come on, show us some of those dance moves, man!'

They all laugh at my expense.

Lauren and Jessica are standing within earshot, shivering in their towels.

'Why was Uncle Vaughn dancing, Dad?' Lauren asks.

Gus replies. 'Beats me, sweetheart. I have absolutely no idea. You better ask him.'

Jenny comes to my rescue by telling them to go and get dressed. They run off to the house.

Angela turns to me. 'Let's do some drawing together, Vaughn. Like we used to. Come on. I've got a spare sketch-book.'

'I don't think there's going to be much time for such luxuries as art. Not if my cultured art expert brother can help it. He seems to have my programme all worked out.'

Gus nods solemnly. 'Yes, Ange, the situation's extremely grave. No time for Vaughn to be prancing around like a poofter doing *art*.'

He assumes a dainty posture, holding a braai fork up like a paintbrush.

Angela laughs. 'Nonsense. I'm sure you can spare him just for a day or two?'

'If he pulls finger, maybe. Actually, it probably won't make any difference, considering his performance yesterday. I'll have to do most of it myself anyway.' He looks at me and laughs. 'Why so grave, professor?'

I sigh irritably. 'A master of the one-liner, aren't you?'

'Well, you'll have to put up with two weaklings then,' Angela says. 'Because I intend doing my bit.'

Gus looks at her across the flames, purses his lips and nods.

Then Jenny commences to hold Angela captive with the gory details of when she met Gus in hospital during the war, after he was shot in the leg – the wound that spelled the end of his army days. 'I tell you, Ange, *that leg*! I swear to God it looked like someone had taken a bloody red-hot skewer and stuck it *right*

102

through him! You wouldn't believe the amount of pus ...' No doubt Angela has heard it all before, but she listens with apparent sympathy. Never one to revel in heroic mutilations (especially before meals) I top up my whisky and join Gus at the fire. The coals are right and he is putting lamb chops and some pumpkin, potatoes and onions wrapped in tin foil on the grid. When he finishes I hand him a fresh beer.

Gus points his braai fork at Jenny. 'Just listen to her go on! Man, she lives to tell that bloody tale! I swear, it gets more gruesome every time.'

'That's nurses for you,' I say. 'Christ, the stuff Beth used to talk about! Blood and guts. Diseases. And always somehow just as you're about to eat.'

Gus nods and laughs.

'You never told me what happened when you got wounded. Angela phoned me in Australia with a few sketchy details, that's all. I don't even know *where* it happened.'

Gus sips his beer and gazes off into space. 'It was in one of the last Rhodesian raids into Mozambique towards the end of the war. We drove a whole bloody armoured convoy of captured Frelimo trucks straight into a Zanla camp at the dawn muster.' He shakes his head and lowers his voice. 'Bloody amazing, boet. The cruel simplicity of it. We took those poor fuckers completely by surprise. They thought we were Frelimo – some of those stupid gooks even *waved* at us as we came in. And we replied by just mowing them down. In their hundreds, man. It was actually pathetic. Most of them just stood there with their mouths open.'

I pause to wonder if I've ever truly known Gus, or if anyone else in our family could have done such things. Rex maybe.

'Sounds pretty damn horrific, if you ask me. Couldn't have been all one-way traffic, though.'

'It was a turkey shoot, basically. There was a bit of resistance. Nothing heavy duty. One of our guys got killed, a few wounded, including me. I caught two slugs in the leg. One broke the bone, the other severed an artery. One minute I was standing up culling gooks, the next I was on the deck with blood spurting out my leg. Not much I remember after that.'

'Jesus, Gus. I don't know how you live with all of this.'

'All of what?'

'Having killed. In such abundance.'

Gus's eyes glint across the fire. 'Us or them, boet. That's all. Us or them.'

I take a deep breath, reflecting once more on the gulf that separates Gus and me. Not for the first time I thank God I had the sense to dodge military service in such a futile and brutal conflict. I vow not to visit Gus's war with him again.

Gus looks up at the stars appearing above the departing clouds.

'There're times when I love this world,' he sighs.

'You scare me when you get sentimental, Gus. What's the plan for tomorrow?'

'We'll head back to the farm. I want to stop off at the church first. They haven't finished digging the new graves yet. The service is in a week's time.'

'I assume it's going to be a quiet affair.'

Gus nods.

A car pulls up at the gate. Lazy Monty, who'd positioned himself strategically in Gus's line of vision when the chops started sizzling, now demonstrates that empty vessels indeed do make the most noise by bounding over to the gate barking lustily.

'Hold the fort, boet,' Gus says handing his fork to me. He goes over to the gate, opens it and follows the car to where it parks in front of the house. Then he comes back accompanied by Bella Gerber. She is looking a little less severe in tight fitting jeans and a T-shirt with Marge Simpson emblazoned on it. Angela gets to her feet and greets her affectionately. I gather that during her many trips back to Zimbabwe over the years she and Bella have become good friends. I raise my glass in greeting. She smiles and says with a wink, 'Hi, Vaughn.'

Gus fixes Bella up with a drink and resumes his duties at the braai.

'What's the story with Bella?' I ask, sotto voce, as the ladies chat away.

'You mean is she available? You're a bit over the hill, boet.'

'Don't be crass, you bloody savage.'

'Bit of a sad story, actually. Bella's had a string of stuffed-up romances. Nearly got married once to an American safari operator, but that fell through. Always seems attracted to the wrong sort of bloke.'

'With her looks there must be plenty more fish in the sea.'

'Not exactly, boet. Not that many blokes left around these parts. Whites, I mean. So maybe there's hope for you.'

I shake my head. 'Christ, gimme a break, Gus.'

Jessica and Lauren come back from the house and sit with the ladies, showing Angela, the real artist, their school art sketchbooks, which Angela makes a big fuss over. Gus finishes the cooking and I help him carry the food to the table in the summerhouse. Jennifer gets up and uncovers some salads and we all help ourselves. We sit there in the dim lamplight eating and talking. I'm next to Bella. At one point she leans over and asks me in a whisper if she could have a whisky. Her musky perfume smells exotic and vaguely pricey, though in contrast I note she is wearing one of those silver dolphin bracelets commonly sported by sentimental teenagers labouring under the delusion that we can all be at one with nature. I get up and fix her a whisky. Sitting down again, I ask how her father is.

'Oh, it's been a hard time for him,' she replies.

'I'm very sorry to hear what happened.'

She smiles and nods. 'It's been hard. Aside from everything else, we've got no income from the farm. With inflation, my father's savings have virtually been wiped out. I'm keeping things going with my job.'

'It must be a struggle.'

'You and Angela were lucky to get out of this place.'

'I know.'

Sensing things are becoming a little sombre, Gus cuts in. 'Hey, what do you call a gay dinosaur?' he asks.

We all look at him.

'Megasorass,' Gus says, laughing abruptly at his own joke.

Needless to say, Jessica and Lauren giggle and Jenny wears that frown that by now I realise indicates she is just as amused as the girls. Bella slaps her thigh and erupts into peals of laughter. Angela – gay Angela – sits there with a little smile on her face, her eyebrows raised. Most disappointing of all is me, however. When Bella slaps my thigh too I laugh like a kookaburra.

*

My ingratiating submission to Bella's gaiety, if I may risk such a term, fills me with shame. I am mortified by my weakness. What impression did I make on Angela? Why didn't I contain myself? Why did I laugh so readily, so vacuously? Gus's insensitivity staggers me. Jokes and jibes about homosexuality have always issued freely from his lips; it amazes me he can be so tactless, knowing Angela. But she has always shown an inexplicable tolerance towards him. She describes him as one of those few who can joke about anything without causing offence. A bit generous, perhaps, although the way he laughs at his own jokes is disarming, I'll admit. Still, it doesn't excuse his insensitivity, for he too experienced the pain of Angela's awakening.

There was an idyllic time when Angela was the most perfect girl in the world. In the eyes of her besotted siblings, she had everything. Not only was she daring and beautiful, but creative too. An artistic talent was the one thing I had in common with her – the one thing that made Gus an outsider, since he possessed not a single creative bone in his body. Yes, I believed it made us kindred spirits and one day solemnly announced my intention to marry her when I grew up. My parents were amused by my innocent infatuation. Gus, then seven, heaped scorn on me. Angela was horrified. Not by my forlorn infatuation, which she quickly dismissed as a childish quirk – no, she was appalled by the mere thought of being a *wife*. As a girl she never showed the slightest interest in the roles ascribed to females. Nan tried hard to instil in her a sense of domesticity. She got Angela to observe when she sewed or baked; she insisted that she lend a hand in the kitchen when there were visitors – all to little avail. Angela was never one for frills and fancies, despite her artistic leanings. She preferred the company of boys and men. Everyone called her a tomboy, but she was more than that.

It was in high school that it began to emerge. The three of us were boarders at Chaplin High in Gwelo. Angela was a bright and popular girl who excelled in most things. No one suspected that behind the confident exterior lay a tormented soul. Homosexuality was ridiculed by both boys and girls, so she went through the motions of being a normal teenager. She tried dating boys and even went out with Tienus Gerber for a spell.

And it wasn't discussed among families. Certainly, Dad and Nan never suspected a thing, even when it began to show. At home during holidays Angela resisted doing domestic chores and insisted on wearing male attire, much to Nan's dismay. When she was sixteen she began wearing her hair short, like a boy. More perplexing to Gus and me, she would sometimes take off on one of the horses and be gone the whole day. We would scour the farm searching for her, but if she saw us or heard us calling she stayed hidden. Sometimes she secluded herself in her room for days at a time, ostensibly to paint or read. Occasionally we heard her crying. Unable to get through to her, my parents dismissed it as the normal emotional idiosyncrasies of female adolescence. Once in a while, when she and I went out drawing together, the guise would slip. 'Why? Why am I different? Why am I made like this?' she would say softly to herself. Only much later did I understand what she meant.

After school Angela went to the Teachers Training College in Bulawayo. My parents had hoped she would go to university, since she'd always excelled academically. But for some years Angela had taken refuge in wildlife painting. She had won several national prizes and it became her passion. She emphatically rejected the notion of university study, even if it entailed a course in Fine Art. Wildlife painting was all she wanted to do. But my father dug in his heels and insisted she get qualified in something, at least. So Angela thought she'd take an easy option and do a teaching course. She dropped out after a year, a major disappointment to my parents. But this was nothing compared with the shock they received when, during that year, Angela arrived home one holiday with a friend called Mavis.

One afternoon, Nan, thinking the girls were out riding, went into Angela's room to put up some new curtains. She found Angela and Mavis together in bed, not, presumably, enjoying a quiet nap. She dropped the curtains and ran.

Later that night, Angela calmly and rationally explained her sexuality to Dad and Nan. Nan, acceptant soul that she was, wept a little but immediately rallied to her side. My father appeared to take it on the chin, in that for a period of some weeks he seemed completely stunned. But, to his credit, he too ultimately came to accept the strange ways of this world.

It was a painful road for Angela. Her relationship with Mavis never worked out, nor did the many others since. She has lived alone for the past eight years. Increasingly, as the e-mails I received from her in Australia revealed, she has longed for the togetherness our family once provided. She once said that nothing, neither her success as a painter, nor the wealth that came with it, compensated for the disintegration of our family. More than Gus and me, she longs for what cannot be restored.

*

Wednesday. I try to phone Beth again the next morning. Michael answers and tells me she is on shift. It's the first time in months that I've spoken with him. I ask him how he is and he answers with a noncommittal 'Good.' He seems completely unfazed about where I am. I give him the Burnside phone number, in case they need to contact me. 'Look after yourself, Mikey, and give my love to your mother, okay?' I say after the meagre conversation has dried up. 'Okay,' he replies. I wonder if he'll do either.

We set off to Shangani. I am attired in a new set of *Hard Yakka* clothes and my *Rhodesia is Super* floppy hat; Angela sports her fancy safari gear. Once again, Gus's music (this time the Eagles) renders any coherent conversation impossible as we drive along. I'd hoped Angela and I might join forces in protest, but to my dismay she sings along in snatches, and I realise this must be an old favourite of hers Gus chose especially. Am I the only one who inherited my mother's love of serious music? Is it too much to expect something a little more inspiring from my siblings? The overturned truck is still partly obstructing the road, though the driver appears to have moved on to better things. Gus looks at Angela sitting up front next to him, one world-weary eyebrow raised, and points at the truck. Angela shakes her head. Where will it all end?

Gus makes his obligatory stop to take a leak, this time on one of the overgrown bougainvilleas alongside the road that provide the drab brown countryside with occasional dashes of magenta. Angela and I sample a turbulent symphony of splashing sounds concluded by a poignant fart. As he gets back into the car, Angela says with an amused frown, 'Gus, you are *such* a barbarian!' Naturally, the barbarian beams with pleasure at this attention.

At Shangani we stop at the tiny Anglican church across the road from the railway siding. Built in 1922, St David's looks quaintly English with its Gothic stone arches and thatched roof. It was the spiritual and social hub of the district until the Club usurped that role in the early fifties (despite the church's opposition to the kind of spirits worshipped there). Anglican ministers used to reside in the small house next to the church, but from the mid-fifties they travelled in from Gwelo or Bulawayo. The incumbent during our childhood was Reverend Davis who caused a bit of a stir in the late sixties when he stopped performing separate services for black and white congregations. His wife ran the Sunday School under a big marula tree adjacent to the church. These days there is once more a live-in priest, a Reverend Dlomo.

Gus introduces us to Reverend Dlomo, an old bespectacled man in a threadbare cassock and slightly-too-large priest's collar, whom we find in the sacristy. Exuding a quiet dignity, he greets us warmly, shaking our hands and repeating our names carefully, before leading us around to the cemetery behind the church. We inspect the progress made by the two gravediggers. Reverend Dlomo explains that the ground is hard and progress is slow – the men have completed three of the required six graves. Gus speaks to the men, who are busy having their breakfast under the marula tree. They give him solemn assurances that the job will be finished in a week.

Reverend Dlomo takes us to a nearby shed where Gus shows us the new headstones he'd had a stone mason in Gweru make from slabs of the farm's granite. Word for word, they have identical inscriptions to the original headstones. Gus's plan is to leave the originals in their place. I'm not sure if this implies there will be another exhumation if things in the country improve – a dismal thought indeed. We take leave of Reverend Dlomo and head for the farm, with *Hotel California* ringing in our ears.

'Those two layabouts are really milking that job,' Gus shouts above the din. 'Hard ground, my arse!'

'Oh Gus,' Angela replies. 'Wouldn't you do the same in their shoes?'

'Probably. The trouble is I'm paying for it.'

Shangani has not had a drop of last night's meagre rain. The lands are as tinder-dry and dusty as before. Angela gazes thoughtfully, wistfully, at the passing countryside. As we pass the squatter camp on the Gerbers' place, she says, 'I feel so sorry for Bella. I asked her if she wanted to come out to Hopelands this weekend. She said she couldn't stand being anywhere near their place.'

'What?' Gus shouts.

Angela turns the music down and repeats herself.

'I don't blame her,' Gus says.

'She says she feels trapped in this country. No future. Nowhere to go.'

'There're a lot of people in that boat,' Gus replies.

'Really, I just can't understand that mentality,' I interject. 'Surely there are options? She and the old man could leave.'

'And go where, professor?'

'South Africa. Overseas. There must be options.'

Gus scoffs. 'Options? Jesus, you've got no idea, boet. The little money the old man has in the bank has been reduced to practically nothing by inflation. Bella's salary just keeps them going – if it wasn't for her, who knows what he'd do? Everyone thinks Zimbabweans can just up stakes and bugger off, as though every country in the world will welcome them with open arms. It's not that simple, man. I can tell you Bella's already tried. She applied to go to Australia a while back, before Tienus got killed, but got knocked back – not enough points, or something. Now it's even more difficult because of the old man. She can't leave him behind.'

'What about South Africa? Don't they have any relatives?'

'South Africa used to be an option. Not any more. There's no work there for people like Bella. And the few relatives they have down south are finding it hard enough to make ends meet themselves, without having extra mouths to feed.'

'There must be some way out, surely? I just can't believe there're no options. You white Zimbabweans should stop complaining so much and do something about your situation. Unlike your poor black counterparts, you're still the ones with choices – whites will always have choices in this part of the world.'

Gus glances at me, a sudden anger in his eyes.

'I'm not going to bother arguing with you, Vaughn. But just don't give me that fuckwit crap about whites, okay? People are going through *real* hardship here, professor! Something you know fuck-all about.'

'Why is it we can never have a discussion about serious things without you becoming abusive, hey? Don't get so damn touchy, Gus. I just want to know why everyone seems to resign themselves to a fate dictated by Mugabe. What is it about this place that instils such submissive fatalism?'

Gus just drums his hands on the steering wheel, ignoring me.

'Oh, come on, Vaughn!' Angela snaps. 'Gus's right. Put your-self in Bella's shoes. What would you do? What *could* you do?'

Stung by the fact that she has rallied to Gus's side, I raise my hands and drop them, exasperated.

At the farm Gus leaves us at the house while he goes off in the Cruiser to find Witness and the 'boys' whose task it is today to fix the fence on the eastern boundary that was torn down by squatters. Angela and I have a cup of tea on the veranda, then we walk around the parched gardens and orchard. Angela, too, is impressed at how Gus has maintained everything. Despite the drought, the apricot and orange trees are laden with new fruit. We amble up to the reservoir and climb up onto the cement wall. Taking off our shoes we let our feet dangle in the water and reminisce about the old days when the reservoir dou-bled as our swimming pool. Angela remembers how she hated the slime on the sides and the water scorpions. She laughs as I recall the epic swimming races in which Gus and I competed for her favour. Gus always won, naturally – but it amuses her to think that my middling success later as a backstroker was born of this idiotic rivalry.

From our vantage point we can see the Cruiser and Ncube's yellow van down in the maize fields. Gus and Ncube are stand-ing together, talking animatedly. Angela explains that she has already met Ncube during two previous visits. She thinks he's a godsend. We watch the Cruiser wind its way back up the hill. As he comes past us to the security gate we can see Gus whist-ling away and drumming his hands on the steering wheel.

Angela laughs. 'He hasn't changed a bit. The only one who hasn't. The world could be falling apart, and still he'd whistle like everything's hunky-dory.'

'His world *is* falling apart,' I reply. 'The carefree facade is wearing thin, don't you think? The way he reacts sometimes.'

'You antagonise him, Vaughn. When it comes to politics, you're like a red flag to a bull. Be careful what you say. He's got a lot to deal with.'

'Oh, I must just accept everything he says? Come on, Ange!'

'Is there any point in arguing with him? You're never going to change him.'

Sad to say, that is a simple incontrovertible fact of life. On the way back to the house Angela pauses at the security gate. She looks down at the ground and heaves a long sigh. Her eyes fill with tears. I know what she is thinking.

'This is where they found Dad,' she says. 'Where they shot him.'

I put my arm around her shoulders.

'Come on, Ange. It's not good to think of it.'

She nods. 'I know ... I can't help it though. This place can be so horrible. Sometimes I just can't deal with it. At least he died instantly. Unlike Nan.'

'Try not to think of it, Ange.'

Gus has bad news. Witness told him another of the men has left and seventeen sheep are missing. He phones the police in Shangani to report the theft. They tell him there is no vehicle available to come and investigate. Gus hangs up and rants, 'Corrupt bastards! What's the bet those cop vans are busy carting my sheep off somewhere!' The air is blue with curses as he throws picks and shovels, a roll of black plastic sheeting and some rope on the back of the Cruiser. Angela says she wants to see Joseph and Anna first, and will catch up with us later. We leave her at the house and go on our way.

We arrive at the graveyard and get straight to work. I have no desire to perpetuate an impression of abject uselessness, but every challenge this place throws my way seems specially designed to bring new humiliations. My prowess as a grave-digger, needless to say, has not improved a great deal since two days ago. I manage a reasonably solid hour of slow digging before beginning to falter. Reaching the point where I can no longer heft the pick above my shoulders, I despair at my phys-ical limits – reaping my brother's scorn, it seems, is destined to be my lot in life. By the time Angela comes walking up with the dogs, I'm prone again in the shade of the gum tree, a spent force – too weak even to resist as Frik licks my face. My sym-pathetic siblings have a good laugh at my expense, before Angela takes up my pick and shovel and to my further embar-rassment proves no slouch with either. She has changed into some rugby shorts and a T-shirt, and I can see by the muscu-lar definition of her legs and arms that she is a gym fiend. In no time at all she has surpassed my efforts with Catherine's grave. Gus, who aside from the odd break for a drink has con-tinued at his steady pace, glances at her approvingly, then at me and shakes his head. Even my contempt for such primitive body language does not alleviate the rout of my already low self-esteem.

The buzzing of insects and the lowing of cattle in the dis-tance, not to mention the rhythmic activity of my siblings, makes me drowsy and I drift off into a fitful sleep, disturbed by horseflies and the raucous natter of two hornbills perched in a tree nearby. It's late afternoon when I wake. Gus and Angela are loading the implements onto the cruiser. Wearily I rise and go over to inspect their progress. Angela has dug to about five feet. In Vaughn's grave a couple of stained bones are poking through the soil. So old and eroded, I mistake them at first for roots. I recoil in fright, not expecting to be confronted so soon with the object of the exercise.

I climb into the cruiser with Gus and Angela and we set off back to the house. Angela is nursing blisters on her hands. I feel some comfort in the knowledge that there is another mere mortal to keep me company.

'It'll get easier,' Gus says, by way of reassurance.

Joseph and Anna surprise us with a roast chicken dinner when we get back. The old people have been hard at work in our absence, cleaning the kitchen and sprucing up the house. After all, they say, it's the first time the three of us have been together on the farm for over twenty years. Anna has arranged some pink bougainvillea flowers (the only flowers currently blooming in the arid garden) on the dining room table, a sweet gesture that impresses even Gus. They wait for us to finish eating, chatting quietly in the kitchen, then they clear away the dishes.

Angela asks them to join us for some coffee on the veranda. They agree hesitantly. Gus frowns, but says nothing. We sit outside and drink coffee and reminisce a bit. Joseph and Anna are uneasy. They nod and laugh on cue, they answer our questions about the old days politely and without opinion. The language they speak, as it always was in this house, is formal – never effusive or too familiar. It seems impossible for them to break the old habits of subservience. Now more accustomed to Australia's egalitarian society, I find it incredible that these two souls can be so intimately connected to us, yet still summon an obsolete protocol to maintain a discreet distance while in our space. I realise the only times we've ever met on vaguely equal terms have been at their kraal – the only space they have ever dared to regard as their own. When they finish their coffee, Joseph quickly goads Anna to her feet and they take their leave. We watch their torch-light flickering along the path down the hill and listen to them chattering away loudly to frighten away evil spirits.

'You shouldn't force things on them, Ange,' Gus says. 'They're too old for change.'

Angela scoffs. 'Oh, Gus! No one's forcing anyone. They're like family. Life's too short to keep up pretences, man.'

'No, Ange. They're too old. It makes them uncomfortable. It turns their world upside down. Like when the professor here kisses and slobbers all over them.'

'God, you're a dinosaur!' Angela laughs. 'Lighten up a bit, brother. You need to reach out a bit. This is the twenty-first century, you know! The world has changed.'

'*Their* world hasn't,' Gus says.

Angela and Gus continue to reminisce about the old days. They talk about how grand it was when Dad and Nan had our neighbours over for a braai and how they'd dance to Bing Crosby and Frank Sinatra out there on the veranda. Good times, emerging from a province of memory ruled by sorrow.

I don't contribute much to the conversation. I just sit there listening to them, sad and happy to be with them again.

*

My parents were enthusiastic entertainers. When guests were coming they would sometimes spend days getting things organised. Under a pernickety Nan, the kitchen took on the frenetic bustle of a ship's galley. Poor Joseph and Anna (and every so often a reluctant Angela) were put through their paces preparing the side dishes and puddings. Nan was fussy about presentation; everything had to be just right. No one else in the district brought out their best silver and crockery for braais. No one else used starched table cloths and napkins. Dad would get the meat from the cold room adjoining the tool shed and cut it up with a bandsaw. Once in a while he did a sheep on the spit, but mostly it was plain old Rhodesian fare – steak and lamb chops. He made sure that enough firewood was cut and that the supply of drinks befitted the occasion – this usually involved a special trip to Gwelo or Bulawayo to check out what specials the bottle stores were offering. He'd spend hours stringing up coloured lights on the veranda and testing them to see if they were all working. Then he'd rig up the gramophone with extension leads and listen to one or two records with a faraway look in his eyes. Music was the only thing that ever made my father sentimental.

Our most frequent guests were the Gerbers. Dad, in particular, got on very well with Oom Jasper Gerber, Tienus and Bella's father – Oom Jasper had served alongside Dad and Rex in North Africa during the war. Then there were our other neighbours, the Thorntons, and Mack and Tilly Griegg whose son, Jeff, lost a leg in a landmine explosion up near Kariba the year I left for Australia. There were the Mapstones, the Pringles and Pug and Shiela Durnford, whose skinny runt of a son turned into Big Bull Durnford. We would be on hand to welcome them as they drove in. Handshakes and gay laughter. The excited chatter of kids.

Those evenings ... clear and fresh and perfect if it had rained during the day. The smell of the land and the ladies' perfumes. The elegant clothes and the coloured lights against the muted land, and the conversations mingling with the ripple of leaves and the quiet breezes through the long grass.

While the men talked shop and the ladies traded secrets, Dad lit the pyramid of wood in the raised stone fireplace nearby. As the wood crackled and popped and sent sparks flying, Angela, Gus and I played with the other kids on the lawn: catches, open gates, touch rugby – boys' games usually, for which Angela showed a distinct flair. We poked sticks into the fire and ran around waving our arms in circles, making fiery patterns against the darkness. We plummeted down a foofy slide from our tree house high up in the flamboyant tree at the bottom of the garden. We gulped down Hubbly Bubbly cold drinks and Willards chips like gannets.

When the coals were ready Dad would braai the meat, beer in hand, turning the steaks and chops over with a long wire fork. When the meat was done, he let it simmer a bit in wine, a little culinary flourish he learned from Nan. Then the guests helped themselves. There was plenty for everyone and seconds for the men who enjoyed their meat, and most did.

And as the guests topped their glasses and the evening progressed, the talk and laughter would get louder and more jovial. A memory of Nan in a red evening gown, slim and pretty, her eyes sparkling and her laughter filtering through the darkness, evoking response from the roosting birds in the trees. A city girl at heart, Nan loved those rich, crowded moments. They all danced to Bing and Frank and the noises of the dark veld. Now, Rex came into his own. He'd pounce upon any lady who had been left idle and launch out onto the floor. Dowdy, self-conscious women became princesses in his arms. I have an enduring image of him, sailing immaculately across the floor, his partner attempting a conservative pirouette or two, stars in her eyes. Doing the tango with Nan, a look of mock sincerity on his face. Nan unable to contain her laughter.

My father liked to dance too, but he was no dancer. His repertoire was limited to a basic slow waltz and his only partner was Nan. As they moved laboriously from one side of the floor to the other, Dad closed his eyes and was transported back in time to when they were younger and hopelessly in love. Nan watched him with a twinkle in her eye. She loved him when he got like this, when he let go.

*

In matters of race, I must be brutally honest. I can only ascribe my incredulity at Joseph and Anna's reluctance or inability to transcend their status as servants to the transforming effects of Australian egalitarianism. As a young Rhodesian, I took their status for granted. Joseph and Anna waited on me, the little white master; they cooked for me, cleaned up after me, as they did for the rest of my family. As domestic servants did for whites everywhere in Rhodesia. Blinkered by what appeared to be the norm, I never seriously questioned this arrangement until my student years in South Africa when, in the revelatory tumult of university politics, the notion that the huge inequalities that existed between whites and blacks were neither natural nor morally sustainable first established a foothold in my naive world-view. But that questioning only occurred within the security of dominance – whites still ruled in southern Africa and the knowledge that things should be different came, I guess, with the unconscious consolation that they weren't.

But my incredulity as to Joseph and Anna's behaviour is born of a certain falsehood. The idea of racial equality as something inalienable was something I fervently embraced in Australia. Yet this transformation can also be questioned in much the same way as my fledgling liberalism at university. It came in the security of empowerment. In this sense, Australian egalitarianism itself rests on shaky ground. I didn't win many friends among my fellow academics when I argued that to claim the moral high ground in matters of race requires the passage of surrender and loss – and few Australians can claim either. I usually made this assertion while under siege for my colonial upbringing, to counter hypocritical allusions to a life of privilege at the expense of black Africans – for what else have white Australians enjoyed at the expense of Aborigines? In Australia, where the indigenous population has been reduced to a powerless minority, it is too easy to claim the moral high ground. One doesn't have to give up anything to atone for the past. There is no test that involves surrender or loss.

A story I heard once of an Aboriginal family wishing to return to the land where their ancestors were buried now strikes a particular chord in me. The graves of their people were situated on a farm in Queensland. The white farmer, fearing this family's visit was a prelude to some form of land claim, barred their entry. They were sent on their way, repelled like invaders, denied access to their ancestors by the farmer's fear of dispossession.

This story suggests that when it comes to the question of land Australians are not all that different from white Rhodesians or South Africans. Would my academic colleagues, so fond of reducing issues of race to sentimental theory, have behaved any differently from the farmer? Only by standing in his shoes could they know. True atonement for the colonial past comes through the surrender of land, and therefore of place. That is the hard reality whites in Africa have had to face.

*

I wake disoriented, elated yet depressed. Last night I had some vivid dreams, all of them of Australia. It takes me a while to place myself. The songbirds do it; the distinctive *Piet my Vrou* and the liquid call of doves, so sweet and gentle to the ear. In Australia one wakes to a raucous cacophony – kookaburras, currawongs, cockatoos, galahs, and the strange warbling of magpies. For the traveller, the soul seems to lag behind, existing in the past. Waiting for birds.

What pleases and depresses me this morning is that I've woken with an erection. I attribute this to having stopped taking anti-depressants, which make me semi-impotent. The physical pleasure of renewed sexual desire is the upside of my mental state. What depresses me is not so much the abject sleaziness of it but more the unequivocal realisation of what I am – a middle-aged man, long starved of female company. Yet another unpalatable pill for Authentic Man to swallow.

Gus is his normal cheery self. For Cro Magnon Man the biological clock does not tick. The sun is just rising, yet he has already been out and about the farm, ferrying the labour and checking on the stock. Angela and I have pulled up a little worse for wear, myself most certainly more so. I shuffle to the breakfast table, somewhat voluble in my discomfort, which is naturally a source of amusement to my siblings. I make a mental note to die rather than fail to lift my game today.

After a quick breakfast of slightly overripe pawpaw and fried eggs on toasted maize bread, we gird ourselves. Angela and I bandage our blistered hands. Angela rubs Deep Heat on my newly-awakened shoulder muscles. Gus lends me a pair of shorts and an old T-shirt, since my *Hard Yakka* strides and long-sleeved shirt have proven too uncomfortable in the heat. The shorts are too big around the waist, requiring me to pull them up high and secure them with a leather belt – a definitive 'naff' look according to Gus. Then we load the Cruiser with two of the contingency coffins and with dogs bounding along behind, drive off into the sunrise towards Long Cross Hill.

The sun and the flies are already out in force when we get to the graveyard. The dogs charge off into the bush, barking like idiots. Gus arranges three plastic mugs on the Cruiser bonnet and pours us some tea from a thermos flask. We sit on our haunches and sip the tea. Over in the distance we can see Ncube's yellow van pulling to a stop in the maize fields and disgorging a gang of women workers. Ncube emerges, gesticulating. He halts suddenly, reaches into his pocket and walks away from the women, cell phone to his ear.

'Hello, Saxon Ncube Incorporated,' Gus announces, mimicking Saxon's deep voice.

Angela giggles. 'Don't be mean, Gus.'

'I'm not being mean. I'll be the first to admit Saxon's a natural-born businessman. Just a pity there's no business. But just try telling him that! It's his undying bloody optimism that amuses me.'

'He's a character all right,' Angela says. 'Zimbabwe needs more people like him.'

'Has he done anything about your sheep?' I ask.

Gus shrugs. 'Last time I spoke to him he said the cops have promised to look into it. I'm not holding my breath in anticipation of any speedy action on their part.' He slugs back the last of his tea and gets to his feet. 'Come on, let's get to work.'

I follow Gus and Angela into the graveyard. We survey yesterday's progress. Gus figures we can easily finish with Vaughn and Catherine today. He suggests we do Vaughn's remains first. He hands me a small builder's trowel and a bucket and we clamber down into the grave. Working from opposite ends, we gently scrape away the soil from what is left of the fragile skeleton. It's unbearably hot down in this confined space; we smear dirt over our faces as we wipe away the sweat. My glasses keep fogging up. The glimpse of my great-grandfather's stained bones has plagued my mind since yesterday. I was not sure I had what it takes to pick through the remains of my family, to salvage what is left, yet in the clear light of day it becomes a strangely objective business. Not least of all because Vaughn's remains are so few: a fragment of the pelvis, the joint of a femur, a few vertebrae, and a section of the cranium including the eye sockets. They are the loam brown colour of the earth. Brittle, ancient, almost dust. One by one, we hand them up to Angela who lays them out on a sheet of black plastic, along with everything else we find – the coffin name-plate, his wedding ring, some bits of metal that Angela recognises as cuff links, an eroded brass belt buckle. We pass up a few buckets of the surrounding soil as well.

There is a sombre moment as Gus lifts up the piece of skull. So small and fragile, yet therein lay a hardy man's soul. The one who brought us to Africa.

I need assistance from my siblings in climbing out of the grave. Much to my annoyance, they drag me out by the arms like a corpse, laughing at my fogged-up glasses. Vaughn's remains seem pitifully little as Gus wraps them up in the plastic and binds them with sisal rope. Angela and I watch him in silence. The birds in the trees seem suddenly loud.

Lifting up the small bundle, Gus is philosophical. 'Symbolic, I guess. But as long as we've got something,' he says. He places them carefully in one of the coffins on the Cruiser and screws the lid shut. Then we take shovels and fill in the grave and reposition the whitewashed stones.

'One down, five to go,' Gus says when we're finished.

We break for lunch under the gum tree. Silently we eat our chicken sandwiches, gazing off into the distance. Gus and I resemble two filthy desperadoes. Rivulets of sweat run through the dirt on our faces. Angela screws up her nose and shifts upwind slightly. 'Phew! You fellows reek,' she says.

Gus belches. 'Nothing wrong with a bit of honest sweat, eh Vaughn?'

I rest my head against the tree, ignoring him. My back aches from all the shovelling it took to fill Vaughn's grave. Yet I am elated – I feel that so far I've contributed well today. The countryside is quiet, except for the sound of the women workers singing down below in Ncube's maize fields.

Angela pours us each a mug of tea from the thermos flask. 'I'm really glad to be here,' she says.

Gus glances at her and nods. 'Thanks for making the effort.

Both of you. It would've been pretty damn lonely doing this on my own.'

Angela hands us our tea. 'Not that it would've stopped you. You're incorrigible, you know. Once you get a bee in that balding bonnet of yours ....'

'If you ask me, Gus, I think you're completely bloody mad,' I say.

'No one asked you, boet, but nice to hear your vote of confidence on this grave occasion.'

Angela laughs and slaps him on the arm. She kisses him on the cheek and Gus blushes with pleasure. He's about to deliver another no doubt flippant remark when suddenly the dogs start a mad racket down among some trees in the cleft of a nearby kopje. Amid the barking, we hear something else – a faint, rattling growl. We look at each other, startled.

Gus puts his tea down. 'Jesus!'

'What is it?' Angela says.

'That, big sister, is one helluva cranky leopard! We better grab those stupid mutts before he makes a meal out of them. Come on!'

Gus leaps to his feet and sprints off down the rocky slope towards the kopje. Angela and I run after him. Or should I say Angela runs – I bring up the rear with a shuffle, my tardy speed less the result of sore muscles than trepidation at confronting, unarmed, one of Africa's fiercest animals. I wonder at the impetuous stupidity of my brother. Does he ever stop to think? What if the leopard is cornered and decides to attack? What will he do? Fight it with his bare hands? Apparently no problem to our portly Tarzan.

Following the sound of the dogs we enter the shaded cleft.

127

Gus slows to a walk and leads the way through a corridor of high rock walls until we come in sight of the dogs milling around under a massive wild fig tree. Gus drops to his haunches and points, his lopsided grin radiant.

'Look at him!' he exclaims in a fierce whisper. 'Isn't he something, hey?'

Angela and I creep forward. I see nothing, just the mottled canopy of leaves and branches high above. The dogs' barking reverberates deafeningly from the walls of rock around us. My armpits prickle with sweat. Impatiently, Gus points again. 'Up there!' he whispers. His myopic siblings stare upwards, glasses glinting. Then, a quick ripple of spots, like leaves in a gust of wind, and it materialises. The prince of cats. Angela gasps in awe. Tightly crouched, poised, eyes bright and deadly, it watches us nervously from its perch next to the decimated carcass of a sheep. As we squat down next to Gus it bares its fangs. My heart is in my mouth.

Angela curses. 'Damn! The most beautiful animal on earth and I don't have my bloody camera!'

The dogs continue to bark as if possessed. The leopard flashes its teeth again and hisses, its long white whiskers bristling. Rhodesian Ridgebacks were once called lion dogs, not due to any particular resemblance in appearance or strength but rather because they were used (sacrificed, to be more precise) in lion hunts in the old days. Somehow the dim instincts of Frik and Tiny have calculated that taking on this incomparably ferocious animal is a feasible, if not potentially enjoyable, prospect.

Gus whistles. The dogs stop barking momentarily. They look at us with silly, joyous expressions, then continue their barking. Gus whistles again, louder this time. He calls them. 'Frik! Tiny! Here!' Reluctantly, the dogs quieten and come to us. Gus grabs their collars. They tremble and whine plaintively. For a few more minutes we watch the leopard, mesmerised by its blank, deadly stare. Silently I acknowledge one of those rare moments in which we find transcendent beauty in fear.

Then Gus says, 'Come on, let's leave him in peace.'

We return to the graveyard, Gus almost dragging the dogs by their collars. We are silent, reflective. I remember clearly the day my grandfather and Rex set off to shoot what was thought to be the last leopard in the district. It had been caught in a trap and they came back with its corpse in the back of the Dodge truck. My grandfather and Rex were grim-faced. No one was happy about killing it. I remember climbing into the truck and touching the hard, inert form of the fearsome beast, and being overwhelmed by a sense of irretrievable loss. Reflecting the mentality of the time, my grandfather tried to justify it. There was no option, he said – the stock had to be protected. The way he said it, you could tell even he didn't believe it. For a while that leopard's skin lay over the chair on the veranda that Gus made at school until my mother persuaded Rex to remove it to his lodge.

At the graveyard Gus asks me to take the dogs back to the house since they can't be trusted to leave the leopard alone. He and Angela resume digging in Catherine's grave; I drive off with Frik and Tiny swanking like gladiators on the back of the Cruiser.

After shutting the dogs inside the security fence at the house, I'm about to return to the graveyard when Ncube arrives in his van. He pulls up alongside the Cruiser and greets me through the dust. He asks for Gus, saying there's an urgent matter to discuss. I hear the bleating of sheep inside the van.

'He's busy at the graves,' I reply.

Ncube frowns thoughtfully.

'It's no trouble to take you there, if you want. I'm going myself,' I say.

He eyes the coffins on the back of the Cruiser and shakes his head. 'The graves are your private business. Just tell him I'll be here tonight to talk.' He gestures behind him with his thumb. 'Tell him also that I found some of his sheep. Five, that's all. I'll take them back to the flock.'

'Thanks, Saxon. Where'd you find them?'

'Next door. The old Thornton place.'

He waves and drives off. I head back to the graveyard. It suddenly occurs to me that we'd been talking in English, whereas the other night we conversed mostly in SiNdebele. For some reason this bothers me. It seems to suggest that Ncube regards me as an outsider, a foreigner. Why should this be of concern? Why should I care what Ncube thinks of me? I continue on to the graveyard, confused by these thoughts.

I find Gus and Angela in Catherine's grave, painstakingly excavating the soil from around her remains.

'What took you so long?' Gus grumbles.

'Saxon pitched up. Says he needs to talk to you.'

'What about?'

'Wouldn't say. He'll come round this evening. He found five of your sheep, by the way.'

Gus looks up at me, eyebrows raised, and nods. 'That's good. I'd more or less written them off.' He looks at his watch.

130

'Come on, professor, there's a couple of hours left. Grab some of that plastic and make yourself useful up there.'

I cut a length of black plastic from the roll on the back of the Cruiser and lay it out next to the grave. Gus and Angela begin passing up Catherine's remains which I lay out carefully. There's virtually nothing of her left, just tiny, fragile pieces of her pelvis and skull that almost crumble to dust in my hands as I place them on the plastic. Soberly I reflect that Vaughn and Catherine's remains comprise almost entirely of dust. Dust to dust. For the first time I understand how literally we are given back to the earth.

Gus and Angela have made a poignant discovery in my absence. The soil of Catherine's remains is sprinkled with tiny silver charms, now tarnished with age. Once the last of the bones has been lifted up to me, they sift carefully through the soil to make sure they have retrieved them all. One by one I place them with the bones – reindeers, edelweiss, a bugle, cute dogs and kittens. I remember my grandfather telling us how Catherine had loved to collect these charms – how the Christmas pudding each year would be a veritable minefield of them, and beware the impatient boy who gobbled too fast. Catherine died in 1938, a year before Vaughn, and it had evidently been a sentimental act of devotion on his part to bury these little keepsakes with her.

Angela, a sop for sentiment, keeps saying, 'It's so sweet. So bloody sweet.'

The sun has gone down by the time we've filled in the grave. Exhausted, we drive back in silence and offload the coffins in the shed. Back at the house we find Joseph and Anna fussing around in the kitchen. They have insisted on doing another dinner – this time a chicken casserole. Anna announces formally that since none of us ever showed any domestic talents, notwithstanding Gus's recent efforts, she and Joseph have no choice but save us from our descent into barbarism.

We shower and sit outside on the veranda with a couple of drinks, enjoying the peace and quiet, almost like old times. For a long while we just gaze silently at the land. The late twilight gloom is deep and intense, the black burgundy earth an impenetrable swathe beneath the first stars. Far off, the weaver birds chatter along the river and baboons bark in the kopjes.

To break our silence I begin discussing the abstract qualities of sunsets with Angela and am a little miffed when, comparing the scene in front of us to the glowing subliminal paintings of Rothko, I discover she knows everything I know about him, and more.

'I think all those Abstract Expressionists believed too much in what painting can do,' Angela says. 'Especially Rothko.'

'Hey, I'm supposed to be the cynic, Ange,' I say. 'I thought you would've admired his belief in art.'

'I do. There's something really beautiful in his belief. He once said that paintings should be a revelation – an unexpected and unprecedented resolution of an eternally familiar need. That's a wonderful ambition, if only it were possible. If anyone demonstrates that art has its limitations – that there's a danger in expecting too much from art – it's Rothko. When he committed suicide it was as though he did it out of fury – fury and despair at having realised, finally, that painting wasn't enough. It could never deliver the spiritual potential he wanted from it. He couldn't live with his failure – his collapse of faith – so he killed himself. Apparently, he was really vicious – slashed his wrists down to the bone.'

'Nice to have some light conversation,' Gus remarks.

'I'm just saying you shouldn't expect too much from art.'

'I don't expect anything from art.'

Angela laughs. 'That goes without saying, Angus.' She turns to me. 'Let's do some drawing together, Vaughn. If our slave-driver brother would be so kind to spare us for a while.'

'Please feel free,' Gus says. 'Vaughn's so useless you'll be doing me a favour, Ange.'

'Oh, rubbish. I thought Vaughn did very well today. Since we're going back to Bulawayo this weekend, I thought we could do some sketching in the Matopos. What do you reckon, Vaughn?'

'Fine by me,' I say.

I'm expecting another philistine critique of my artistic abilities from Gus but just then Ncube pitches up in a cloud of dust. Gus goes down the stairs and quietens the dogs. Anna comes out to see the cause of the commotion. Ncube climbs out of the van and waves at us on the veranda. He greets Angela by name.

'Nice to see you, Saxon,' Angela replies. 'You missed a lovely sunset.'

Ncube glances behind him at the last glimmer of light along the horizon as though he's forgotten such things existed.

'Yes,' he says. 'Very pretty.'

Anna gives a loud sigh and mutters, 'As if that baboon knows what is pretty!'

'Don't worry, Mama,' Ncube laughs. 'I won't stay long.'

'What's up, Saxon?' Gus asks.

Ncube's face becomes serious. 'We must talk, umngani wami.'

Gus puts his hand on Ncube's shoulder and escorts him to the security fence where they stand talking, out of earshot. Anna goes back inside muttering to herself. Angela leans over and gives me a long, tight hug.

'I've missed you, little brother,' she says. 'How are you?'

'Fine.'

'Really?'

'No. My life's a complete mess, frankly.'

She assumes that quizzical expression I adore. 'Want to talk about it?'

'No.'

'Oh, Vaughn! Spare me your feeble stoicism, please.'

'You never liked effusive males, as I recall.'

Angela laughs and loosens her arms around me. 'We all mellow with age. There's nothing wrong with men opening their hearts now and then. Come on, you can talk to me.'

I take a swig of whisky. 'I don't know, Ange. This whole damn business is affecting me more than I imagined. I shut out the past all these years. Now I just can't escape it. Losing the farm ... I know it's inevitable – I'm resigned to the fact – but it's as though we're losing the last tangible remnant of our togetherness. As though the farm itself is a grave we won't ever be able to visit again. Only we can't exhume it and take it somewhere else.'

Angela sits back. 'That's one way of looking at it. But think of it this way: As far as you and I are concerned, all the farm amounts to, as you say, is a remnant of togetherness, not togetherness itself. For Gus, of course, the farm means more because he has invested it with much more than just the past. But for us, it's only a memorial to something that has been lost already.'

134

'But is that all it amounts to, Ange? Just a place of fading memories? Don't we need this place to be accessible – to confirm our existence, our past? Isn't that where our sense of belonging comes from?'

'Mmm ... I don't know. Losing the farm is tragic – I'm not ignoring that. But, for me, I need much more than a place of memories to visit every so often. I need people. I need family. I need togetherness *now* – not just a fading memory of it.' She heaves a long sigh. 'I also struggle with the past, you know. I could never shut it out, though.'

'It's like I've been numb for twenty years. Like I've been under some anaesthetic.'

'It was your way of coping, Vaughn. We all coped with what happened as best we could. We all took that time – that togetherness – for granted. Then one day it was gone, and we had to contend with the loss.'

'God, it still seems like nothing is left. Just a huge hole in our lives.'

'No, you shouldn't talk like that. I hate hearing you talk like that. We still have each other. We're still a family.'

'Yes, but dispersed like chaff around the world.'

Angela smiles and nods. 'I wish we all could be together again. In one place. I think Rhodesians must be the most scattered bunch of people in the world.'

We sit looking at the dark forms of Ncube and Gus at the security fence. At one point we hear Ncube's phone ringing and his raised voice as he talks to someone about cement – apparently he is doing some renovations to his house in Gweru.

'I'm really worried about Gus,' Angela says. 'It's just a matter of time before the veterans take over the place. I just hope no one gets hurt. I hope his stubborn streak doesn't get him into trouble. I also worry about what will happen to the workers, especially Joseph and Anna.'

I nod. 'I get the impression Witness and his crew are pretty much resigned to the inevitable. They seem to be hanging in here just as long as they can. They'll cut and run if things turn bad. Joseph and Anna are another story, though.'

Angela sighs. 'I really want to do something for them. They're like family. They deserve more from us. I thought of buying them a house in Bulawayo or Gweru – a decent place, not in a township. Somewhere safe.'

'I can't imagine them living in Bulawayo or Gweru.'

'I just don't want to see them getting attacked and driven off the farm with nothing. Or worse, getting killed. I know Gus can't afford it – his finances are looking pretty shaky right now.'

'If you go ahead, I'd like to contribute.'

'Vaughn, I'm single with lots of money. I know what your divorce cost you. I don't need your money.'

'I want to, Ange. I really want to. Joseph and Anna *are* family.'

Gus and Ncube come walking up to the house. Ncube waves at us, shakes Gus's hand and drives off. Gus climbs the stairs, a stony look on his face, and goes through to get another beer. He returns and sits down with a deep sigh.

'Nothing's ever bloody straightforward in this country,' he says. 'Saxon says he bumped into Mtunzi at the Club last night and it seems things didn't go too well. He reckons Mtunzi got drunk and aggressive and accused him of being a sell-out – of standing in the way of his "operations". He basically gave Saxon an ultimatum: ditch me or else.'

'What was Saxon's response?' Angela asks.

'Saxon tried to bullshit the prick that he needs me – needs my know-how – to keep going.'

'Doesn't seem like bullshit to me,' Angela says. 'Saxon's dependent on you for more than just know-how. Your land, your machinery – your tractor, ploughs, irrigation equipment – he's completely dependent on you.'

'But that's beside the point, Ange. Saxon's viability as a farmer means absolutely bugger-all to Mtunzi. Taking over the farms has never been about good agriculture. It's all about Mugabe keeping power. Mtunzi doesn't give a shit about farming.'

'So where does this leave you now?' I ask. 'I mean, will Saxon stand by you? Can you really trust him?'

'Saxon won't shaft me. We'll just have to wait and see what Mtunzi does.'

Angela sighs. 'Oh Angus, is it really worth it?'

'I'm surprised you even ask, Angela.'

Anna comes out to announce that dinner is ready. We file through and take our places at the table. The mood is sombre. Gus is lost in thought, distracted by his conversation with Ncube.

'It's time all you bloody antipodeans came back to Britain,' Angela says half-jokingly. 'To the mother country.'

Gus just looks at her bleakly. The phone rings in the passageway and he goes to answer it. We hear him turn on some light-hearted banter. Then he calls, 'Hey, Vaughn! It's for you.'

I notice the wink he gives Angela as he sits down.

It's Bella.

'Hi Vaughn,' she says. 'Hope I'm not interrupting anything?'

'Not at all.'

'Gus tells me you're coming back on Friday. I thought you might want to have dinner with my dad and me on Saturday. Papa's dying to hear about Australia.'

'I'd love to, Bella. What can I bring?'

'Just yourself.'

Gus and Angela are grinning like two weasels when I get back to the table.

'*I'd love to, Bella,*' Gus mimics. '*What can I bring?*'

'Shut up, you buffoon,' I say, sitting down.

'I notice we don't get invited to dinner at the Gerbers,' Angela says.

'Wonder why that is?' Gus muses.

'Don't be childish, you idiots. Bella says the old man wants to hear about Australia.'

It sounds so stupid even I laugh as I say it.

*

We get an early start on my grandparents' graves and by the time Gus decides to call it a day at three in the afternoon we've made better than expected progress. Gus figures another day's work ought to see the job done. And then begins the task none of us wishes to confront – our parents. But that will have to wait until Monday. Tonight, Gus reminds us, we have Jessica and Lauren's school concert on our itinerary.

Although I still ache in every joint and my hands are covered by a pox of blisters, I glow with a sense of wellbeing. A sign, no doubt, that I am over the worst of my physical tribulations. Indeed, as far as the digging is concerned, I've improved enough to hold my own against Angela – believe me, a proud achievement for any flaccid male academic of my age – though our combined efforts still lag behind Gus, the behemoth.

Late in the afternoon we stop again at the church in Shangani on our way back to Bulawayo. Reverend Dlomo informs us that the two gravediggers went AWOL yesterday afternoon, leaving one grave undug. Gus shakes his head and gets cranky. In an impetuous and undemocratic reaction, he tells Reverend Dlomo that if they don't come back and finish the job by Tuesday next week *we* will do it. Silently I pray for the safe and speedy return of the absconders.

On the way back to Bulawayo Angela tells Gus of her plan to look after Joseph and Anna.

'Jumping the gun a bit, aren't you?' he says. 'Can't imagine Joseph and Anna in a three-bedroom house, watching TV.'

'It's not as though they've never seen a house before,' Angela replies. 'They've been running ours since the year dot. I just don't want them to come to any harm.'

Gus lapses into silence. Pit bull mode.

'I'm not asking you for any money, Gus. It's important to anticipate what might happen. You've done it with Jenny and the girls ...'

'Are you saying I don't care about Joseph and Anna? Who the hell has been looking after them while you two have been swanning around overseas?'

'Angela's not saying anything of the sort,' I intervene. 'We just want to do what we can to look after them.'

'Oh, so you're in on it too, Chickenheart?'

'I think it would be a wise move, under the circumstances.'

Gus makes the sound of a bugle. 'Tally ho! Let's pop into Africa and rescue the natives, shall we?'

'Don't be stupid, Gus,' Angela says, peeved. 'We don't need your bloody permission, you know.'

Gus scratches his unshaven jaw. 'It never bloody ends, does it? No one can just get on with their damn lives without others interfering. I'll tell you right now, Joseph and Anna don't want to live anywhere else. If you took them off the farm they'd just shrivel up and die.'

We come to the overturned truck. Gus stops and walks around it, shaking his head. He whistles as he pisses against it. Back in the car, he rummages around in the glove box and slaps his Creedence tape in the cassette. As we drive, he sings in a woefully off-key voice:

I seeya bad-a-moon-a-risin'
I seeya trouble's on the way.

The three weary gravediggers arrive back at the Burnside house in the evening. We shower and dress smart-casual for the girls' concert. Then Gus and I settle down to a drink on the front veranda which is enclosed by a solid, though ornate, burglar screen. Angela and Jenny are helping the girls get ready.

Gus's mood has not improved. The talk about Joseph and Anna has touched a nerve. 'Isn't it bloody depressing?' he says. 'Every prediction Ian Smith made about this country falling into the hands of the kaffirs has come to pass. Doesn't that amaze you, professor?'

'I thought Smith predicted white rule for a thousand years.'

'You know what I mean, smart-arse. Every bloody warning he gave about what would happen if whites *didn't* rule has come true. Tyranny, chaos ... where are you clever bastards now, who ridiculed him back then, hey?'

'Snap out of it, Gus. Rhodesia run by whites never had a snowball's chance in hell of lasting a thousand years. The problem with Zimbabwe is Mugabe, not the black Zimbabweans. Direct your anger at him, not at a whole race of people.'

Gus gives me a chilly smile. 'Still banging the same drum, hey? Despite all the evidence in front of your eyes. And when the next dictator does the same thing? And the next? How many Mugabes does it take for you to realise these people cannot run a chicken raffle, let alone a country?'

'I don't want to argue with you, Gus. But please don't come at me with your bloody bigotry. If Africa's awash with dictators that's just the way it is. You're exhausting, you know – one minute you extol the virtues of your pal Saxon, the next you're vilifying Africans *en masse*. I've told you before, cut your losses and leave. You're just part of an inexorable tide of history. A tide that's going out.'

'What kind of gutless crap is that? Face it, man, if it was whites doing what these savages are doing you bloody hippies would be marching down the street with placards. But because it's kaffirs ... somehow it's all explained away as a perfectly understandable fucking historical tide.'

'It's pointless arguing with you, Gus. You won't listen to reason. What will it take before you wake up to the realisation that it's over? The time for whites in Africa has gone. When is it going to penetrate that thick skull of yours that Africans don't want you here? You might find this hard to stomach, Gus, but they actually don't need you either. They've had a gutful of white paternalism.'

'Fuck off, Chickenheart. I have a right to be here, as much as any munt. I'm just not a bloody coward who runs when things get bad. Tell me, is there anything that you'd actually stand up and fight for, hey? No, you fucking gutless wonders are all the same. Sleep with the enemy and then run when the shit hits the fan.'

The violence in his voice is unnerving. I get up and walk down into the garden, glass of whisky in hand, trying to contain my own anger and confusion. I look up at the massive spray of stars above that only seem to confirm the futility of our human squabbles. Then Gus comes up behind me. He puts a hand on my shoulder.

'Sorry, boet' he says. 'I was out of line. I didn't mean it.'

'Yes, you did.'

He takes a deep breath. 'Look, I know I go off the handle sometimes. You've got a right to speak your mind. It just sticks in my craw, that's all. I can't stand what's happening to this country ... I hate it when people try to rationalise it.'

I sigh wearily. 'The future lies in the hands of black Africans, Gus. It's for them to determine, not you.'

Gus waves his hand to dismiss the subject. 'Let's just forget it, boet. I'm sorry I got out of line. You've got your beliefs. I've got mine. Let's just leave it at that, okay?'

'No, it's not okay. I've just about had it with you, Gus. If you want me to fuck off back to Australia, just tell me and I'll go.'

'Vaughn, please ... just forget what I said. Having you and Ange here means a lot to me.' He squeezes my shoulder again.

'Come on, man, let's grab ourselves another grog. How's that for a plan?'

We go to the concert in Jenny's car, a lovingly-maintained '82 model Ford station wagon. Jessica and Lauren, who are done up to the nines with lipstick and dark mascara, cavort in the back. Jenny explains that every year Bulawayo Christian Girls High holds a fund-raising variety concert in conjunction with the local private boys' school, St Patrick's. The venue alternates between the schools – this year it's at St Patrick's. There are hordes of kids standing around in groups as we park the car in the school grounds. Jessica and Lauren immediately rush off to meet their friends. We file into the hall and sit on hard school chairs under the glare of fluorescent lights and President Mugabe, whose ubiquitous portrait hangs above the stage. The hall is abuzz. Finally, St Patrick's headmaster climbs the stairs to the stage and welcomes the audience. He finishes with an inane joke about how Hollywood movie directors would be scrambling for their chequebooks if they had any inkling of the up and coming talent in Bulawayo. A stoic ripple of laughter.

The lights dim.

The concert takes me by surprise. Expecting something quite mundane, I'm instead moved and intrigued by what I see. In this neck of the woods, it seems time has stood still. Aside from the fact that the majority of the performers are white, each pantomime, each cautious little skit on the foibles of teachers, each recited poem, and finally the inept pop band, plunges me into the past, into the Victorian values of my own school days. A small Indian boy with a lisp gives a stirring rendition of Rudyard Kipling's *If*. Jessica and Lauren are in half-a-dozen performances, including a reasonably amusing extract from *As You Like It* (which I remember having to do myself at Chaplin High in 1970). They are both in the choir whose angelic rendition of *Onward Christian Soldiers* at the end has everyone tapping their feet and singing along.

The audience appears to clap almost hysterically after each act. I'm charmed and disturbed by this strange Victorian delusion, poignant yet profoundly depressing because I can think of nothing quite so anachronistic. These youngsters are in a time warp. Soon, if they are to follow the exodus of people leaving the country, they will be thrust into a world in which, for better or for worse, Tom Brown's School Days are over, and Tom is now a human rights lawyer acting for Iraqi refugees.

Still, I shower praise on the girls as we drive home and even recite a bit from *King Lear* that I remember from my school days. This magnanimous act precipitates a most unfortunate avalanche of old school songs and poems from Angela and Jenny – I swear, Coleridge and Tennyson have a lot to answer for. It is excruciating and Gus gives me a recriminatory glance. Only Gus maintains his dignity, mostly because the performing arts were never considered safe territory by any self-respecting heterosexual Rhodesian male in *his* school days. No doubt, the only thing he remembers from those days is the rugby war cry.

When we get home Gus hands Angela and me some formidable wads of local currency. Angela pretends to collapse under the weight of hers.

'It amounts to bugger-all,' Gus says. 'A bit of pocket money to get around over the weekend. I'm going back to the farm tomorrow. I've got things to sort out with Saxon. Jenny doesn't need the car tomorrow – you could go drawing in the Matopos, if you still want to.'

Later, perusing the bookshelf in the lounge, I find Stuart Cloete's *The African Giant*. I fall asleep while reading the first chapter, the tone of which is curiously reminiscent of tonight's blast from the past.

*

Most whites in Bulawayo still refer to the Matobo hills as 'the Matopos', another faint reminder of colonial Rhodesia's penchant for corrupting African names for places. Despite the fact that I applaud the restoration of correct African terms to sites, I find it difficult to conform to the new names and, like Angela, find myself reverting to what is familiar. But while it is sometimes simpler to use the familiar terms of the past, I realise it carries also a refusal to accept the present – to accept the implications of what has taken the past's place. I convince myself that for me, a visitor passing through, it's of no great consequence. But for those who live here it becomes a sign of intransigence. A badge of despair for the present.

The family's trips to Matobo started with my great-grandfather, Vaughn. Grandpa John said he could remember going out there in an ox wagon for a week each year, where they would camp under the stars. Vaughn and John felt strongly about Rhodesians paying respect to the man who was buried there, Cecil John Rhodes. My father continued the tradition, although our sorties into this rugged wilderness a short drive south of Bulawayo were more for rest and relaxation than doffing our hats to the nation's founder.

Matobo is an awesome geological wonder that suddenly rears up from the monotonous Matabeleland plains and swallows you into its midst. One minute you are driving through the tedious acacia bush and savannah that surrounds Bulawayo, the next you are enveloped by a vast maze of exfoliating granite eruptions, breathtaking and eerie in their immensity. Mile upon mile of mountainous grey domes bursting through the earth, colossal boulders piled and scattered in random profusion, stained with washes of green and orange lichens. In this pristine wilderness the troubles of the world – even the troubles of Zimbabwe – seem puny and irrelevant, despite the fact that there are government officials at every main site, waiting like trap-door spiders in tattered old army tents with rolls of tickets to prey upon Zimbabwe's few remaining tourists.

Angela drives, stopping every so often to take photographs. We pass small herds of wildebeest and zebra in grasslands between the maze of outcrops. We spot baboons, dassies and klipspringers. As luck would have it, we come across two white rhinos grazing a short distance from the road. Angela stops and loads her camera. Then, ignoring my pleas for caution, she climbs out of the car and sneaks off like an Apache downwind through the bush, getting to within a few metres of the beasts. She returns after expending her film, jubilant, waving the shed skin of a black mamba she has found lying in the grass. She laughs when I reprimand her for such foolhardiness.

We arrive beneath World's View, Rhodes's burial site. After paying the official camped at the base of the hill, we hike slowly up the granite dome to its crest. We pause at Rhodes's grave. As far back as I can remember, there always was a wind blowing up here among the great round boulders that surround the grave.

It's an extraordinary anomaly, this site. A hundred years ago they railed Rhodes's body all the way up from Cape Town to bury him here, his chosen place, carved deep in Africa's stony heart. His grave is without embellishment. The simple inscription on the bronze cover reads: *Here Lie the Remains of Cecil John Rhodes.* No dates, no lofty citation. Whereas in the past this site was a place of pilgrimage, we are now completely alone. A short distance away there is another similar grave, although this one is not surrounded by great boulders. This belongs to Leander Starr Jameson, Rhodes's devoted though impetuous lieutenant. And further along is the Memorial to the Shangani Patrol, a contingent of white soldiers who were wiped out by Lobengula's warriors during the Matabele Wars. Heroes of the past, all slaves to a dream that turned into a nightmare for their dispossessed kith and kin.

We sit out of the wind in the lee of some rocks next to the Shangani Memorial and gaze quietly into the distance. The chaotic jumble of hills extends before us in layers of hazy greys and blues as far as the eye can see. The wind whistles and hums around the rocks. Angela starts drawing. I watch her as she begins by throwing the group of boulders around Rhodes's grave against the sky with the endlessly diminishing hills in the background. A true traditionalist, she applies the formulas of Constable and Turner – a low horizon to create a sense of vastness, even the suggestion of aerial perspective where her background lines seem faint and indistinct in contrast to the hard, sure lines of the foreground.

I simply don't know where to begin and out of professional embarrassment walk off on my own to another sheltered spot. I cannot remember when I was last challenged to work in such a conventional way. Despite what Gus may jest to the contrary,

147

I am amply blessed with a natural drawing ability; in fact, unlike Angela, who has worked hard over many years to hone her skills, drawing had come so naturally to me that at a young age I found the tedium associated with straight observation un-bearable. Conventional realism, to me, never explained the heart of anything – it only explained what I could see already, before I started drawing. Why draw what can be captured by a camera in an instant? That's why I moved into distortion and abstraction, so things might have a parallel life in art. But that was a long time ago – in another lifetime, it seems.

There on that rock in Africa's stony heart I despair at the waste of my life. I curse myself for having relinquished my belief in the intrinsic value of my God-given skills, to have capitulated so meekly to the facile trends of contemporary art. In this Angela has shown so much more intelligence, despite the fact that I show disdain for her work. The scene before me seems unimaginably complex – it seems a lifetime of tedious labour will not be enough to complete such intricate detail. If I had some oil paints perhaps I might make a stab at it. Before I stopped painting, I had developed a loose, expressive manner of working with transparent oil washes, the accidental effects of which might have suggested the intricate geological layering that lies before me.

Instead, I find myself drawn to the simple block-like form of the Shangani Patrol Memorial that, from my vantage point below, now looms against the sky. Something about its brood-ing silence and the obsolete narratives told by its bronze plaques seems strangely befitting. I begin to draw the monu-ment. And as it takes form on my paper, I notice the other things begin to fit in too – the granite rampart on which it is situated, the oblique glimpse of the hills in the background. It has provided a perspective within which to see the rest.

And it's at this point that I realise my existential dilemma. Despite the fact that I was born in Africa, I realise how *unAfrican* I am. Angela too. We will never be able to approach Africa without looking through the filtered lens of Europe – Angela with her artistic formulas invented and perfected by Europe, me with my need for a familiar historical edifice against which to see and measure the continent that bore me. When I was younger such a realisation might have been profoundly disappointing – how I had promoted myself as 'African' in my student days, when others still clung to the title of 'European'! Even in Australia, the delusion that I saw the world from an African perspective persisted. A South African colleague from the English Department at Hunter Valley University once described his longing for Africa as 'a miserable postcolonial affliction'. He'd come to realise that the Africa he longed for was, in fact, Europe's Africa – not the sentimental umbilical fantasy that whites, like ourselves, had concocted in our hearts. What we really longed for, he said, was for the time when whites had a sense of hope and security, a time when they *owned* Africa. That time was gone forever, and the lost white tribe, now dispersed and dispossessed, was left in a contradictory limbo of moral awakening and existential regret.

Such was my denial that I pitied my colleague, his confession almost too honest for me to bear. Now I realise that he spoke for me, especially me.

I do four finished drawings, one from each aspect of the Monument. This takes the best part of the day. Angela ambles over a few times to see what I'm doing. She seems puzzled and intrigued by my choice of subject. She's been trying to capture a sense of an unspoilt Africa – Africa uncontaminated by intrusion. It occurs to me that Rhodes probably had a similar idea when he chose his burial site – he had changed Africa forever, but he wanted to be laid to rest in the untouched heart of what he'd sought to overwhelm.

When I put these thoughts to Angela over a picnic lunch, she frowns. 'Damn it, Vaughn, you always make it too complicated! The traditions are just a means to an end. What ever happened to the idea of straightforward enjoyment in painting? Not everything has to be loaded with political slants and perspectives. You can still have an innocent eye, you know.'

'There's no such thing as an innocent eye, Ange. We always construct a view from a cultural vantage point. And in doing so we create a reality that doesn't exist – at least, in the eyes of others outside our culture. What may be real to us is just fiction to others.'

Angela laughs. 'So what? Isn't that what makes the world interesting? Different cultures offering different realities? Lighten up, you miserable sceptic. You don't need to apologise for how you see the world!'

'It doesn't bother you that our art exposes us for what we are?'

'What do you mean?'

'I mean that it reveals how unAfrican we are – that we don't belong here?'

'Oh, Vaughn ... you poor lost soul. When are you going to stop agonising over what we are?'

'That's the point, Ange! We don't know what we are. We exist in some limbo between identities. That's what our art tells me.'

Angela raises her hands, exasperated. 'For heaven's sake!

You were born here, Vaughn! That makes you African. White African – yes. Powerless in your place of birth – yes. But still African! I don't know why you make it so damn complicated!'

'Come on, Ange. We were Europeans who owned a piece of Africa. Did we ever call ourselves African then? No. But now that we've lost Africa, we lay claim to Africanness! The brutal fact is we can't be African unless we have a place in Africa that we can call our own.'

Angela sighs. 'Vaughn ... sometimes you disappoint me. Since when did you become so materialistic? I'm sick of the whole idea of *owning* Africa. A more reverent view of our relationship to this continent is long overdue, don't you think? It's time we thought in terms of Africa owning us.'

I shake my head. 'That's nice and romantic, Ange, but I don't think the likes of Mugabe would be swayed but such a naïve fantasy. He has some pretty firm ideas about our Africanness.'

'A deranged bigot, blinded by hate – why bother what Mugabe thinks?'

'Because he calls the shots in this country.'

Angela laughs dryly. 'Relax, little brother. Not even Mugabe can change the fact that we're African. We don't need to prove anything – it is just simple *fact*. And we don't have to apologise to anyone – we've already paid dearly for what we are. Do me a favour, Vaughn. Paint for pleasure, okay? Try it just once.'

As we head back to Bulawayo, I feel a curious relief, as though poison has been purged from my system. I glance at Angela's profile as she drives, Roman-nosed, faintly haughty. It depresses me that now I must share her again with the world.

*

Since Angela and I spent longer than anticipated in Matobo, I am a bit late for my dinner date at the Gerbers. Bella and her father, Oom Jasper, live in a modest, though comfortable home in Suburbs, not far from the park and museum. As I drive Jenny's station wagon up to their gate in Clarke Street, a blaze of security lights come on. It was my intention to leave the car outside, but the gates open and I drive through the glare of lights into the dark yard beyond.

Bella is there on the front porch, dispatching an unruly pack of guard dogs to the back garden and attempting to close the gate with a remote control. The batteries appear to be flat and it takes several attempts before it works. I climb out of the car and walk up the path to the porch. Bella is looking positively virginal in a long white cotton dress. She has her hair drawn up at the back like one of Alma Tadema's Grecian nymphs. Since I don't wish to convey the impression to Oom Jasper that Australians are a nation of slobs and layabouts, I, too, have put a little time into my appearance, having shaved and dressed in my most presentable ensemble – beige longs, a blue shirt and my trusty Harris Tweed jacket with its leather patches on the elbows.

'Sorry I'm late,' I say, kissing her cheek.

She looks at the bottle of wine in my hand. 'You shouldn't have.'

'Draytons,' I say. 'All the way from the Hunter Valley for that very special occasion.'

She laughs and beckons me inside to where Oom Jasper is sitting in a lounge filled with cigarette smoke and family memorabilia. Oom Jasper had always been a tall, powerful man – he once played rugby for Rhodesia, lock forward as I recall – but now he is thin and frail. There is a brown nicotine stain on the ceiling above his chair and another above the chair to his left which I guess had been Mevrou Gerber's – they had both been chain smokers. The pair of bifocals almost slips off his nose as he leans forward on his walking stick to get to his feet.

'Sit, Papa!' Bella says. 'Vaughn doesn't expect you to stand on ceremony for him.'

'Nee, God, meisie!' Oom Jasper wheezes. ''n Man moet maar staan. Hey, Vaughn! Hoe gaan dit, ou seun?'

I can vaguely understand Afrikaans but could never speak it. 'I'm fine, Oom Jasper,' I reply, shaking his hard old hand. 'Nice to see you again.'

Oom Jasper pushes his bifocals back up his nose and studies my face. 'Jesus tog, ons word almal oud! When last did I see you, Vaughn.'

'I can't remember, Oom. Must've been back in the early seventies.'

Oom Jasper groans tiredly and sits slowly down again. 'Ja, so gaan die lewe, né? Kom, Isabella, maak vir die manne 'n dop!'

'What would you like, Vaughn?' Bella asks. 'Beer? Brandy? We'll have the wine with dinner. Vaughn brought us some wine all the way from Australia, Papa.'

Oom Jasper glowers at her. 'Wine from Australia! Is this what the world's come to?'

'A beer will be fine,' I tell Bella, handing her the bottle of wine.

While Bella goes to the kitchen to fix our drinks, I sit next to Oom Jasper in Mevrou Gerber's chair and we reminisce a bit about the old days. My eyes stray to the photographs on the walls of the family in happier times. Mostly, my eyes seem to gravitate towards the pictures of Tienus, the good Afrikaner son, in his rugby kit, in his RLI uniform, standing next to a prize Aberdeen Angus bull at the Trade Fair. I can't bring myself to mention him.

Bella comes back with the drinks. She and her father are having brandies. They both light cigarettes and offer me one, which in a moment of masochistic solidarity I accept. We toast to each other's health. Oom Jasper asks me how things are going on the farm. I explain how far we've got with the graves. 'Bloody ridiculous state of affairs,' he mutters.

'Let's not spoil the conversation, Papa,' Bella intervenes.

'Ja, but what have we come to when the dead cannot even rest in peace? Ag, but you're right, meisie. Let's not get upset about things we can't change. Tell me about Australia, Vaughn. I knew some Aussies up in North Africa during the war. Rough as hell, but bloody good soldiers. I always wondered what kind of country made blokes like that.'

I reach into my jacket pocket and take out some photographs. 'It's a big place, Oom. But these will give you some idea.'

Bella drags over a coffee table for me to put the photographs on. She sits on the floor at her father's feet. One by one I show them shots of Newcastle, my small miner's cottage in the suburb of Wallsend (where I moved after my divorce), the university, the beautiful beaches, the farming hinterland of the Hunter Valley. I also have some pictures of the trip Angela and I made to Alice Springs, where we'd seen Ayers Rock and the Olgas. Oom Jasper has plenty of questions about farming. He is impressed by how Australian farmers manage to work huge properties with so little by way of manpower. I show them one photograph of Beth and Michael and briefly explain the debacle of my marriage to get it out of the way. Oom Jasper takes the photograph and studies it carefully, shaking his head sadly. 'Ja, seun, so gaan die lewe,' he sighs.

Bella is intrigued by my modest home in Wallsend.

'Newcastle used to be a real working-class town,' I explain. 'Coal mining. Iron and steel. The homes are nothing special.'

Bella draws on her cigarette. 'It's amazing. You don't have burglar guards! And your neighbour too!'

Oom Jasper sits back when I finish showing the photographs and blows a thin stream of smoke at the ceiling. 'You made a good move, Vaughn.' he says. 'You used your bloody brains and got out of this place before it was too late. This is not a country for civilised people.'

'Ag, Papa. It's no use talking about it.'

'I wish you'd pack up and go to Australia too, Isabella. Make a new life for yourself. You're still young enough. Talk some sense into her head, Vaughn!'

Bella sighs impatiently. 'You know I've already applied and didn't have enough points, remember?'

'Ag, man, that was years ago. You should keep trying.'

'Ja? And who's going to look after you, Papa?'

'Don't worry about me, meisie. You just look after yourself. There's no future here for you. Jy kan mos 'n plekkie maak vir my daar in Australië.'

'You know I won't leave you, Papa.'

Bella looks suddenly wistful and for an instant I think she is going to cry. She gets up, straightens her dress and goes through to the kitchen.

Oom Jasper sighs, watching her go. 'I'm serious, Vaughn. She's wasting her life here because of me. Talk to her, seun.'

I shrug, uncomfortable at being drawn into their personal affairs.

Oom Jasper gives me a frank stare. He points to the photograph of Tienus with the prize bull. 'My life is finished,' he says. 'It finished with Tienus. He held all my hopes and dreams. He was the one I entrusted to take care of our farm for the Gerbers of the future. He was the seed that would multiply here in Africa, who would pass on our name. Now that's all finished. Bella's a good girl. She deserves a better life than this.'

I sit there smoking with him, unable to find an intelligent word to acknowledge the rout of his life. Then Bella calls us through for dinner. I help Oom Jasper to his feet and we go through to the candle-lit dining room and sit down in the gloom. Oom Jasper says grace. Bella dishes us up a plate of beef curry and rice and we help ourselves to sambals. At her suggestion I open the bottle of Draytons dry red and pour everyone a glass. We again toast each other's health.

'Jesus, I can hardly see what I'm eating here, meisie!' Oom Jasper grumbles. 'Let's have some bloody light on the subject!'

'Ag, Papa! Don't spoil the atmosphere. Candles are nice, man!'

'There is still such a thing as electricity in Zimbabwe, you know. When they remember to switch it on.'

We tuck into the curry which is perfect – thick and hot enough to bring out a mild sweat. I notice Bella glancing at me as I eat. Perhaps it's the wine, or just the haze after of a long, good day, but in the yellow candlelight she exudes a strange, contradictory beauty. In her dark green eyes lurk a predator and a victim.

I engage Oom Jasper in some light-hearted discussion about the Rugby World Cup (of which I have a passing knowledge, but absolutely no interest). He laments the 'changing of the guard', meaning the decline of the Springboks, and reminisces about the time when the Bokke reigned supreme. Not partial to the golden age of apartheid I change the subject by asking Bella about her work at the law firm. She shrugs and tells me it's nothing exciting – her firm is mostly involved in matters of industrial property law. But since the economic situation has become so terrible, she says, the partners are thinking of opening a branch in South Africa – a prelude, she suspects, to closing down in Zimbabwe. Since 'Brains Trust' Mugabe has begun to turn his attention from farm invasions to white and Asian businesses, most of the still-viable companies are looking for ways of getting their assets out of the country.

'Our company's not in great shape,' Bella sighs. 'They've already started retrenching people. It's just a matter of time before I'll have to consider my options. Which are zero.'

'I've told you, meisie. Don't waste your time with this bloody country! It doesn't deserve good people who work hard. You work hard only so the thieves in government can keep their snouts in the trough.'

'The country deserves good people, Papa. What it doesn't deserve are the thieves.'

'Well, it's pointless waiting around, hoping it will change.'

Bella turns to me. 'There's an interesting exhibition on at the National Gallery, Vaughn. I was wondering if you wanted to go tomorrow.'

157

'I wouldn't have picked you for an art lover, Bella.'

'I may surprise you yet, Professor Bourke. It's a show of photos of Bulawayo from the fifties and sixties. From a black perspective.'

'Strange choice of subject. I'd love to go, Bella. Are they open on Sundays?'

Bella nods. 'I'll pick you up tomorrow morning. Would you like to come too, Papa?'

Oom Jasper waves his hand dismissively. 'I'm afraid I've got no interest in art. Besides, I have a black perspective of my own!'

We polish off the bottle of wine. Oom Jasper has become drowsy and mellow. We finish the dinner with a fruit salad (with fruit from their own trees in the back yard) and ice cream and then have coffee in the lounge. After this, Oom Jasper makes a great show of stretching and yawning and gets laboriously to his feet.

'I must get these old bones to bed,' he wheezes. 'I'll leave you to talk. It's good to see you again, Vaughn. Please stop by again before you go.'

'Of course I will, Oom.'

We watch his slow exit from the room. Then I say, 'I suppose I'd better call it a night too.'

'You don't want a small drop of brandy in your coffee?' Bella asks.

I affect serious deliberation. 'Since you mention it, I might just be a devil.'

Bella giggles and goes off to collect the brandy from the kitchen. She doses our coffees with a more than liberal 'drop' and offers me a cigarette. We sit back smoking and drinking. I tell her about the graves and show her the state of my hands.

She touches a blister gently and says, 'Ag, shame, man.' Hoping to tap into that gullible reverence some women have for the artistic personality, I tell her about my revelatory experience in Matobo with Angela. I probe her eyes for glints of admiration. They stare back, amused.

'You don't look like an artist, you know,' Bella says.

'Oh? And what do I look like?'

'I don't know. You just don't look like an artist.'

'Nice to know I'm so nondescript. And how should an artist look? A beret? Minus an ear?'

Bella laughs again, slapping my arm gently. 'You're still handsome, Vaughn. To me, anyway.'

I'm immediately assailed by the memory of those green eyes scanning my pitiful physique as I lay next to the pool in my hung-over state. The fact that she is lying through her teeth, however, now seems of little significance.

After the coffee we, ominously, opt for a small nightcap of Oom Jasper's homemade 'mampoer' – a liqueur that I can best describe as saccharine paint stripper. We continue to smoke and make small talk. And, of course, the nightcap soon expands in girth and, before we know it, we're both wearing sombreros, as appears to be the fashion in Zimbabwe these days. Bella puts an old Neil Diamond record on the stereo. Despite questions in my mind as to old Rhodesians and their taste in music, we sing to each other: *You are the sun; I am the moon. You are the words; I am the tune. Play ...*

Somewhere in the fog of it all, I admonish myself: Vaughn, my boy, you are turning into a complete reprobate. What is it about this place – about these people – that propels you to cavort about like a drunken oaf? Like some irresponsible boor unblessed by a fully functioning brain? Is this my authentic self finally emerging? With all the mixed drinks of the evening I've managed to get myself well and truly beyond the pale, which, strange to say, appears to be no deterrent for Bella. If my befuddled observations are correct, it is indeed Bella who more than generously tops up my drinks. And who lights the never-ending stream of cigarettes? Led astray, I'm putty in her hands. By the time I lean over and kiss her, I am convinced beyond any doubt that we are kindred spirits, completely meant for each other. Yes, Frida Kahlo and her emaciated Diego Rivera. We roll around on the couch a bit, planting sloppy kisses on each other's faces and necks. Somehow my hand slips accidentally under her white dress and rests on her bottom, which, I'm pleased to note, is firm but fleshy to the touch. Giggling heartily, Bella transfers my groping paw to her breasts. She allows me a spell of exploratory fondling before gently pushing me away.

'Ag, Vaughn,' she says in a hoarse, tremulous whisper. 'Stadig oor die klippetjies, man.'

Whatever the hell that means. But even in my drunken state I cannot deny that I'm relieved this tomfoolery has come to an end. That I might have needed to prove myself beyond this point has been a niggling worry.

That last thing I recall is scraping Jenny's car on the gate post as I reverse down the drive.

*

I wake the next morning to the sound of the family going off to church. I'm still dressed in my evening ensemble, sweating and disoriented. For half an hour I lie there like death warmed up, cowering beneath a barrage of tacky flashbacks. The sudden recollection of the liberties I took with Bella brings me into a contradictory state of mortification and sleazy half-arousal. Is this what I have become? A pathetic roué? Unable to stomach my wretchedness, I change into my swimming trunks and go through to the kitchen to make some coffee. Angela is sitting at the breakfast table, reading a book. I manage a cheery greeting. She looks up and scrutinises me as I stand there, head bowed, waiting for the kettle to boil.

'Jesus, I hope Bella's still in one piece, because you certainly aren't.'

With no defences to muster, I can only grin stupidly.

'Bella's my friend, you know. I hope you didn't take advantage of her.'

'Come on, Ange. We just had a few drinks.'

Angela smiles, one eyebrow raised. 'I'm sure you did. By the way, Jenny's pretty pissed off with the scratch on her car. You better get it fixed, or you'll be forever in the dog box.'

The memory of it thrusts into my consciousness like a corkscrew. That long metallic scrape and Bella convulsing into laughter as she waved me goodbye at the gate.

'Oh God, that car's a relic. It's just a little scratch.'

'Cars are like gold in this place, Vaughn.'

'Don't worry. I'll get it fixed.'

I pour myself some coffee and go down to the pool. Filled with alcoholic remorse I sit with my feet dangling in the water, pondering my miserable life. I drink the coffee in a couple of gulps, remove my glasses, then slide into the water. I blow the air from my dank lungs and sink to the bottom of the pool. There I lie thinking of how drowning is said to be a pleasurable death. Then I kick to the surface and swim to the shallow end. It's nearly nine o'clock and already the sun is hot. I lie face down on the slasto with one blistered hand dangling in the water, close my eyes and pass out into a dreadful swirling world in which demons bark at me like baboons. Authentic Man.

I wake to a slap on my backside and a familiar giggle.

'Ag, arme ou ding,' Bella laughs. 'Licking your wounds again, I see.'

I open one eye and see her blurred form crouched over me. I roll over and retrieve my glasses. In focus, Bella looks fresh and pretty. I groan and roll back onto my stomach. What is it about this world that no one but me seems to suffer the ill effects of alcohol? Bella runs her fingers up my knobbly spine which makes me shiver with pleasure.

'How are you feeling, old man?' she asks.

I smile with fake bravado. 'Bloody shocking. Are you here to torment me? Or to lay a charge of harassment?'

She laughs and kisses me on the cheek. Her perfume nearly makes me swoon. 'Have you forgotten our arrangement?'

'Arrangement?'

'The exhibition, remember?'

'Oh Christ. Yes, I did forget. I'm sorry.'

'We can go some other time if you don't feel up to it.'

I sit up. 'No, no. Give me ten minutes and I'll be ready.'

She cups a gentle hand to my stubbled cheek. 'You sure?'

I nod and get to my feet, my knees clicking. We walk back to the house. As we pass Jenny's car, Bella stops and inspects the scratch. I stand there with an inane look of guilt. She giggles and gives me a quick hug which, I confess, is an elixir.

Bella chats with Angela as I shower and dress. I can hear

them laughing from the bathroom. It seems I've spent my whole life trying to get others to take me seriously, to no avail. It pains me to see my self-respect peeling away to reveal a tawdry clown. It's something I will have to address.

We climb into Bella's early-model Volkswagen Golf and head into town. Along the way we pass the family returning from church. I notice an icy expression on Jenny's face that I realise won't thaw until her car is fixed. Gus grins lopsidedly as he sees the two of us.

We park outside the National Gallery in the centre of town. A beautiful old three-storey flagstone building that once housed government offices in colonial times, the Gallery is now in dire need of maintenance. Nevertheless, the exhibition called *Bygone* is astonishing. The works, all photographs from the fifties and sixties, are of Bulawayo's black society at its leisure. Scenes at beerhalls and dances, weddings, families and friends standing in front of township shacks, young blokes lounging in cars or taxis. A smiling old man with his trousers clipped up around his calves astride a new bicycle. Happy people, well fed, well dressed. Young couples in their finery. Marriage photographs. Children's birthdays. School plays. As Bella and I walk through the rooms on creaking wooden floors, I wonder at the curator's intention. I'm stunned by the (inadvertent?) message these images give. They are, without exception, a record of happier times. Nothing could be more extreme than the contrast between the people inside these photographs and the miserable Breughelian processions outside in the street.

It's a brave message that declares: Look how things were in the times of colonial oppression. And look at how things are today. In other words, look at how our president and his government have betrayed the people of Zimbabwe by making the time of oppression a time to long for!

I'm mesmerised by the brilliance of this protest and as I explain my interpretation to Bella she nods thoughtfully, her eyes also wistful for a lost time.

Afterwards, we have lunch at the Churchill Hotel. I talk animatedly about the exhibition. Mugabe's greatest crime is that he has proven Ian Smith right, I say, mealy-mouthed. A flicker of irritation crosses Bella's face. She is about to say something, then a curtain descends behind her eyes. She just reaches over and strokes my hand. I tell her I'll be stuck on the farm with Gus and Angela during the week. I ask her to come out to the farm if she can get away from work.

'I don't want to go near our place,' she says.

'I know. I understand. It's just an idea. I'd like to see you.'

'I'll see,' she says. 'Maybe. I'll definitely come to the funeral.'

*

It's still dark when we leave for the farm. Just as dawn is breaking we drop in at the church in Shangani to find the last grave has been dug. We continue on to the farm. Up until now Gus has refrained from subjecting us to his barbaric music. Now, as he rummages around for a tape, I finally muster the will to protest.

'Can't we listen to something else, Gus?' I say. 'The radio or something?'

Gus looks at me with fake concern. 'You wanna hear the radio? Okay, let's have the radio.'

He turns on the radio. By malevolent coincidence a recent

speech by the president is being broadcast. In his peculiar, dainty way of speaking, Mugabe is castigating Zimbabwe's whites.

'*These crooks we inherited as part of our population. We cannot expect them to have straightened up, to be honest people and an honest community. Yes, some of them are good people, but they remain cheats. They remain dishonest. They remain uncommitted even to the national cause …*'

'Oh, turn it off, please!' Angela says. 'It's too early in the morning to listen to that racist crap.'

'But, Ange, the professor wants to listen. You don't think it's crap, do you, Vaughn?'

I raise my hands in defeat. 'Play your bloody music, Gus.'

Back at the farm we load up the Cruiser in preparation for another day's digging. Witness and the other workers turn up at the gate just as the sun is rising. As usual the dogs give them a rousing reception. Angela and I drink coffee on the veranda as we watch Gus give instructions to the group. It seems Gus is now down to six men. We watch as they clamber onto a trailer behind the old Nuffield tractor. With Witness driving they bounce off down the road.

Gus climbs the steps to the veranda, muttering, 'Two more have gapped it. Witness said some of Mtunzi's mob pitched up at the compound this weekend and threatened them. Why the hell I even bother, I don't know.'

'Good question, Gus,' I say.

He gives me a sour look and knocks back his coffee in a gulp. Frik and Tiny sidle up to him, campaigning for a run. We climb into the Cruiser and head off to the graveyard with the dogs galloping behind. Angela is in a cheerful mood.

'Remember when we used to go on holidays down to Cape Town,' she reminisces. 'Those endless bloody car trips! How we used to drive Dad and Nan crazy with our fighting. And our singing! Remember our singing?'

Gus and I laugh and nod our heads. Angela begins singing:

One little elephant began to play
Upon a spider's web one day
He thought it such tremendous fun
So he called for another little elephant to come.

Laughing, Gus joins in. And, scarcely believing I could be party to such silliness, I throw back my head and along with my siblings begin bellowing out an endless succession of verses.

Two little elephants began to play
Upon a spider's web one day
They thought it such tremendous fun
So they called for another little elephant to come ...

On and on we go, yelling ridiculously at the top of our voices. We are in hysterics by the time we get to the graveyard. Gus's cherubic features are bright red and tear-streaked. Angela clutches at her stomach, in silent paroxysms of laughter.

Yes, a moment of levity, only possible amid bleakness ...

While the dogs hive off among the kopjes we grab our picks and shovels and get straight to work. Angela and me in Janice's grave, Gus in John's. I loosen the soil with the pick while Angela shovels. Despite sore hands still taped up with plasters, we are in much better shape than last week. The flies come out and cling to our eyes and mouths. The soil reeks of humus, sour and musty. Gus whistles as he labours away in John's grave. He grunts each time his pick thumps into the ground. As I listen to his rhythmic digging it reminds me of his peculiar penchant for repetitive physical action. How, as a boy, he could mindlessly bowl spinners at the veranda wall with a tennis ball for hours on end. That endless *thump-thump* that would irritate me so. Everyone except me would compliment him for his perseverance. Practice makes perfect, my grandfather used to say. Perfect morons, I used to think.

Gus reaches John's remains first. Angela and I follow up shortly after with Janice's. As with Vaughn and Catherine, there is not much to sift through. Just the skulls and major bones remain. The coffins have completely disappeared, except for the brass handles and name-plates. Painstakingly, we retrieve the remains and lay them out on black plastic sheets next to the graves. A modest sum. Rings, buttons and buckles. A metal ring which we deduce is from the stem of John's pipe. Their silver crucifixes. An array of brown bones. At last the skeletal anatomy I learned as an art student is finding a purpose of sorts. I'm able to name each fragile bone fragment as I arrange them: a right femur, the radius of an arm, an almost complete scapula. This I do silently so as not to seem pedantic to my siblings.

Gus passes up buckets of the soil that surrounded the skeletons which I pour among the bones. Dust to dust.

Once we have the coffins screwed shut and loaded back on the Cruiser we sit resting under the gum tree, reminiscing about the old couple. Our grandparents were blessed with many harmless eccentricities. Gus recalls going fishing with them down at the river. Granny Jan would wear a big white bonnet on these occasions. John would bait up her hook with earthworms, cast in her line and return the rod to where she sat high up on the river bank like a Voortrekker vrou, well away from the water – she had an inordinate fear of drowning. If she caught a fish it would suffer the indignity of being reeled across the ground all the way to her chair – the Groot Trek, as we jokingly described it. I recall how during the day they'd sit together out on the veranda observing the mundane proceedings of farm life, always handing out loads of advice to anyone who would listen. The huge pair of buffalo horns mounted on the wall above Granny Jan made her look like some fierce pagan goddess – a sight that amused everyone no end.

Angela laughs. 'They were a formidable pair all right! Remember how religious they were! Grandpa's morbid predictions for our fragile souls. God, he was so funny! Remember how he'd tell us the end of the world would come by fire. How the sky would catch alight and a blinding sheet of flame would incinerate the forests and boil the seas. That was how God would punish mankind.'

'It used to scare the shit out of me,' Gus says.

Angela shakes her head. 'I remember when they used to sleep in the room opposite mine. They'd take a thermos flask to bed with them and every night they'd wake up at God knows what hour, light a candle and have a cup of tea. They'd always leave their door slightly ajar and I could see their shadows on the wall and hear them laughing and talking. And every night, without fail, Granny Jan would haul her potty out from under the bed and have a pee. From my room I could see the gigantic shadow of her bum descending down the wall as she squatted.'

'How bloody terrifying!' Gus says. 'No wonder Grandpa was so obsessed with the shadow of doom!'

We laugh. It's been a day of laughter. It seems an eternity has separated us from the last time we laughed together like this.

We fill in the empty graves and replace the stones. Gus whistles and calls for the dogs but they have strayed too far afield to hear. So we wait; there is no hurry to get back. After an hour or so the dogs appear, covered in blackjacks and spider webs, saliva flecked over their faces. Frik has been rolling in some dung and is evidently very pleased with himself. Gus admonishes them like naughty boys. Tomorrow you're staying home, he chides.

It's late afternoon when we wind our way back to the house. It's been a good day. The best I can remember with the three of us.

*

Today the mood is sombre. There's no laughter or frivolity as we make our way to the graveyard again. The sun fingers the top of Long Cross Hill and the air is cool and filled with birdsong. Gus sniffs the air as we drive. He scans the clouds along the horizon and tells us he senses rain. Angela says she had a dream last night where it poured. The river was flowing in a torrent and the farm was bright green, like in England.

As we pull up at the graveyard, Angela, seated between Gus and me, kisses each of on the cheek. First Gus, then me.

'Nothing is ever perfect,' she says.

I'm not sure what she means. But everything about our task

today will carry unanswerable things. The story of our parents has lurked behind our lives all these years, too painful and dreadful to deal with – something we may never come to terms with. We sit for a while under the gum tree, drinking coffee, silently contemplating the task ahead. The surrounding bush teems with birds – doves, finches, barbets, bee-eaters, grey louries. Ground hornbills make their distinctive booming calls as they search the rocks for lizards. I feel a twinge of envy when Gus removes his cap and prays – if only I could find such solace. Angela watches him too, a pensive smile on her face.

Down below on the plain we see Ncube's van wending its way through the maize fields. It stops near the river next to the irrigation pump and disgorges its cargo of women. We can hear their distant laughter and chatter as they pick up their badzas and head off into the fields. Ncube emerges from the van yelling instructions.

Gus swigs back the last of his coffee, gets up and enters the graveyard. He stands at Rex's grave, his hand resting on the tall granite shard, his head bowed. We follow and Angela stands next to him and puts her arm around him. She leans her head against his shoulder. Gus just nods, his lips drawn tight. Without a word he turns to the other graves, and we begin our final task.

After removing the whitewashed stones, we start to dig, Angela and me working at opposite ends of my father's grave, Gus alone with my mother's. Soon I'm drenched in sweat, but for the first time I feel my body has the strength and stamina to endure. I wield my pick and shovel like a machine. Relentless, methodical. While Angela rests every so often, I keep working. We don't speak. Gus whistles tunelessly as he digs.

We strike an unexpected difficulty. Thick roots from the nearby gum tree have spread underground through the graves. It seems the tree has wrapped itself around my parents, holding them to this place. The violence with which we hack at the roots seems desperate and forlorn, born of a reluctant treachery. It seems directed at the very bonds that tie us together, that hold us to this earth. I'm filled with a sense of futility in what we're doing. The pragmatic logic of it is not enough to dispel my unease – what will we unearth in ourselves by exhuming these remains? A final rout? I wonder if my siblings harbour the same misgivings. Doggedly, we continue.

We spend the morning chopping out roots. They are piled in bits and pieces alongside the graves like dismembered limbs. Around noon we rest. We eat sandwiches with dirty hands. Gus sits on the running board of the Cruiser tapping a knife against his dirty velskoens while Angela and I rest our backs against the wrought-iron fence. I try to readjust the plasters that have come loose on my hands. Some of the blisters are bleeding.

'It's a real pity to have to do this,' Angela says. 'It's so peaceful here – such a nice place for them to rest.'

Gus and I just nod.

Angela sighs. 'I hate the way death can be so arbitrary, so indiscriminate. They deserved better.'

'Ja, but that's what they got,' Gus says bitterly.

Angela gestures at the graves. 'I never thought one day I'd be doing something like this. I still miss them. The way they were. Such a bloody waste.'

Gus jabs the knife in the ground. I'm struggling to breathe beneath a sudden wave of emotion. I get up and walk away up the hill, my breath coming in strained sobs. I keep my eyes on the distant horizon, trying to thrust the thought of them away from me. But I can't.

One Sunday evening, barely a year after I arrived in Australia, Gus phoned me. When he told me what happened – he gave no details, just the bare fact – I felt a sudden, lurching vertigo, as though I was teetering above an abyss. The finality of fact was something I was not equipped to deal with. That one could not meddle with this fact, that it was irrevocable, was a realisation that removed the earth from beneath my feet. And when his letter giving the details reached me two weeks later, I tipped over into the void and never stopped falling.

I see it, as I have seen it ever since, clear and distinct, as though I was there.

My father walks through the twilight to the security gate. He fiddles with the lock. Then he pushes the gate and it yawns open. He waits for Joseph and Anna to leave so he can lock the gate behind them. The dogs, three ridgebacks, stare at the bush, transfixed. The bush is dark, impenetrable. It's quiet and still. Peaceful. Then stars begin shining in the bush. Tiny bursts of light. My father doesn't hear the shots. He drops to the ground, dead before the gunfire tears the stillness asunder. The dogs run in circles, barking madly. Nan puts down her drink and runs to the end of the veranda. She leans over the wall. She screams out my father's name when she sees him on the ground. Men are emerging from the shadows, each emitting a star of light. She feels two terrific jolts in her chest and stomach and is flung backwards. Bits of cement spatter off the pillar into her face, cutting her. The air crackles with gunfire. She gets to her feet and staggers back into the house. She sees Joseph and Anna watching her come into the kitchen, stunned, terrified. She wants to say something, but she has no strength to breathe or speak. Her strength has seeped out of her to the floor at her feet ...

The sound of a vehicle intrudes on my thoughts. I turn to see Ncube's van making its way up the overgrown track to the graveyard. I welcome this diversion and go back to join the others. Ncube parks near the Cruiser and comes over. He greets us and squats on his haunches next to Gus. 'Mayibabo!' he sighs.

'What's wrong, Saxon?' Gus asks. 'What are your wives up to now?'

Ncube smiles, his eyes downcast. 'My wives are a small problem, umngane wami. I ran into Mtunzi on the way to the farm this morning.'

'And?'

Ncube holds his palms out in a gesture of defeat. 'I was hoping that Mtunzi might have forgotten our conversation in the Club last week. He was very drunk that night. But he's a hard man with a good memory. I can manage hard men, Angus, if they are on their own. But Mtunzi knows he has the police, the army, even the president behind him. He told me I am the only reason that they have not taken this farm. He said he no longer has patience, that I must decide whose side I am on.'

'I hope you're still on my side, Saxon,' Gus says.

He means it in jest, but it sounds like an accusation. Ncube glances sharply at him, a flicker of anger in his eyes.

Gus reaches across and puts a hand on his shoulder. 'I trust you, Saxon. Never for a moment would I question where you stand. But tell me, I thought your friends in the police had fixed things with Mtunzi.'

'Under pressure friends can change, umngane. My friends tell me I am sleeping with the enemy. They say there must be no white farmers on the land. Some of them even say there must be no white people in this country. In any case, the police are nothing to men like Mtunzi, who are a law unto themselves. Mtunzi says the question is not *if* your farm will be taken, it is *when*. I believe he is waiting for you to finish with the graves. Then he will act.'

Ncube pauses. He glances at Angela and me. 'You should take precautions not to expose others to danger, umngane.'

'It was too good to last,' Angela says. 'Everyone else around here has been chased off. Why should you be any different, Gus?'

Gus just nods and jabs the ground with his knife.

'I'm sorry I can do no more, umngane,' Ncube says.

'It's okay, Saxon. I appreciate what you've done. We'll just have to wait and see what happens.'

'Christ, Gus, why wait?' I plead. 'It's obvious what's going to happen.'

Gus gives me a withering look. 'I didn't say *you* had to wait, Chickenheart.'

Ncube gets up. He looks at the cumulus clouds building on the horizon. 'It better rain soon, or my mielies will die.'

He departs. We sit for a while in silence. Then Gus gets up and disappears behind some bushes. We hear him pissing. He comes back and starts digging again. Angela looks at me. I shrug and we follow suit. Gus is distracted as he works. His tuneless whistling has ceased. Every so often he stops and stares sullenly into the distance. We continue for a couple of hours, then Gus decides to call it a day. We pack up and return to the house.

It seems Gus intends to spend the rest of the day brooding alone on the veranda. He has retreated into a fortress of silence. After a while the tension becomes unbearable so Angela and I decide to leave him to his deliberations and pay Joseph and Anna a visit. Lightning flickers along the northern horizon as we walk down to the kraal. There is a crackle of thunder, tauntingly distant. It's early evening when we reach the kraal. Anna has a fire going in front of the huts and is stirring a pot of sadza. Another pot of stew with chicken feet protruding from it simmers at the edge of the coals.

'Utshonile, Mama!' I call.

Anna straightens up and smiles. 'Ngitshonile, utshone njani wena?'

Angela laughs. 'Yes, Mama, we have spent the day well. If you can call digging up graves a pleasant pastime!'

Anna shakes her head. 'Ai, ai, ai! You should not interfere with the dead. What has this world come to.'

Joseph emerges from his hut and greets us. He fetches some chairs and we sit around the fire. We talk about the possibility of rain. Anna lifts the pot of sadza off the fire and insists that we have something to eat. We know it will be futile to refuse, so while we talk we scoop sadza out the pot with our blistered hands and dip it in the pot of stew. After the day's exertions it is delicious. Joseph sips at a gourd of beer. He offers us some and laughs when we decline. The only one in our family who could stomach African beer was Rex.

After some pleasantries, Angela and I broach the serious business.

'Old people,' Angela says. 'You have had a long life on this farm. You are like family to us. You have cared for us all these

years, now it is time for us to care for you. You know that evil
has stalked this land for a long time. First, in the war when our
parents were murdered. Then when Mugabe set his Gugura-
hundi loose in Matabeleland. And now the war veterans. You
have seen what has happened to all the other farms in this area.
The same will happen here. Even my stubborn brother Gus
knows this, otherwise he would not be removing our family
from their graves.'

Joseph and Anna just sit there, listening quietly.

I continue. 'We worry what will become of you. You have
heard what has happened to the workers on other farms. Many
have been beaten, some killed. These are evil men who do this
but they have the power to do what they wish, and no one can
stop them. Not even Ncube.' Anna draws herself up at the
mention of his name. 'I know you dislike Ncube, but you must
realise he is the reason this farm has not been taken yet. But
even Ncube can't stop this happening.'

'That's right,' Angela says. 'He admitted this himself to us
today.'

'That Ncube is a pisi, a hyena!' Anna mutters.

'Be still, Mama,' Joseph says. 'Listen to what they have to
say.'

'We worry about you and want to look after you,' Angela
goes on. 'If you remain on this farm we cannot help you. So we
wish to make this proposition: We will buy a house for you in
the town, in Gweru or Bulawayo, away from the trouble. We
will buy a good house for you so that you can live your lives in
peace. We will send money to you from overseas, so you are
never hungry or in need. If you move to this house then we can
help you. If you stay here we cannot help you.'

There is a long silence. Then Joseph asks, 'And what will become of Angus? What will he do if the farm is taken?'

'You must not worry about Angus,' I say. 'Angus can take care of himself.'

'Angus cannot live without the farm,' Anna says.

'He will have to learn to live without the farm.'

'What do you think of our offer, old people?' Angela asks.

Joseph looks across at Anna. 'What do you think, Mama?'

Tears begin streaming down Anna's face. Angela gets up and puts her arm around her shoulders. 'Oh, Mama, we did not come here to make you cry,' she says.

Anna sighs. 'What will we do in a town? Away from the bones of our ancestors?' She points at the darkening land. 'Long before this farm our people were buried in this ground. I do not want to die in a strange place.'

Joseph nods and turns to face us. 'I know you make this offer from the goodness of your hearts, and for that I thank you. But we are too old to move to a new place. If evil must come then so be it. I want my bones to rest in the same ground as my ancestors.'

Anna nods her head. 'Ngiyabonga, my children – thank you. Joseph speaks for me. This is our place here.'

It's almost dark as we make our way back to the house. Lightning still flickers weakly along the northern horizon. The thunder is almost inaudible. We avoid the subject of our failure to persuade Joseph and Anna to move. We've resigned ourselves to the fact that we can't force them off the farm against their will. Angela begins to wax lyrical about the evening landscape. Pointing at the bald kopjes still visible in the gloom, she says, 'The old Ndebeles in Mzilikazi's time used to call this place Amakhandeni, the place of heads. Don't you think that's beautiful? Such a poetic view of the world.'

'Beautiful and apt. The place of stone heads and stone hearts.'

'Why is it that the cruellest places are the most beautiful?'

'I don't know. Because they are reminders of our mortality?'

'You have a dark view of beauty, Vaughn. To me, those hills could be old craggy matriarchs, our protectors, watching over us. Or shy maidens waiting for darkness to roam for lost lovers.'

I scoff. 'Matriarchs! Shy maidens! This country's symbols are male, Angela. It belongs to men. Cruel men.'

'Stupid men, you mean?'

'Cruel men are not necessarily stupid.'

Angela laughs. 'In my book they are.'

Gus is still on the veranda when we get back, a row of beer bottles at his feet. Angela and I collapse into chairs, exhausted. 'Help yourselves to beer in the fridge,' Gus says. We shake our heads, too tired to get up. Gus laughs when we tell him Joseph and Anna's response to our proposition. 'Told you,' he says smugly. 'You've forgotten how fatalistic munts are.'

Gus is slurring slightly. Angela tries to keep things upbeat. She recounts a story about a German client who commissioned her to paint a dramatic scene of a charging 'baffellow', claiming to have experienced such a horror while on safari in Kenya. When she was finished he was pleased with the result, but suggested that Angela's rendition of the buffalo was a touch too exaggerated. It turned out that he'd actually been charged by a wildebeest.

'Typical!' Gus scoffs. 'People overseas haven't a bloody clue about Africa. Especially when it comes to the munts. No one understands what a mess these bastards are making here. You have to live here to know what's going on.'

Angela reaches across and puts her hand on his arm. 'Yes, but there's nothing you can do about it, Angus.'

'Africa needs to go back to the Africans,' I say. 'Let them get on with whatever they have to do with it.'

Gus shakes his head. 'That's bullshit. I'm African too. Kaffir to the core, that's me!'

'Oh please, Gus,' I implore. 'Be sensible, man! Forget about who is bloody African and who isn't. Face up to reality. There's no future here. The only way no one's going to get hurt is for you to pack up and walk away. Let go, for God's sake.'

Gus's eyes blaze. 'Vaughn, just shuddup with your gutless crap, okay?'

I slap my hands down on my thighs in frustration.

'Vaughn's right,' Angela says. 'Don't take out your frustrations on him. Let go, Angus. You *have* to let go!'

Gus gets to his feet and walks away from us. He puts one leg up on the veranda wall and glares out at the darkness. 'No one's asking either of you to stick around. You're free to bugger off whenever you like. No one's stopping you.'

'Oh Gus, man,' I say.

He turns and jabs a finger in our direction. 'Don't give me that bloody crap about giving Africa back to the Africans! I'm bloody African, okay? White, black – what does it matter? I belong here. This is my place. I don't care what the fuck you two think you are – I know what I am!'

As I begin to reply he shuts me up with a wave of his hand, and goes down the stairs out into the desolate garden. There he stands in the darkness looking up at the stars.

'God, I hate this bloody place,' I say.

Angela looks pensively at Gus, then turns to me. 'Don't let him get to you, Vaughn. It's the beer talking. He doesn't mean what he's saying.'

'Yes, he does. And I'm sick of it. I'm sick of him and all this damn rubbish about being African too.'

'Put yourself in his shoes. Without the farm he's nothing. What's happening is sad for us, but for Gus it's tragic. Truly tragic.'

'I understand that, Ange. But it doesn't change the obvious fact that he's going to lose it. And the longer he hangs on, the more he stands to lose. Christ, it's so bloody exasperating trying to reason with him!'

The phone rings and Angela gets up to answer. She comes back and says, 'It's for you.'

I go through to the phone, thinking it must be Bella.

It's Beth.

'I tried the house in Bulawayo,' she says, 'but Jenny told me you were on the farm. How are things going, crazy man?'

'Pretty crap. Can't wait to get out of here.'

'I was watching an SBS programme last night on the farm seizures. Pretty horrific what's going on there. That's why I thought I'd give you a ring.'

'Thanks Bella ... er, Beth ...'

'Who the hell is Bella?'

'Sorry, I got mixed up. Bella's an old family friend ...'

Beth laughs. 'You don't have to make excuses any more, Vaughn. We're divorced, remember? Good to hear you're, how shall I put it, socialising again.'

'How's Mikey?'

180

'Mikey's fine. That's also why I phoned. He's found a nice girlfriend who seems to be pulling him into line. She's got him interested in school again. He wants to finish his Year Twelve. He's even talking about university.'

'That's great, Beth. That's really fantastic ... such a relief to hear!'

'It's early days yet. But I honestly think he's turned the corner.'

'Well, that's brightened a pretty bleak day. Does he ever mention me?'

'He talks about you, Vaughn. Often.'

'And you? How're things with you?'

'Oh, you know. I wouldn't be happy unless I was working my backside off.'

'It's so good to hear from you, Beth.'

'Are you safe there? After that programme last night ...'

'I'm safe. We're all safe,' I say.

I return outside and sit for a while with Angela. When we go to bed Gus is still there in the garden staring at the stars.

*

Deep in the night I wake from a restless sleep, troubled and afraid. I think of how secure I felt as a boy, lying in this same bed, listening to the night sounds. I cannot remember ever feeling threatened by the world outside. Now, outside, the night begins to roar. My heart pounds. I struggle to breathe. The space around me seems too heavy to bear. I have always thought of space as a passive void, something we invade. But here it invades us, imposes upon us. Here, it bestows power or loss. We are helpless to its manipulations. The power to determine our existence is taken from us. Everything is thrown into confusion. Unreality becomes reality. The unacceptable becomes acceptable. Life is shorn of sacrosanct dimensions – its very insignificance the source of profound fear.

In this space, I seem to stumble around like a blind man. Solid ground gives way. I grasp at familiar things, but they are things from the past. Things that no longer exist.

*

I wake at first light, listless. Outside I hear Gus talking to Witness and the men. He tells them what animals must be rounded up for dipping. The tractor starts up and drives off. The men shout and laugh on the trailer as it bounces behind down the hill. The dogs bark at the fading noise.

Gus whistles as he stomps through the house to the kitchen. I hear him rustling up some breakfast on the stove. I shower and dress in my borrowed shorts and T-shirt. When I go through to the kitchen Angela is there, warming her hands around a mug of coffee. Gus is in better spirits. He chats away about mundane things as he dishes up some mielie meal porridge. We eat the porridge and some toast with fig jam.

'No rain last night,' I comment.

Gus shakes his head. 'No, but at least there was some hope. That's all we need sometimes.'

As we go outside to the Cruiser he puts his hand briefly on my shoulder, about as big a gesture of affection as is possible between Rhodesian males.

'Sorry I got short with you last night, boet,' he says.

'It's becoming a bit of habit, don't you think?' I reply.

'Bear with me, boet,' he says. 'Bear with me.'

We are just getting on our way when we see Witness on the tractor driving flat out up the hill towards us. Gus pulls over to the side of the road and waits until the tractor draws up alongside. Through the dust Witness doffs his hat at Angela and me.

'Kuyini, Witness?' Gus asks. 'What's the matter?'

Witness looks scared. He gabbles something. Gus indicates for him to switch off the tractor. 'Speak slowly, Witness. Khuluma kacane.'

Witness gathers himself. 'Trouble, nkosi. Wellington is injured.'

'What do you mean injured? What's wrong with him?'

Witness shakes his head. 'Woza please, nkosi. Wellington is hurt. Woza. Please come and see.'

'Ngaphi? Where?'

Witness points towards the far pastures.

Gus curses as we follow the tractor down across the river. He explains that Wellington had recently been moved to better grazing in the farm's northernmost pasture which borders the Fort Rixon road. 'This is what bloody happens when you don't keep tabs on things,' he mutters. It's a slow, frustrating drive behind the tractor. Finally we reach the pasture. The men are huddled together next to the unhitched trailer near the water trough. They stop talking as we arrive. Witness kills the tractor engine and points over at a thorn tree in a far corner of the pasture. There is an eerie silence, broken only by the squeak of the windmill next to the water trough as it catches a fickle early-morning breeze.

Under the thorn tree there looks to be a large red ant heap.

But as we follow Witness closer we see it's the bull, lying on its side. As we approach, Wellington lifts his head and emits a deep, dreadful groan. Gus takes one look and says, 'Fuck' and marches off back to the Cruiser. Angela turns away, ashen, her hand across her mouth. I can only stand there watching as the bull squirms weakly on the ground and emits its terrible groans.

They have slashed the hock tendons. They have gouged out its eyes. One eye still hangs like a squashed grape from its socket. They have built a fire alongside its rump and butchered the meat as it cooked.

Gus returns from the Cruiser with his revolver, a look of fury and disgust on his face. He goes up to the bull, points the revolver at an empty eye socket and pulls the trigger. Angela and I jump at the report. Doves burst from the trees like grey flack. The bull defecates in its death throes. It shudders and flops, then lies still. The shot echoes in the distant kopjes.

Witness has taken off his hat and is shaking his head.

'Butcher the meat and take it up to the cold room,' Gus says, without looking at him. 'Forget about the dip today. Make sure this meat doesn't go bad. Uzwile na?'

'I understand,' Witness replies. 'Sorry, nkosi.'

Gus just grunts angrily. He sticks the revolver in his pocket and takes Angela by the elbow. 'You okay?' he asks.

She nods, still with her back to the carcass.

My legs feel rubbery as we walk back to the Cruiser. The men next to the trailer watch us as we climb in and drive off.

*

We uncover their remains in the afternoon. Around the bones the soil is dark grey. Flesh and blood turned to dust. Slowly, methodically, we work together to lift the bones from the soil along with the small items that remain – their wedding rings, a broach, buckles, my father's Swiss Army knife. There are remnants of my father's leather shoes. Gus retrieves a small pewter box lying next to my mother. It contains her glasses, an eroded deck of cards and a small crystal sherry glass. He hands the box to me. It was his idea to bury her with these things, he says. I struggle to maintain my composure as I hold this trace of her. I can see her, out on the veranda in the evening, playing Solitaire and sipping her sherry, chatting quietly with my father. Angela's eyes brim with tears when I pass the box to her. We don't talk about my mother's smashed pelvis or the hole in my father's skull.

A fearful gestalt.

PART III

UNSPEAKABLE FREEDOMS

Saturday. There are more people than expected at the funeral. Gus had wanted a simple graveside ceremony with just the family in attendance but Reverend Dlomo talked him into having a full service; such an unusual occasion, he argued, is a sad indictment of the times and therefore demands the unequivocal support of the church. Since then word has got around: a crowd of at least two hundred people have turned up. Most I don't recognise – I gather many are MDC members. There are not enough seats in the small church and some have to stand. The children too young to follow the service play outside around the marula tree. As we wait in the afternoon heat we can hear their shouts and laughter.

It is meant to be a no-frills affair. Aside from a small bouquet of wilting flowers on each of the six coffins positioned in a row in front of the pulpit, the church is unadorned. Angela wears a simple black dress with a carnation pinned to her lapel. Gus wears his grey Sunday church suit that looks several sizes too small. I, too, wear a nondescript grey suit that in the past twenty years has only ever seen the light of day at my wedding and at university graduation ceremonies. We sit in the front pew, along with Jenny and the girls. Jessica and Lauren seem cowed by the sight of the coffins. Joseph and Anna are seated behind us with Ncube. Anna has set aside her disdain for Ncube for the time being, since he gallantly gave them a lift to the funeral. Joseph is wearing the new sports jacket I gave him; Anna is resplendent in the table cloth with the Australian map

189

which is drawn around her shoulders like a shawl and clasped together with a large safety pin. Bella and Oom Jasper Gerber sit next to them. Bella looks prim in a long green dress with a black bow on her breast.

Across the aisle from us there are some of our former neighbours: the Thorntons, Grieggs, Mapstones and Pringles. All pushed off their farms and now living elsewhere. Big Bull Durnford, who played for Chaplin High's first rugby team with Gus, is there, looking as beefy and prosperous as ever. He runs a twenty-four-hour armed response security firm in South Africa, apparently a booming industry these days. Most of the congregation are white, but we are surprised by the number of black folk present, mostly older people who remember my family from the old days.

People greet each other, old acquaintances are renewed. It is stiflingly hot and the men sweat profusely in their suits while the women fan their faces with service leaflets. Outside, insects sing. A train squeals to a stop at the station nearby. The church's small Gothic stained-glass windows cast dappled patches of colour on the congregation. These windows were imported from Britain a few years before I was born and installed with great fanfare by the Bishop from Salisbury. As a boy I gazed in awe at them every Sunday. They were beautiful, magical. The colours of heaven amid the drab browns of Africa. Now they are reminders of the erosion of innocence, of self. Of the lost belief that good will prevail.

An elderly black man in a faded navy blue double-breasted jacket and a pair of tennis shoes from a pre-Borg era totters in through a side door. He lovingly removes the threadbare red velvet cover from the organ, seats himself and begins to play.

The organ is slightly out of tune and two keys are dead. Undaunted, the grizzled veteran puts his heart and soul into an ensemble of hymns. He sways in his seat and turns, smiling, to the congregation in the midst of dramatic flourishes to gauge our approval. The music sounds weird and funky. Each time he hits a dead note there is a dull click that sets my teeth on edge. Finally, he delivers a dramatic, disjointed crescendo as Reverend Dlomo, calm and dignified in his robes, enters from the vestry and stands at the altar. In his deep voice he greets the congregation:

'Grace and peace from the Lord be with you. We have come together to thank God for the lives of these members of the Bourke family before us and to lay to rest their mortal remains. Those who die in Christ share eternal life with him. Therefore in faith and hope we turn to God, who created and sustains us all. Let us reflect upon the lives of these departed souls and the circumstances that have brought us together today.'

The congregation sits, heads bowed. The laughter of the children outside filters in.

Reverend Dlomo continues: 'Loving God, you alone are the source of life. May your life-giving Spirit flow through us, and fill us with compassion, one for another. In our sorrow give us the calm of your peace. Kindle our hope, and let our fears give way to joy, through Jesus Christ our Lord. Amen.'

We sing a tortuous version of *How Great Thou Art*, after which Gus is called upon to deliver the eulogy.

Mopping his brow with a handkerchief, Gus climbs the steps to the pulpit. Never one for sober speeches (though quite adept once properly fortified) he fumbles his way through an impromptu welcome, then reads from prepared notes.

'This has been a tough time for us. Some of you who have farmed here will know what I mean. Years ago, we would never have dreamt it might one day be necessary to move the remains of our family from their place of rest, in the land they loved and worked so hard to make their own. As most of you will remember, these were hardworking, honest people who deserved their place of rest in this country. Years ago, it seemed the right to rest in peace in the soil of our land was beyond question. What my family has gone through is what countless others have experienced already or are experiencing now. But this is our moment, and the time has come for us to mourn what this moment means for us. But it is also a time to remember and celebrate the lives of my forebears. To celebrate who they were and what they contributed to this community. I remember when I was a kid, Oom Jasper Gerber saying Shangani wouldn't be the same without the Bourkes. It filled me with pride then, and it fills me with pride now. It's nice to know we at least meant something to this community, just as this community meant everything to us. Unfortunately, Shangani, as we knew it, no longer exists. Just as many old farming communities around the country no longer exist. It doesn't take a genius or a visionary to understand what families and communities mean to this country. Without them everything falls apart. One can only wonder what will come in their place?

'This is a sad occasion, yet it has its blessings. It's good to see familiar faces, some that have been missing from Shangani for a long time. I'm also grateful that my sister Angela and my brother Vaughn are here – it's been a while since the three of us were together. I'd like to thank them for helping me with the task of moving our loved ones to safer ground. On behalf of the family I want to thank you all – each and every one of you – for your attendance. We had no idea so many of you would turn up.'

Gus smiles and glances at his old pal, Big Bull Durnford. 'Had I known some of you were coming, I'd have alerted the breweries!'

Ripples of laughter. Gus resumes his seat next to me. Reverend Dlomo waits for the laughter to die down before commencing his sermon.

'Dearly Beloved, many of you will remember my predecessor from the diocese, Reverend Davis, with whom I had the honour of a deep and long-lasting friendship. Reverend Davis always spoke in affectionate terms of these six dear souls before us that he buried on the farm called Hopelands. Today it is my sad duty to commit these same dear souls again to the earth – thankfully not too far from the land they loved. Such are our times that such a duty is necessary ...'

Here he is interrupted by a demented Mozart jingle from Ncube's cell phone. Ncube feverishly grasps for the blasted thing in his pocket and switches it off, mumbling apologies. Anna and Oom Jasper on either side of him give him withering stares.

Reverend Dlomo gazes patiently towards heaven, then continues. 'As I was saying, such are our times that such a duty is necessary. When the departed cannot rest in peace in their graves, or when their loved ones are denied access to the graves of their ancestors, it speaks of an evil beyond comprehension that plagues this land. Those who perpetrate this evil will one day account to their Maker for the tragedies they have brought to so many. Of this there is no doubt. But let us ...'

Again, he is interrupted, this time by a sudden angry murmur from the congregation. I turn to see a group of men, ten or so, entering the church. They saunter noisily to the back near the baptism font. One is smoking a cigarette. I recognise Mtunzi as he leans against the wall with one foot resting on the base of the font, casually gripping the lapels of his beige jacket in his hands. Blind or indifferent to the disturbance he has caused, he jabbers away with the man called Yengwa, from our previous acquaintance on the road.

Livid, Gus starts to get up but Ncube leans over the pew and pushes him down firmly. 'Leave it, umngani,' he says.

'What are they doing here?' I ask.

'Pretty obvious, isn't it, boet?' Gus growls. 'Just a bit of your garden variety intimidation.' He turns to Ncube. 'Saxon, I swear, I'm not putting up with this bullshit. Not today.'

'Calm down, umngani,' Ncube replies. 'This will be resolved peacefully.'

The congregation has grown quiet.

'You men! What is your business here?' Reverend Dlomo demands in SiNdebele.

Mtunzi, affecting blank surprise behind his black-rimmed glasses, breaks off his conversation with Yengwa. 'Business? Our business is to celebrate,' he calls back. 'For us, it is Christmas time!'

His men smirk and laugh.

'You desecrate this place with your presence. You!' Reverend Dlomo points at the smoker. 'How dare you bring your vile habits into my church! Have you no respect?'

Amused, the smoker stares back at Reverend Dlomo. He takes a drag on his cigarette and blows a plume of smoke into the air.

194

Reverend Dlomo gestures at the coffins. 'Have you no respect for the dead? When you violate this space, you violate the dead! Do you understand the gravity of your actions?'

His words seem to have an effect on some of Mtunzi's men who drop their eyes and shuffle uncomfortably.

'Leave these people in peace!' Reverend Dlomo cries, his voice wavering. 'You have created enough evil! Hamba! Leave this holy place!'

Mtunzi motions at his men to stay put. His face deadpan, he replies calmly in English. 'Enough of your hocus-pocus, old man. Carry on with your sermon. I'm sure that the words of God are soothing to the ears of these old Rhodesians.' He points at the frightened blacks in the congregation. 'And to these dogs who wish to be the slaves of white men again.'

Gus gets to his feet, muttering, 'Bloody swine! I've had enough ...'

Big Bull Durnford and some other men, including old codgers like Oom Jasper and Joseph, begin to rise with him. Angela and Jenny plead with Gus to sit down. Ncube's huge arm reaches over my shoulder, grabs Gus by the coat tails and pulls him back into his seat. Then Ncube stands up. He waves the others back to their seats.

'Let me speak with these men,' he says to Reverend Dlomo.

Reverend Dlomo nods and gestures for him to proceed. Ncube squeezes his way past Oom Jasper and Bella out of the pew. The congregation is hushed as he makes his way to the back. The old organist, groomed to cope with interruptions, strikes up a rendition of *Abide with Me*.

Ncube approaches the group. He offers Mtunzi his hand in greeting but Mtunzi ignores him. Ncube speaks in hushed

195

SiNdebele while the congregation watches uneasily. The old organist has managed to turn *Abide with Me* into something vaguely reminiscent of Jimi Hendrix's Woodstock version of *Star-Spangled Banner*. Ncube and Mtunzi argue. Mtunzi assumes the haughty, amused look of an academic – arguments just child's play to him. The smoker grinds his cigarette out on the floor. Finally, after what seems an eternity, Mtunzi beckons his disciples and they slowly saunter back outside, laughing and talking. We hear a vehicle start up and drive off.

Ncube resumes his seat. There is a buzz of talk as we wait for Reverend Dlomo to recommence. I glance behind me at Bella and Oom Jasper. The old man is staring grimly down at his service leaflet. Bella returns my gaze. She gives a strained smile, then looks away.

Reverend Dlomo gazes into the middle distance above the congregation's heads. The congregation becomes silent, then he continues. 'As I was saying, before we were so rudely interrupted, those who perpetrate the evil in this land will one day account for the calamity that has befallen our nation. May that day come soon, dear Lord God, for your people are suffering. May that day come soon ...'

'Hear, hear,' someone in the congregation murmurs.

Reverend Dlomo pauses. 'Still, let this not be a moment of bitterness or hate. It is not for us to judge. As Angus has asked us, let us rejoice in the memory of these departed souls. The size of this congregation is an indication of what these good people meant to this community. And let us also rejoice in the commitment of the remaining Bourkes to honour and care for their loved ones. This commitment speaks of a love and faith that transcends the storms of life ...'

He goes on to talk of Jesus calming the waters of Galilee in the face of the storm, urging us to find solace in a spiritual life, '... for the world has turned its back on this place and there is nowhere else to turn'.

After the service the coffins are carried out to the cemetery. They are light, needing just one pallbearer on each side. Gus and I lead the procession with Vaughn Bourke's remains. The congregation follows behind. We place the coffins next to the graves that are now marked by the new headstones. One by one, they are lowered into the graves. We bow our heads as Reverend Dlomo performs the final obsequies, casting a handful of soil onto each coffin:

'Almighty God, our heavenly Father, you have given us a sure and certain hope of the resurrection to eternal life. In your keeping are all who have departed in Christ. We here commit once again the mortal remains of our dear brothers and sisters, earth to earth, ashes to ashes, dust to dust, in the name of our Lord Jesus Christ, who died and was buried, and rose again for us ...'

As he finishes, the black women in the congregation spontaneously begin an Ndebele hymn. Their men join in with the chorus and the air is filled with loud, solemn harmonies. Angela weeps.

At this moment, Africa claims me, and I turn my head and weep too.

*

Afterwards, everyone stands around talking while the two gravediggers begin filling in the graves. Gus, Angela and I go about thanking people before seeing them off in their cars. There is a ritualistic bit of backslapping between Gus and Big Bull Durnford. Gus invites Big Bull to overnight at the farm; Big Bull declines, saying he's on his way to Harare to visit some relatives, but promises to drop in on his way back to South Africa in a week or so. Ncube departs in his van with Joseph and Anna, promising to come by the house later. We find Reverend Dlomo talking to Angela, Bella and Oom Jasper in the shade of the marula tree near the car park. Gus thanks Reverend Dlomo and shakes his hand. We chat informally for a while, avoiding any talk about the future. Angela and Jenny have persuaded Bella to come out to the farm for the night. Since Oom Jasper adamantly refuses to go near his old farm, I'm elected to drive him back to Bulawayo in Bella's car.

Oom Jasper chain-smokes throughout the hundred-kilometre stretch back to Bulawayo. Despite having sworn off cigarettes, I have one or two myself, since he offers. Oom Jasper loosens his tie and wheezes and coughs as he chats about the old days. He has a store of funny anecdotes and a way of punctuating them with a sad 'Ja, so gaan die wêreld, seun. So gaan die wêreld.' I listen without saying much as we drive along. The overturned truck is still there, though it has been dragged to the side of the road and is no longer obstructing traffic. Oom Jasper inspects the wreck with a jaundiced eye, takes a deep drag on his cigarette and shakes his head. 'Ag, no man,' he complains. 'Just look at that! Hell, it's enough to make a grown man cry. Is there anything these people can't break?' He gestures with an open hand at the truck, as if it sums up all of Africa's woes. I can't help but laugh at the look of incredulity on his face.

As we near Bulawayo he turns to me suddenly. 'So, what's the story with you and Bella?'

I'm at a loss for words. 'I'm not sure what you mean ...'

'Ag, seun, I've seen that girl moping around with bloody spaniel eyes.'

I've always prided myself on a better than average imagination. But nowhere in my head can I conjure up an image of Bella moping around with spaniel eyes.

'Well, Oom, that's a bit of a surprise. I had no idea ...'

'I know my own daughter, Vaughn. Bella's all I have left in this world. She's the apple of my eye, that girl. But she's been unlucky with men, and time doesn't stand still. I want her to have a good life. I want her to be safe. In this country that's impossible. Take her away from here, Vaughn. Please, get her out of this bloody country, man.'

'Oom Jasper, we've hardly ...'

'I know she won't leave because of me. I'm too old to start again in another country. I've had my time. Tell her not to worry about me. I will survive. Tell her once she's in Australia, then she can bring me over too. I know she'll go if you put it like that to her.'

I'm speechless. Oom Jasper coughs and catches his breath. Then he reaches across and puts his hand on my shoulder.

'I'm sorry to embarrass you, seun. I won't ask you again.'

With that he resumes his earlier banter about the old days. We reach the house in Clarke Street and I help him to the door. Oom Jasper can only take a few steps at a time before resting on his stick. The dogs mill around our legs. Oom Jasper brandishes his stick and chases them off, but not before one of them, a nasty critter with yellow eyes, nips me on my thigh. 'That bloody Jakkals,' Oom Jasper wheezes, 'he's always been otherwise. But the kaffirs are scared of him, that's why I keep him.'

199

He stands at the door and waves as I drive off.

I stop off at the house in Burnside to pick up some extra beer (as Gus instructed) and to shower and change out of my suit. I dab some Dettol on Jakkals's bite on my thigh, which has drawn blood. Then I head back to the farm, my head full of the complexities of life.

By the time I get back to Hopelands the shadows from the distant hills are reaching across the plain. The house is bathed in a fading yellow glow. Bella, I discover, is hardly in spaniel-eye mode. I can hear her high-pitched laughter from the gate as I drive up. They are sitting out on the veranda, the evidence of moderate alcohol abuse in the form of empty bottles plain to see. Gus, Jenny and the girls are sitting together on a sofa, holding their stomachs. Ncube is standing with one leg up on the veranda wall, cackling away at the sight of Bella who is con-vulsed into unbridled hysterics. I must say, the sight of Bella in such a state is quite disturbing – to me, the object of my desire should be more demure, like those helpless waifs in Pre-Raphaelite paintings. Angela sits smiling to one side, sipping her wine. She raises her eyebrows at me as I come up the steps, as if to say, lo, the descent of man.

I carry the extra beer through to the kitchen and fetch a cold one for myself from the fridge. Joseph and Anna are there; Joseph is arranging some salads on a tray while Anna stirs a pot of sadza on the woodstove.

'Litshonile, old people,' I say. 'You work too hard. Why don't you join the others outside?'

Anna shakes her head at the sound of merriment outside. 'Hayi! Today is not a day for laughter. That Ncube! He laughs on any occasion.'

Poor Ncube. Of all the revellers, he's the one singled out.

'It's been a long day,' Joseph says. 'We will finish here and go.'

I return to the veranda and sit at the top of the stairs, next to Bella, my back against the pillar. The laughter is tailing off.

'Nice to see everyone in a state of quiet reflection,' I say. 'Commensurate with today's sombre occasion.'

Bella reaches over, wiping her eyes, and slaps my knee. 'Hey, big guy! You've just missed a classic joke! Saxon, you're a star, man!'

'Pray tell,' I say. 'Or is it too filthy for decent folks like me?'

'Go on, Saxon,' Bella pleads. 'Tell it again.'

Ncube shakes his head. 'No, once is enough.'

'Oh, Saxon, man! Gus, you tell it then.'

'Nah, Vaughn's too much of a prude,' Gus scoffs.

'Oh, come on, Angus!' Jenny says.

'Okay, but don't blame me if it sounds lame,' Gus says. He calms himself by taking a deep breath and a swig of beer. 'Okay, there's this businessman dictating a letter to his secretary – you know, him sitting behind his desk, she sitting there taking notes. The businessman finishes dictating and the secretary gets up to leave. At the door she pauses and says, "Excuse me, sir, but did you know your armoury door is open?" The businessman is puzzled by this comment but eventually discovers his fly is open. The next day he dictates another letter. At the end of it he asks the secretary, "Miss, when you noticed the armoury door was open yesterday, did you also notice a soldier standing to attention at the door?" The secretary ponders for a second, then says, "Actually, to tell the truth I didn't notice that at all. What I did notice, though, was a tired old veteran lying asleep on a duffel bag!"'

Once again, the merry throng convulses into laughter. I sit there patiently, shaking my head. It seems the last thing left to do for ordinary folk in Zimbabwe is to get drunk and laugh at puerile jokes. Bella leans over again, grabs my cheeks and pulls my lips into a smile. 'Come on, smile, party boy! Let's boogie!' she laughs. 'Hey Gus! What's happened to the music?'

'Is Uncle Vaughn going to dance?' Jessica asks.

That, too, tickles everyone's fancy. Ncube claps his hands and guffaws. Gus ruffles Jessica's hair. 'You never know, babe. Once that boy gets a couple of drinks in him ...'

'Won't you put some music on?' Jenny tells Jessica and Lauren.

The two girls jump up and run inside. The weaver birds are roosting down at the river. Far off, I can hear the *clonk clonk* of a cow bell. How nice it would be just to have the gentle evening sounds, I think, fearing the inevitable onslaught of Gus's sad seventies Pop collection. If we are to have music, why not something quiet, something minimalist? Erik Satie perhaps. Or better still, a Chopin *Nocturne* – something my mother would have liked.

'Thought we'd have a little braai tonight,' Gus announces.

'Just for a change,' Angela says.

'Well, we've got a ton of Wellington to get through. Might as well get started.'

Angela shakes her head and shivers.

'Joseph and Anna are pretty grumpy,' I say.

'They were sitting out here earlier, before you pitched up,' Angela replies. 'They beat a retreat once the booze started flowing.'

Gus has rigged up a stereo set in the lounge, next to where

we're sitting. We hear *Hotel California* starting up. Jessica and Lauren push open the windows and the music blasts out into the evening air.

'Ag, pragtig!' Bella says.

'Not so loud, man! We're not deaf!' Jenny shouts.

The girls giggle and turn the music down. Gus puts an arm around Jenny, a sentimental gleam in his eye. He stifles a belch.

'Jeez, you're so crude, Angus!' Jenny chides, laughing.

'Shall I start the fire, umngani wami?' Ncube asks.

Gus raises his beer. 'Thanks, Saxon. If you'd be so kind.'

While Bella talks with Angela, I join Ncube down at the stone fireplace nearby. Drink in hand, I watch as Ncube lights the kindling, then piles the bigger wood on top. He blows on the wood to get the flames going. *Tequila Sunrise* begins floating across the muted veld. I take a deep swig of beer, enjoying the moment. Yes, even the music suddenly seems right, I'll confess. The dogs, Frik and Tiny, stand to one side, eyeing Ncube suspiciously. Frik gives a single, uncertain bark. Ncube chuckles and pats Frik's head.

'When the good Lord gave out brains he must have forgotten you,' he says.

Frik smiles up at Ncube, as if in agreement.

'What was Mtunzi's business coming to the church?' I ask.

Ncube pauses before replying. 'By coming to the church he was saying to everyone there – your time is finished. You have no more purpose in this place. He's been waiting for your brother to finish with the graves. I worry now for what lies ahead.'

'What about your friends in the police, Saxon?'

'My connections are limited, umngani. I don't hold much

sway these days. When I talk to my friends they nod their heads, but I know they are too scared to be seen sympathising with a man who is an MDC member and has white friends. In this country such sympathy can cost a man his life.'

I sigh. 'I know, Saxon. It's impossible. Can't you try to persuade Gus that the situation is hopeless? It's time to let go.'

Ncube smiles. 'Your brother is a stubborn man.'

'I know, he's a bloody mule. But maybe you can get through to him. I certainly can't.'

'I've already spoken to him, but it's like talking to a tree. Vaughn, you should remember that your brother, stubborn or not, is a man of principle. Angus is not afraid to stand and be counted. He is a man who deserves respect.'

'Thank you for helping him. He'd have lost the farm by now.'

Ncube puts his hand on my shoulder. 'You should not thank me, umngani. The country should not be this way.'

Joseph and Anna emerge from the house and take their leave. As they walk down to the gate, Ncube waves at them but receives a hard stare from Anna in reply.

He chuckles. 'That Anna! I'm back in the dog box!'

We stand there next to the fire, watching the sunset. Jessica and Lauren, our self-appointed disc-jockeys, have rummaged through Gus's records and found an old *Bread* album. Up on the veranda Jenny and Bella applaud their choice with sentimental wails. Jessica and Lauren begin dancing with each other, laughing and doing little pirouettes. Gus and Jenny also begin dancing, Gus demonstrating some nifty footwork. The girls squeal with pleasure, watching them. Bella runs down the stairs and grabs my arm. 'Come on, big guy, let's shake a leg!' she says. She leads me up onto the veranda where I commence a tentative waltz with her. She laughs and kisses my neck. I close my eyes, savouring the moment. The angels appear to be smiling down on us. When I open my eyes, Angela and Ncube are sailing past in each other's arms. Angela glances at me and winks. Just as well Joseph and Anna are not here to witness *this*, I think.

'It's so lovely out here, Vaughn,' Bella says in my ear. 'I'm glad I came.'

'I'm glad the funeral's over. Now we can all get on with our lives.'

'When are you going back to Australia?'

'Thursday week. I can change my ticket if I want.'

'Why would you want to change it?'

'I don't know. Maybe something will convince me to stay a bit longer.'

Bella looks at me. I catch a glimpse of the spaniel. 'Let's do something crazy tonight,' she says.

'Like what?'

She points to Long Cross Hill, silhouetted against the evening sky. 'See the cross? Let's sleep up there tonight.'

'Christ, Bella. Do you realise there's a leopard lurking out there?'

'Come on! Be crazy. Fuck the leopard.'

'I don't think I could quite manage a *ménage à trois*.'

Bella laughs, slapping my arm. 'You fool, you! Come on, don't be a sissy, man! Let's do it!'

The helpless Pre-Raphaelite waif slips even further from my mind's eye.

'Okay,' I say.

She puts her head against my chest and we dance some more. A cool breeze is coming off the plain and the evening sky fills with stars. As we dance, I watch the others. The girls holding hands, Gus and Jenny smooching. Ncube and Angela laughing as they try out fancy moves. It's all so beautifully sweet and sad – a glimpse of something that I wish could last forever, but has already been lost. I feel like I'm floating, such is the weight that's been lifted from my shoulders. Then the music ends and while the girls go to change the record we gravitate to our respective gender clans. I join Gus and Ncube down at the fire. Whitney Houston bellows out from the lounge. Gus wags his big arse and sings along as he turns the meat. *Ooh, I wanna dance with somebody.* Frik barks. Ncube cackles at the sight of Gus.

I ask if Bella and I can use the Cruiser for our nocturnal adventure.

Eyeing me across the flames, Gus says, 'Didn't have you figured for an outdoors type, professor. Why don't you two just sleep in one of the rooms? No one's gonna mind, boet.'

'What? Together in the same room?' Ncube asks innocently. 'What for?'

'I take it that's a yes, Gus?'

Gus holds his hands out. 'Who am I to stand in the way of love?'

'I still don't understand,' Ncube says, his brow bunched in thought. 'Sleeping together. Now why would two people do such a thing? What purpose is served?'

'With Vaughn, who the hell knows?' Gus says.

I blow my cheeks out, exasperated. 'Fuck off and grow up, both of you!'

Ncube claps me on the back, causing me to spill some of my drink. The two of them laugh like schoolboys.

Later, we take the chairs down and sit in a circle down around the fire. We eat what has become our usual fare – steaks, chops, sadza and salads. The dogs lie on either side of Gus, knowing who's the soft touch.

'I think I'll have to go to detox when I get back to Australia,' I say. 'To wean me off meat.'

'Me too,' Angela agrees. 'God, I feel a complete carnivore!'

'Nothing wrong with a bit of meat now and then,' Gus replies sagely.

'It's been lovely having you here,' Jenny says. 'I hate the thought of you going so soon.'

'Despite the scratch on your car?' I ask.

Jenny laughs wryly. 'Yes, despite the scratch. We miss family so.'

Gus nods. 'Tell that surfer son of yours to come and visit us sometime, boet. It's time he got to know his cousins. Tell him there's some work to be done on the farm that his father never got around to.'

If only that was possible, I think.

There's a long silence, then Angela says, 'Of course, you're all welcome to come and stay with me in England. Wouldn't you like that, girls?'

'Oh, ja!' Jessica and Lauren cry in unison.

'Thank you very much,' Ncube pipes in. 'So kind of you to offer. Can I bring my wives too?'

We laugh. Bella puts her hand on my arm. Gus throws a couple of chop bones at the dogs. 'Who's for some more meat?' he says. 'Come on, there's plenty.'

'Mayibabo!' Ncube says. 'No more of your bull, Angus! I'm right up to here!' He gestures at his throat.

There's a moment's silence, before we all laugh at his pun. Ncube offers me a cigarette and we light up.

'I could do with another gin,' Jenny says.

'Now you're talking,' Bella concurs, holding up an empty glass.

We recharge our drinks and sit there talking and laughing, happy and sad in each other's company, knowing the purpose for our togetherness has come to an end.

The time slips away. Ncube leaves, despite Gus's invitation to sleep at the house. Bella and I load up the cruiser with a mattress and some blankets, a bottle of whisky, cigarettes and a thermos flask of coffee. With Bella still in her long dress, we set off across the plain towards the distant hills, the headlights of the cruiser burning long shafts through the bush. We wind down along the river, then turn up into the hills. We weave through thickets of msasa and gondi trees that look spooky against the black night. Bella sings quietly as I drive. I think about what Oom Jasper had said, and where this will lead me. A strange contradiction besets me. It worries me that I don't care.

The headlights catch the headstones as we pass the graveyard. I drive the Cruiser as high up the base of Long Cross Hill as I can. We're both pretty tipsy and laugh as we lug the mattress and things up the steep bare dome of the hill. I shine a torch to illuminate the way. Bella struggles in her long dress. She slips and falls, grazing her elbow, so she takes off her leather-soled shoes and climbs the rest of the way barefoot. The cross looms tall and black against the starry sky. It's a fairly strenuous climb and we reach the top breathing heavily. We place the mattress on a flat ledge of rock near the cross. There is a cool breeze blowing, filled with the dry scent of the surrounding bush that laps at the hill like a black ocean. I take the torch and go back down the hill to gather some wood. While I stumble around among the trees, the torch catches the sudden glimpse of a night adder as it slithers into a crevice. I pause only for a second to consider the complications of a snake bite, so assured am I the spirits are with me tonight. I return and build a fire and we sit there on the mattress with a blanket around our shoulders gazing out at the spray of stars and the black land below. We sip neat whisky and smoke, listening to the muted cries of night birds and animals in the trees below.

'This is so lekker,' Bella says.

I nod, aware of a sudden sense of loss.

'How do the Aussies say lekker?' Bella asks.

'Oh, they've got a few equivalents – bonza, ripper, beaut, corker, cracker.'

'I'd love to see Australia.'

'You would?'

'Ja, it sounds so nice.'

'It takes a bit of getting used to. After living in Africa. Living anywhere after Africa takes getting used to, I guess.'

'Anything is better than Zimbabwe.'

I swig at my whisky, feeling it burn through my body. 'Oh, yes ... that's hit the spot!'

Bella laughs and leans close against me. Unable to shake off the nagging sense of loss, I gesture out at the black land. 'You know, it's a hell of a thing to think that soon this won't belong to us. That the Bourkes will be gone forever from this place. Ripped from the soil, literally.'

'I know,' Bella says quietly. 'I've been through it.'

'When I left Rhodesia I tried to deny my emotional attachment to this place. Especially after my folks were killed. I tried to convince myself that Hopelands – the physical place – had no real significance. I honestly believed that if I never came back it was no big deal. But I was never able to sever the umbilical cord. Subconsciously, there must always have been a sense of security in knowing that the farm was still here – that I could go home if ever I needed to. It's ironic ... I've only begun to realise that now that it's all gone. Now it's as though we – the Bourkes – have been cast out of the Garden of Eden, never to return.'

Bella sighs. 'Ja, it is special, this place. I think some of us will roam the earth forever looking for something like it. Not realising we're really looking for the past. I just want to look forward, Vaughn. I'm tired of the past.'

'Unfortunately we're the product of the past. Of our memories.'

I lean over and kiss her, first on the cheek and then on her lips. Her lips part and we fall back on the mattress. In a manic hunger her mouth seems to devour me, her body writhes beneath her clothes against mine. I feel the wetness of her tears against my face. Her hands clasp at my skin. If it were not for the effects of whisky, she might have terrified me. I run my hands beneath her dress, feeling her soft breasts and hips. She sits up and pulls off her clothes. I cast mine aside and she sits astride me. I push myself into her and she rides me, leaning forward with her breasts dragging over my chest. I clasp her thighs and pull myself deeper into her. Then we roll over and she wraps her legs around my back and we rock and heave.

Bella cries out and rakes at my back with her nails, coming in a short, violent spasm. When I come she sighs and laughs gently and says she loves me. I lie there with her head on my chest, gasping for air, realising in the post-coital glow that I do care.

*

I wake early the next morning to the staccato bleating of guinea fowl and the first dove calls. The sun has not yet risen and the land below stretches out in black-mauve to the distant lighted horizon. I get up and walk naked up to the cross. I stand there shivering in the morning cold and, still half-crazy with happiness, thank God for being alive. Authentic Man at last. The earth seems to answer with a sudden flush of greens and golds. Like a chameleon it adapts to its heavenly condition.

Bella calls my name. I go back to her. She is wrapped in the blankets, smiling at the scrawny savage wearing only glasses who approaches in the half-light. I pour two mugs of coffee from the still-warm thermos flask. We sit together drinking the coffee. She asks how I got the bite mark on my thigh. 'Your bloody dog, Jakkals,' I say. She holds her hand to her mouth, affecting shock, then giggles.

We make love again to prove it was no whisky fluke.

By the time we have loaded everything back on the Cruiser, the sun has broken free of the horizon and is rising hot and white in the sky. I'm about to start the engine when Bella grabs my arm and points. 'Ag, Vaughn, look!' she whispers.

I look at where she's pointing. Nothing but trees.

'There!' she whispers again, fiercely.

Again, just bush. Then, a tiny flicker of movement and I see the leopard in an msusu thicket, not thirty metres away. He stands there in the dappled shadows watching us, his tail twitching. We sit motionless, transfixed by his stare. A small eternity of wonder passes. I wonder if angels are confined to humanly form. Then, as though it's his regal cue, he strides out across our path, his splendid spotted coat bright and shining in the sunlight. We sit mesmerised as he stops in front of the Cruiser and stares at us again with green eyes as uncaring as the stars in the night sky.

Then he lopes off into the trees and disappears.

*

We leave the farm around noon, Bella and me following Gus and the others. The dust billowing out behind the Cressida makes it difficult to see, so we drop back to avoid the worst of it. There is barely a breeze and the dust hangs in the hot, heavy air. As we cross the bridge, I glance back at the house on the hill, but it's gone, hidden by dust. Bella leans forward over the steering wheel, watching out for potholes. She smiles as I slip my hand under her blouse and run it over her back.

'I'm trying to concentrate,' she says. 'You're not helping, you know.'

When I move my hand away, she laughs and says, 'That doesn't mean stop!'

She almost purrs as I continue. I fiddle with her bra strap but, never adept at the technical riddles posed by female garments, give up trying to get it undone. With my free hand I turn on the radio and search through a barrage of static for a station.

'Don't bother,' Bella says. 'The aerial's buggered.'

'I just want to hear some news. Any news. God, I feel as though I've been stranded on a desert island. I've absolutely no idea what's been going on in the world.'

'Ag, Vaughn, what's there to hear, hey? Afghanistan, Iraq, terrorism ... I'm sick of it.'

Though we've dropped back to where we can no longer see the Cressida, the dust seems to get thicker. I'm busy contemplating how much I might have preferred the simple word 'broken', or even the more exotic 'kaput', to have issued from such sweet lips, rather than 'buggered', when, as we come over the slight crest that marks the old boundary to the Gerbers' farm, Bella slams on the brakes. We skid to a halt, almost colliding with the Cressida.

As the dust settles we see a group of men, perhaps a dozen, standing around the Cressida, talking to Gus. Two women wearing red berets stand officiously in the middle of the road, one holding a hand-painted sign that reads, STOP – WAR VETREN AREA. We can see Angela through the back window with her arm around Jessica and Lauren. Most of the men are carrying sticks and knobkerries. A few are armed with axes and pangas. Two have old Rhodesian army-issue FN rifles. Gus emerges from the Cressida and walks around to open the boot. He waves at us to stay put. The vets begin rummaging around and removing things from the boot. The one doing most of the talking is Terror Yengwa.

'Oh God,' Bella says. 'Oh God, oh God.'

I take her hand. 'Don't worry. Gus will handle this.'

Two of the vets, one with a rifle, come sauntering over to our car. Bella begins to panic, her breath coming in quick gasps. I

squeeze her hand and tell her to stay calm. To my embarrassment, my voice has a slight quaver to it. The men approach our
windows. I recognise the man with the rifle – one of Mtunzi's
goons at the church, the one who was smoking. He comes to
my side and indicates with a spiral gesture for us to wind our
windows down. We comply and the men inspect us and the
car's interior with sullen stares.

'Sakubona, amadoda!' I greet, trying Gus's cheery approach.
'Ai! Kuyatshisa lamuhla – it's hot today. How can I help you?'

The same sullen stares. The man with the rifle tells Bella to
switch off the engine. She complies.

'You are trespassing,' he says.

'Trespassing? Trespassing where?'

'This is veteran property.'

'What are you talking about? This is a bloody public road,'
Bella says in a voice that has found more steel than mine,
despite the fact that the other man, who is carrying an axe, is
leaning on her door, his face less than a foot from hers.

The man with the rifle responds angrily to Bella answering
him in that tone. 'Be quiet, you! This road – this land – belongs
to the veterans! All of it! You are trespassing now!'

I hold out my hands placatingly. 'We must be mistaken then.
We will remember next time.'

'No "next time!" Who are you? What are you doing here?'

He knows who I am. This whole mob knows who we are.
This has been planned. They've been waiting for us. The utter
helplessness of our situation begins to dawn on me. When I see
Gus remonstrating with Yengwa in front of us, I am filled with
dread. Vaguely I hear him. 'What the hell are you doing? Hey!
That's my property – put it back!'

If a game must be played, so be it.

'I am Vaughn Bourke.' I say. I gesture at Bella. 'This is my friend who lives in Bulawayo. I am visiting from Australia.'

'Bourke?' the man says. 'You must go back to Australia, Bourke. What is your friend's name?'

Angrily, Bella sticks her hand in her bag between our seats and pulls out her driver's licence. 'There!' she says, waving it at both men. 'I'm Isabella Gerber, a citizen of Zimbabwe!'

The man with the rifle takes the licence and scrutinises it. He points at the entrance to the Gerber farm, fifty metres up the road. 'Gerber? You are not the Gerber who belongs here?'

'I *am* the Gerber who belongs here,' Bella replies.

Both men, no doubt among the many murderers of her brother, gaze at her blankly. Then the man with the rifle tosses the driver's licence back into the car.

'Open the back,' he instructs.

Bella climbs out the car and opens the boot, which contains just her overnight bag which is promptly confiscated and placed on the side of the road. The other man meanwhile reaches through the window and takes her handbag. In a blind reaction, I grab at it. 'Hey! Let go of that!' I shout. A brief tug of war ensues. Bella comes running around and attempts to push the man away. 'You fucking thief! Get away!' she cries. The man gives her a backhand clout across the face that sends her sprawling into the road. Still holding onto the bag I feel the hard metal of the rifle barrel ram against my head. I turn and look into the wild, blood-suffused eyes of the man behind the rifle. Eyes that now have fixed their quarry. Limply I let go of the bag and look away, frozen with terror.

Out of the corner of my eye I can see the other man quickly

rummaging through Bella's bag. He removes her purse, inspects its contents, and puts it in his pocket. Then, with a casual flourish, he flings the bag at the feet of the women in berets. Dropping the sign, they dive on it. One of them rises, holding the bag aloft, laughing.

I still have the rifle to my head. The barrel is up hard against my ear, pushing my head to the side. Ahead of us, Gus stands there watching the commotion. And in the stupid, dumbstruck look in his eyes, I realise our true helplessness. It occurs to me that he has never imagined such a predicament in which he is powerless to act, where others who rely on him to save them cannot be saved. A predicament for which he is responsible. More than anything else in the world, I want him to lose that shock in his eyes. I am his little brother, relying on him to ward off the bullies. I want him, the soldier, the Selous Scout hero, to save us.

Bella shouts, 'Hey! Leave him alone! Put that gun down, you bloody idiot!'

A scuffle behind the car. She cries out. I turn to see her grappling with the other man. He strikes her again and throws her to the ground. The man at my window rams the rifle hard again into my temple, forcing my head forward. The serrated end of the flash guard digs into my skin. I hear Bella crying. I can't see her. I can only see Gus ahead of me, and the terrified faces of Angela and the girls through the rear window of the Cressida.

'Please, don't do this,' I utter meekly.

The shock in Gus's eyes has changed to rage, to livid slits. He bunches his fists and begins to stride towards us. Yengwa moves to stop him and Gus sends him reeling with a punch to the head.

Angry shouts. A blur of violence. Frightened screams from the car in front. Yengwa and his men start climbing into Gus. He is felled with a blow from a knobkerrie to the head. He lies on the ground holding his arms up to protect his head as clubs and sticks rain down on him. Yengwa exacts particular revenge. Jenny and Angela burst out of the car and attempt to pull the men away. They are shrugged off like insects. Forever burned in my memory, the hysterical faces of Jessica and Lauren in the car.

I have no idea how long this goes on for. A minute, a few minutes.

A thunderclap. Everything stops. Silence. My first thought is that Gus has been shot. Fear surges through me. I think, Christ, this is it, we are gone. But then Mtunzi comes striding up the road, brandishing a smoking automatic pistol. He fires another shot into the air. He calls off the dogs. The dogs obey. The rifle is withdrawn from my head. I touch my cheek and my fingers come away smeared with blood. The two men at our vehicle join the others. I climb out, my legs shaking. Bella is sitting on the ground behind the car, her blouse half torn off. She gasps for breath like a stunned bird. Her jaw is bruised. There is a small swelling on her lip, crowned with beads of blood. I help her back into the car.

Gus is getting slowly to his feet. He wipes blood from his face with his sleeve. Mtunzi backs him up against the Cressida, prodding the pistol in his chest.

I go towards them, my hand raised. 'Enough. Please, this is enough.'

Mtunzi waves the gun at me. 'Go back,' he says.

'Get back in the car, Vaughn,' Gus says, panting through bloodied lips.

'No, this has gone too far. Please, for the sake of decency, this is enough.'

My words, uttered in a daze, sound completely stupid, bizarre.

Mtunzi smiles, affecting a puzzled look. 'Decency? Did your forefathers think of decency when they took this land from us?' His cultured English seems surreal. He taps Gus on the chest with the gun. 'No, decency has never been in much supply here. Pain and suffering, yes. But as much as it gives me pleasure to inflict pain and suffering on you whites, in return for that which you inflicted on us, killing you brings me too much attention. When we killed Gerber the whole world was on my doorstep, interfering with our operations here. Strange, isn't it? I can kill a thousand black people, and no one bats an eye. One white, and everyone is clamouring for justice.'

Mtunzi gestures with the gun at Angela and Jenny who are back in the car, trying to calm the girls. 'And when white women are involved, there is even more trouble. You should thank me, Bourke. Who knows what could have happened to these women had I not come to your rescue. Your girls are pretty and innocent. Imagine if they were violated. Fucked by my men. A terrible thought, not so? But such things can happen in this world. It can happen just like this!'

He snaps his fingers.

'Women and children, that's your style, Mtunzi,' Gus mutters.

'Don't test my patience, Bourke. This is just a taste of what will happen if you decide to come back. I will kill you myself if you put one foot on this land again. Don't doubt what I'm saying. If you want to die I will assist you to that end, with pleasure.' Again, he prods Gus in the chest with the gun. 'Do you understand me, Bourke? I wish to be clear on this matter.'

218

Gus just glowers at him.

Mtunzi shakes his head. 'You better understand me, Bourke. You have taken the remains of your people out of this earth and buried them at the church. I say good riddance. The church is the rubbish dump for whites in this country. Now it is time for you to go.' He points his gun at me. 'You too! Go, and don't come back!'

Glaring at Mtunzi and his men, Gus limps around the Cressida. I go back to Bella's car. Bella is sitting with her head on the steering wheel, eyes closed, her mouth clenched. I put my hand on her shoulder and tell her to shift across to the passenger seat. She shakes her head, but then complies. I get into the driver's seat. Ahead, I see Mtunzi give a contemptuous wave of the hand and Gus's car start to move forward. I am shaking so much I stall as I try to take off. I start the engine again, revving loudly, and take off with an unexpected wheelspin. As we pass Mtunzi and his mob, they laugh and brandish their weapons at us. There is a loud bang that makes me nearly shit myself as one of them strikes the roof of the car with a knobkerrie.

'Ja, and fuck you too!' Bella mutters at their laughing faces. Once past them she bursts into tears.

'Are you okay?' I ask, stupidly.

She turns away and nods.

A few kilometres further on, Gus pulls over. As we stop behind him, he gets out and limps off into the bush to urinate. We wait, listening to the splashing of his piss. He emerges, zipping up his fly, and hobbles over to Bella's window. His face is covered in cuts and bruises. A deep gash under the hair next to his ear still bleeds. One eye is half-shut with swelling. 'Are you guys okay? Are you all right, Bella?' he asks.

219

Bella nods her head and blows her nose. With one hand she is holding her torn blouse together at the shoulder.

'I'm okay,' she says. 'How're the girls?'

Gus wipes the blood running down his face near his ear with a sodden sleeve. 'Jenny and Ange are all right. The girls ... Christ, I don't know. Still in a bit of shock, I suppose. Bloody bastards. I'm sorry, Bella. What about you, boet?'

I shrug. 'By comparison, I had the armchair treatment. You better get that cut seen to, Gus.'

Gus shakes his head. 'I'm okay. Those bloody bastards. Shit, I really don't know ...'

Bella gets out and inspects the dent on the roof. Then she climbs back in and says angrily, 'Fucking kaffirs. Let's just go, please.'

We drive on. As we near Shangani Bella says, 'Fuck this! Get me out of this country, Vaughn. I hate this place. I hate these people. Please, get me out of this bloody country, okay?'

The hate in her eyes makes her a different person.

*

At Shangani Gus pulls over again, just before the main road. Jenny, the former nurse, has found some bandages in the glove box and administers some first aid to Gus's head. She argues that they should go straight to the Mater Dei Hospital in Bulawayo to get some of his cuts stitched. She wants his ribs and leg looked at; she suspects fractures. When Gus refuses she loses her temper and storms off up the road, shouting obscenities back at him. A group of people waiting at a bus stop in the shade of some trees at the nearby petrol station have

220

been watching the scene. Some of them exclaim 'Aibo!' at the ripe language. Angela runs after Jenny and brings her back to the car. Gus looks shocked. I surmise it's not often that Jenny flies off the handle like this.

A sign of the times is that no one mentions a word about going to the police. It is taken for granted that will be a waste of time, and probably make things worse.

The shock of it shows in different ways. By the time we reach Bulawayo Bella has gathered herself to the point where she behaves as though nothing has happened. She even insists that I come round to her place for dinner, and looks surprised and a little hurt when I decline. When we get to the house in Burnside, Gus and Jenny are still going hammer and tongs. Bella turns down my invitation to come in when we see Jenny stomping off into the house in tears. Not partial to a long dose of high family tension, I reverse my earlier decision and promise to drop in at her place that evening.

I go inside to find Gus and Jenny still arguing behind the closed door of their bedroom. The maid, Gladys, goes through the motions of wiping down the kitchen table, a worried expression on her normally cheerful face. She has come in voluntarily today (Sunday being her day off) because the family was away yesterday – even domestic jobs are scarce these days and Gladys is no doubt anxious to demonstrate her reliability. Jessica and Lauren have taken refuge in their bedrooms. I find Angela sitting alone in the lounge, staring at one of her paintings. Elephants clustered around a baobab tree against a golden sunset. She looks dazed.

'Jeez, these things are such clichés,' she says. 'They say nothing about the *real* Africa. I really need to move on with my art.'

I sit down next to her. 'To what? Silly conceptual installations? Painting with dung? Chopping cows in half? Somehow I can't quite see you as a contemporary artist.'

Angela laughs. 'Don't be facetious. You're the one who thinks my painting's kitsch.'

'Yes, and I'm the last person you should listen to. There's nothing wrong with your painting, Ange. There's nothing wrong with trying to depict an ideal world – don't *you* lose faith now!'

Angela's eyes suddenly fill with tears.

I put my arm around her. 'Hey, come on, big sister. Don't start drizzling now.'

She smiles and puts her arms around me and cries softly on my chest. I just hold her, saying nothing. I think of how lonely she has been in this world. The muffled argument goes on in the bedroom. After a while, Angela straightens up and blows her nose.

'At least there's one person's shoulder I can cry on.'

'I'll always be there for you, Ange.'

Her eyes fill again. She shakes her head. 'I'm sorry.'

'Don't be sorry. It's been a shit day.'

Angela sighs and blows her nose again.

'What's going on with Gus and Jenny?' I ask.

'Jenny completely freaked out in the car. Says she's leaving. Going back to Britain, with or without Gus.' Angela pauses, then gestures at the closed doors of Jessica's and Lauren's rooms. 'It's been quite a day for those poor girls. First, seeing their father being beaten up, then witnessing their parents going at each other's throats. God, I don't think they've ever heard Jenny swear like that before.'

'I hope Jenny means it. It's the only way anyone will ever prise Gus's big arse loose from this fuck-up of a country.'

Angela nods. 'I agree. But she always ends up doing what Gus wants in the end.'

'Maybe not this time. Talk to her, Angela. Gus is going to get himself killed at this rate. She listens to you.'

We sit for a while, listening to Gus and Jenny. Mostly we hear Jenny, carrying on in a plaintive, high-pitched whine. 'Look at your face, Angus! Look in the mirror, for God's sake, and tell me everything's going to be okay!'

Monty, a sensitive soul beneath his brutish exterior, is whining and scratching at the kitchen door.

'Bella also freaked out,' I say. 'She wants me to take her to Australia.'

Angela raises her eyebrows. 'Take her to Australia?'

I nod.

'What? As a ... a *wife*?'

I laugh. 'I suppose so.'

Angela laughs too. 'I'm sorry. I'm just a bit ... *marry* her? She asked you? And you said yes?'

'Not as such. Indirectly, she did. She just asked me to get her out of here. So did Oom Jasper yesterday. I didn't say yes or no. But that's what's implied. It's the only sure way she could get into Australia.'

'Are you sure about this, Vaughn?'

'Christ, I don't know, Ange. We're like chalk and cheese. But I don't think compatibility's high up on Bella's agenda right now. She just blurted it out in the heat of the moment, after that bloody business on the road. It's quite bizarre, really. To be honest, I can't believe she's serious about me.'

'Bella could do a lot worse. So could you.'

I sigh. 'I don't know. I'll do it just to get her out of the country, I suppose. But the rest of it ... I don't know if I can live with someone so filled with hate. I got a glimpse of it today – it changed her completely. I can understand why she hates, but it's something I can't handle. I just can't carry that sort of baggage again. I've been away from this place too long.'

Angela nods. 'We've both been away too long. We've got used to living in safe, stable countries – we don't have this bloody chaos in our faces every day. We have the luxury to be normal.'

'It's the same with Gus. I just can't identify with his racist bullshit. I'm completely out of my depth here. Right now, all I want to do is climb on a plane and get the hell out of here back to Australia. Back to sanity.'

'It's your life, Vaughn. Do what you think is right. But don't be too judgemental about Gus and Bella. Don't ditch Bella because of a few epithets she utters out of fear. Believe me, it's fear in her heart, not hate. You have more in common with Bella than you think.'

I sit back, looking at Angela's painting. Elephants, baobabs ... Christ, how I envy her! Not for what she paints, but for the dream she pursued. For me, life seems just one confused blur, nothing certain, nothing defined, nothing achieved ...

The argument stops and Gus emerges from the room, his battered face flushed with anger. He limps off down the passageway, muttering to himself. We hear him on the phone, talking to Ncube.

'No, they're all okay ... Ja, that's right, Saxon. Make sure Witness gets the dipping done tomorrow. I'm relying on you. No, that comes first ... ja, those bloody Herefords are full of ticks, man ... Okay, we'd better meet in Shangani and figure out a plan. Tomorrow, at your place, okay? Oh, and Saxon, make sure the dogs are fed ... No, they won't bite you, for Christ sake. They bite kaffirs, not honourable African gentlemen like you.'

I look at Angela. She rolls her eyes and smiles.

Gus hangs up and comes through. Were it not for the pitbull look in his eyes he would seem almost comical with his bandaged head. 'Who's for a bloody drink,' he grunts. Angela shakes her head. I put up my hand. Gus limps through to the kitchen. I lean over and whisper to Angela not to mention anything about Bella and me. We hear Gus telling Gladys she can go home. He lets a worried-looking Monty inside and comes back with two beers. He hands me one and sits down with a sigh. We drink straight from the bottle. Gus strokes Monty's head on his knee. 'Hey, you old parasite,' he says. 'Ever get the feeling the world is just one massive bowl of vomit?'

'What does Saxon say?' I ask.

'Not much he can say at this stage. Says he'll see if he can talk to Mtunzi.'

I throw up my hands. 'Oh Christ, I give up! Talk about what? The time for talking is over, man! Face facts, Gus. If what happened today hasn't woken you up, what the hell will?'

Gus opens his mouth to say something, but fills it with beer instead.

'Is Jenny okay?' Angela asks.

Gus waves his hand dismissively. 'Ag, you know what women are like. Make a big deal about everything.'

'It is a big deal,' Angela says. 'You should listen to her.'

'Don't *you* start on me now.'

'Think about it, Angus. Think about what happened today. Those people could've done anything they pleased with us. With your wife and daughters.'

'Ja, well they didn't.'

Angela gives an exasperated sigh. 'It's the end, Angus. It's time to move on. To some place where you'll be safe – where *your family* will be safe.'

But Gus's jaws are into something he won't let go of. He flattens half his beer in one swig. He belches. 'I said don't start on me, Ange. In any case I've got no money to go and start up again somewhere else. All I have is what's here!'

'There's nothing here, for God's sake! I've got more money than you need. Than all of us need. I'll buy you a farm in Britain, in Australia – anywhere you want. Please, listen to me!'

'I don't want your charity. I don't want to farm anywhere else.'

I butt in. 'Have you ever thought of what Jenny and the girls might want?'

'Look, both of you, if you're going to sit here telling me to throw in the towel, then you might as well fuck off back over-seas! I don't want to hear it, okay?'

Angela's eyes flash angrily. 'You stubborn bastard! You better wake up to yourself, Angus. And soon! There are other people involved in this. Not just you!'

She gets up and marches outside, slamming the door. Through the window we see her go down to the summerhouse next to the pool. Gus gets up too, wincing with pain. 'You want another beer?' he asks. I shake my head. He gets himself another beer and gingerly sits down again.

'So, tell me, Chickenheart,' he says. 'What's it like being a non-vertebrate?'

By three o'clock he has passed out in his chair, a pile of bottles and a snoozing Monty at his feet.

I go to my room and fall into a fitful sleep, exhausted by the highs and lows of the past twenty-four hours. I wake around six, take a shower and get dressed for the evening. Jenny and the girls have emerged from their bedrooms. Her face red-eyed and puffy, Jenny goes about noisily preparing dinner, banging cupboard doors and shoving dishes around. The girls are subdued, shadows of their normal happy selves. I tell Jenny of my plans for the evening. To my surprise, she gives me the keys to her car, since the Cressida is low on fuel. Though I'd made partial amends by pledging to have the scratch on the station wagon fixed, I'd assumed it was forever out of bounds.

I try to make light of it. 'Maybe I could match up the scratch on the other side.'

She gives me a bleak stare. 'Write it off, for all I care.'

As I drive off, I can see Angela still sitting in the summerhouse. There are clouds building up on the horizon but I don't give the possibility of rain much thought. Too much hope is not good for you in this place.

Bella is there to assist in my safe passage into her house, through the lethal pack of dogs that mills around the car as I'm let in through the security gates. Oom Jasper is sitting in his chair in the lounge, with a cigarette and glass of brandy, watching a one-day cricket match between South Africa and Australia on cable TV. He is wearing a jacket and tie.

'Christ, you bloody Aussies are giving the Proteas another hiding!' he says by way of greeting. 'Ag, Bella, maak vir hierdie bliksemse Aussie 'n dop, skattie.'

'Not much of a choice, I'm afraid,' Bella says. 'Brandy or beer.'

'Brandy, thanks.'

I go through to the kitchen with her where she fixes us both a brandy and water. The swelling on her lip has subsided and she has disguised the bruise on her jaw with makeup. She flicks her eyes in the direction of the lounge. 'I told him I got drunk last night and bumped my head,' she says. 'I didn't want him getting upset.'

We go back to the lounge and sit down. Oom Jasper switches the TV off. 'I'm sick of watching you bloody Aussies win,' he says. He looks at his watch. 'We'll have to wikkel, Bella. You better find Vaughn one of my ties.'

'Papa's treating us to dinner at the Bulawayo Club,' Bella says. 'He's been a member for forty years.'

'I thought they only accepted Englishmen,' I jest.

'Ag, seun, these days they accept even kaffirs!'

'Papa! Mind your language. You know Vaughn's a liberal.'

Oom Jasper shakes his head. 'Ag ja, skattie. It's a shame, hey?'

'Please don't go to any expense on my account,' I say. 'At least let me contribute.'

Oom Jasper waves his hand dismissively. 'Nee, wat! I've got a few bob left in the bank. I might as well spend it while I'm still breathing. Kom, julle. Let's drink and go.'

We gulp our drinks down. While Bella hunts for a tie, Oom Jasper glowers fiercely at me over his bifocals. 'What's this I hear about you getting my daughter so drunk she bangs her head?' he demands, wagging his finger at me.

I sit there at a loss for words. He cackles with laughter.

'Only joking, seun! Jussus, but you're a serious bloke, hey! I know Bella's in control even when she's drunk. She has a mind of her own, that girl.'

'You're not kidding,' I murmur.

Oom Jasper eyes the semi-circular cut on my temple.

'Looks like you didn't do too badly yourself,' he laughs.

Bella comes back and festoons me with one of Oom Jasper's ties, a bright yellow and red floral number, inadvertently post-modern in effect.

'Ag, don't you look smart, hey?' Bella says.

It's a short drive to the centre of town. Being a Sunday night, the Club is full. While we wait for a table in the dining room, Oom Jasper gives us a guided tour around the old dinosaur of a building, pointing out items of interest with his walking stick. Built on the spot where Cecil John Rhodes used to slake his thirst in a frontier saloon, the Bulawayo Club is a strange colonial relic – strange in that it still exists in a place like Zimbabwe. It quite literally has the feel and smell of Rhodesia – that reek of floor polish, black waiters in spotless uniforms, a bygone time where white men gathered to bask in the distant glow of Empire. A time in which the catastrophes of today were inconceivable. Rhinoceros and antelope trophies line the dark wood-panelled walls, along with an ornately framed painting of Queen Elizabeth and, throbbing from the wall like a proverbial sore thumb, the dour visage of his Excellency, President Robert Gabriel Mugabe. Upstairs the walls are lined with photographs of yesteryear: Prince Philip and prime ministers officiating; the Club in colonial times with the big Rhodes statue standing close by, now removed, Oom Jasper tells me, to an ignominious spot under some jacaranda trees behind the National Museum. There are glass cases of old silverware, crockery and cigar cases. Shaking his head wistfully, Oom Jasper recalls the good old days when women were only allowed into the Club through a side entrance and restricted to certain areas, and when the only way blacks gained entrance was as waiters, cooks or cleaners.

A waiter calls us to our table and we sit down and order from the menu. We all opt for roast lamb. Bella and Oom Jasper order brandies, I have a whisky. We smoke and drink. Despite my afternoon nap, I feel drained, exhausted.

'So when are you off back to Australia?' Oom Jasper asks.

'Thursday next week, Oom.'

'You must be looking forward to getting the heck away from this place, hey?'

I shrug. 'I've got mixed feelings, Oom.'

'Ag, I tell you, Vaughn, this place is not for decent people. You did the right thing leaving. You had your head screwed on properly, man.'

The reason why I left Rhodesia – that smug protest against the Smith regime – now seems ludicrously ironic because Oom Jasper has me pegged for a visionary, one who'd foreseen the horrors of Zimbabwe.

The old man points the glowing tip of his cigarette at me. 'Ja, man. You had your head screwed on. He's a clever boy, hey Bella?'

Bella smiles at me and winks. 'He's a genius, Papa.'

'People here were just unlucky, Oom,' I say. 'Unlucky Mugabe became such an idiot. Zimbabwe could've been the real jewel of Africa.'

'And who's to say Nkomo or any other kaffir would've been

any better. Nee, seun. 'n Kaffer bly 'n kaffer. Bloody bastards, all of them!'

Bella glances around at the other diners. 'Papa! Not here!'

'I'm afraid I have to disagree with you, Oom,' I say. 'If it was Nelson Mandela running the show here, Zimbabwe would be a different place.'

'Mandela! Ag nee, man! You wait and see what happens to South Africa down the road. It will be the same story, I promise you. Already that Mbeki has made a mess of things. You watch!'

I'm about to reply but Bella cuts the air between her father and me with her hand. 'Come on, you two – let's change the subject,' she says.

The waiter comes with our food. Thankfully the conversation shifts to safer ground. As we eat Oom Jasper and Bella talk about the holiday trips they used to make to Beira in Mozambique in the old days. How they had stayed in bungalows on the beach and eaten like kings in the seafront restaurants. 'Before that country also went to the dogs,' Oom Jasper grumbles. We have a trifle for desert. Then we order another round of drinks, which proves one too many for Oom Jasper.

'You're a good bloke, Vaughn. A boy after my own heart. You come from a good family. I meant what I said yesterday ...'

'Papa, please don't embarrass Vaughn.'

Oom Jasper takes a deep drag on his cigarette and tears start streaming down his cheeks. 'There're not many good people left in this world, seun. Look after my daughter, please. Bella's happiness means everything to me ...'

'Papa, asseblief ...'

He mops his eyes with a serviette. 'Ja, I know, Bella. I'm sorry. We're all going to bloody pieces these days, hey?'

I feel I've been drawn and quartered as we go out into the humid night air. Oom Jasper brushes aside a persistent beggar as we climb into Bella's car. 'Don't ask me for money – ask your stupid president!' he snarls and is surprised when the beggar replies, 'My president can go to hell!' Oom Jasper relents and gives the man a few banknotes.

'Ngiyabonga – thank you, my father,' the beggar says as he shuffles off down the road.

As we drive back we see lightning to the north of the city. Oom Jasper mutters, 'Another bloody false alarm, I bet.' Back at the house, the old man has a cup of coffee, yawns elaborately, then goes to bed. Bella and I sit together in the lounge while thunder rumbles outside. The lights flicker and go out. Bella sighs, 'Not again!' She feels her way through the dark to the kitchen and comes back with a lighted candle which she places on the coffee table next to the couch. She sits down again and puts her arms around me. When we kiss I taste a hint of blood as my tongue lingers on the inside of her swollen lip. Then she lays her head on my chest.

'I'm sorry about my father,' she says. 'He worries too much about me.'

'So he should.'

Bella lies back on the couch and rests her legs over mine. 'I'm sorry about today. I wasn't myself when I asked you to take me to Australia. I've no right to ask you anything. I couldn't leave Papa anyway.'

'He wants you to go. Yesterday he asked me himself.'

'And what did you say?'

'Nothing. It's not my decision to make.'

'Who would look after him? He's got no one else.'

'He could come to Australia too. All of that can be sorted out, once you're there.'

Bella shakes her head and lies gazing at the ceiling, blinking back tears. I flounder before saying, 'Come with me, Bella. There's no future for you here.'

'It would mean getting married.'

'What the hell. We'll do whatever we have to do.'

Bella laughs. 'That's about the most pathetic proposal I've ever heard!'

I lean over and kiss her. 'Let me do something good. For once.'

Outside, it starts raining, first a few big spattering drops, then it comes down in a roar. We go outside onto the veranda. The noise is so loud on the corrugated iron roof we can't hear each other speak. We stand there breathing in the overpowering fragrance of the drinking earth, wondering what lies ahead.

*

I dream we are on the back of my father's Dodge truck, driving across the open veld. It's raining and the truck splashes through deep puddles of water. The raindrops taste sweet in our mouths, like the nectar from trumpet creepers. We hold out our hands, trying to grab the long grass as it whips past. Angela sings into the wind:

Que sera sera, whatever will be will be
The future's not ours to see ...

233

Impervious to pain, Gus laughs as the grass, thick as canes, strikes his hand. Angela stops singing, abruptly. Her fingers are streaming with blood. Gus takes her hand and sucks the blood. I expect to hear my father yelling at us, 'Damn it! How many times have I told you kids the grass will cut you!'

But we are not children, and there is no one up front driving the truck.

*

I wake early to the soft purr of rain outside. I make myself some coffee in the kitchen and go out to the veranda. The garden glistens with water. The bare soil has turned a deep sodden sienna. The pungent, long-suppressed smell of wet humus – sweetly sexual as it combines with the scent of jacaranda and frangipani blossoms – comes wafting in. In the distance, Bulawayo sparkles in the early light. To the south, a piece of rainbow hangs like half a promise.

Gladys arrives at the gate beneath a tattered umbrella. As she lets herself in Monty comes bounding up, barking his stupid head off. When Gladys scolds him he retreats shamefacedly back to his basket under the back awning.

'Sakubona, Nkosi,' Gladys greets as she passes me on the veranda.

'Good morning, Gladys. Nice rain, isn't it?' I reply.

'Beautiful rain, master.'

'Gladys, please, you must call me Vaughn.'

'Yes, master.'

Some things never change.

The rain appears to have had a pacifying effect on everyone

in the Burnside household. Gus and Jenny appear to have patched things up. I see him give her a big sloppy kiss near the garage just before she takes the girls off to school. He gives each girl a hug which puts a smile on their faces. When Jenny gets back we sit around the breakfast table, having coffee. Gladys sings in the scullery as she washes the dishes, no doubt relieved to see a semblance of normality restored.

The reason for the change of mood soon becomes clear. Last night, they explain, Angela had come up with a possible solution to the problem. She had suggested that Gus and Ncube draw up a legal agreement in which title to the farm is handed over to Ncube until such time that political normality is restored in Zimbabwe. Ostensibly, then, Ncube would become Hopelands's caretaker owner. Gus could still have a say in the farm's running, but from the sidelines. Of course, such an agreement would have its risks, but it would be better than losing the farm outright to Mtunzi's thugs. Gus must have finally realised his back was to the wall because, to Jenny and Angela's surprise, he grudgingly agreed, promising to put the proposition to Ncube, providing Jenny would stay in Bulawayo and not leave for Britain as she'd threatened. Whether or not it is legally possible to draw up such an agreement, or whether Ncube will agree to it, remains to be seen. But at least a potential solution is on the table, and Gus has made the vital compromises. I'm so overjoyed to hear this that I leap up from my chair and give him a bear hug – an irrational act that causes Gus to wince not just from yesterday's injuries.

While we're on a roll, I spill the beans about Bella and me. Gus and Jenny seem to take it in their stride. Gus is his usual flippant self. He raises his coffee mug, half a lopsided grin across his swollen dial. 'Oh well, here's to you, boetie boy. What difference will one more disaster make?'

'Angus! Don't be so rude!' Jenny exclaims. 'I think that's the best news ever. When's the big day, Vaughn?'

'God, Jenny!' Angela laughs. 'They've only just decided.'

'As soon as we can – this week, if possible,' I say.

'This week!' Jenny cries. 'Oh Vaughn, man! Where's your sense of occasion!'

'Bella and I don't care how or where we get married, just as long as she's my wife by the time I get on that plane next week. Something quiet and simple. A magistrate will be fine.'

Jenny's eyes roll. 'A magistrate! Over my dead body. You'll love our little Anglican church here in Bulawayo. I'll talk to our minister ...'

'What about old Dlomo?' Gus says. 'I'm sure he could fit you guys in without much notice.'

'I'll ask Bella,' I reply. 'It's up to her.'

I tell them Bella will talk to her bosses today about leaving; she's confident they will understand and let her go at short notice.

'What about Oom Jasper?' Jenny asks. 'She's been his guiding light ever since they left the farm.'

'Once she gets permanent residence he can come out as a last remaining relative. We can send him money from Australia in the meantime.'

'We'll keep an eye on him, anyway,' Gus says. 'He won't starve.'

'I think it's wonderful,' Angela says. 'The poor girl's got no future here.'

'Why don't you take Bella down to the Falls this weekend?' Gus suggests. 'Where you can dust off your old conjugal skills.'

'No man, Angus, don't be rude!' Jenny exclaims, laughing nonetheless.

Gus affects innocence. 'What? I'm being serious. I'll bet Vaughn's a bit out of practice when it comes to, er ... connubial etiquette. Am I right, boet?'

I heave a long sigh. 'Always nice to hear from an expert. But I'm sure Bella will want to spend time with Oom Jasper.'

'I think it's a great idea,' Angela says. 'Let's all go. Oom Jasper can come along too. Come on, I'll stand you all to it.'

Gus shakes his head. 'Defeats the purpose a bit, don't you think? To have us and the old man breathing down their necks while they're on the job.'

Jenny giggles. 'Angus! Jeez, you've got a one-track mind. How did I ever marry you!'

'No, I suppose you're right, Gus,' Angela says. She bursts out laughing. 'It's just, Vaughn you're so ... so *old*! I'm forgetting it's your *honeymoon*!'

I heave another sigh. 'Ha. Ha. I'm sure Bella won't mind, my dear spring chicken.'

'No, I'm sure Bella *will* mind. Of course she'll mind.'

'I'll put it to her anyway,' I say.

Angela sighs. 'I'd just love to see the Falls again. Once more.'

The way she says it makes us fall silent.

*

'*Married!*' Beth exclaims over the phone.

'It sort of just happened, Beth.'

'Sort of just happened? How does getting married at your age sort of just happen?'

'It's the easiest way of getting Bella out of the country.'

'Oh, so now you've become a refugee saviour, have you? Rescuing Zimbabwean damsels in distress?'

'I know it may seem ...'

Beth laughs. When it comes to the foibles of my life, she has a way of laughing that makes me feel two feet tall.

'Nice to see you're taking this in a positive spirit.'

'I'm sorry, Vaughn. It's just so ... so *sudden*! Are you sure you're doing the right thing? More important – are you sure *she's* doing the right thing?'

'No, not really.'

'Does the poor girl have any idea what she's getting herself into?'

'Beth, be serious ...'

Beth takes a deep breath. 'No ... you're right. I'm sorry ... God, you're one for surprises! I'm happy for you, you crazy man. I really hope it works out for both of you. Really, I mean it. When are you coming back?'

'Next week. I'm hoping to get her on the same plane.'

There's an uncomfortable silence.

'Are you sure you're okay with this, Beth?'

'Look, Vaughn, you don't have to justify anything to me. Don't worry, I'm absolutely fine with it – it's good to see you making a fresh start. I just hope it works out. I hope ... what's her name – Bella – will give you a reason to get your life back on track. Will you be going back to the university?'

'I suppose so. It's time I got my act together.'

'It's time you stopped wasting your life, mister. Get back to your painting – I wish I had your talents.'

'You give me too much credit, Beth. How will Mikey take it?'

'Mikey? I don't know. He always set a lot of store in us getting back together, as you know. But I think he'll be fine.
You're not the only one with a new lease on life these days. His
new girlfriend's been such a blessing. He's been back at school
a week. Apparently, she's got him off the weed too. He's doing
okay.'

'That's good to hear, Beth.'

'I'll break it to him gently. I'm sure he'll be okay – enough
water's gone under the bridge by now, I think. Maybe, when
you're ready, you and Bella could come up to Brisbane for a
visit.'

'For sure. Give Mikey my love, okay? How're you keeping,
Beth?'

She laughs. 'Oh, I'm the afterthought, am I? I'm good,
thanks for asking. No romances on my horizon, unfortunately.
Once bitten, twice shy.'

'I think I've contaminated the entire male race.'

'You think too much. Just look after yourself, crazy man.'

*

The week is a blur. The rain continues in intermittent showers.
Bulawayo shines under roving shafts of light, cleansed of its red
clinging dust. The countryside seems to gulp and swill; streams
and dongas flow again, tanks and dams fill and overflow for the
first time in years. A bright flush of green appears overnight.
Zimbabwe's plants are like its people – give them half a chance
and they will thrive.

Despite our misgivings, Gus returns to Shangani, bandaged
head and all, to meet with Ncube. When Ncube tells him all

is well on the farm, he breaks a solemn promise to Jenny not to return to Hopelands and sneaks back via the Nalatale Ruins road. He even spends the night on the farm and phones to tell us of the good falls of rain and that the near-empty dam is filling fast. He tells us that he discussed handing over title to Ncube who agreed it was possibly the only way to stave off the inevitable.

Jenny is furious with him. 'You bloody idiot!' she yells on the phone. 'You promised not to go back! I give up with you, man. Nothing gets through that thick skull of yours, does it? Not even a knobkerrie! Knickers in a knot? Don't tell me I'm getting my knickers in a knot! You'd better watch your step, sonny boy! You never bloody listen to anyone, do you?'

Jenny puts the phone down and glares at me. She shakes her head, hands outstretched helplessly. 'You bloody men! Imbeciles!' she exclaims.

Why she looks at me I've no idea, since I'd be the first to agree that Gus's pigheadedness exists in a league of its own. But when Gus returns the next day, pale and nauseous, he finally agrees to have his injuries checked at the private Mater Dei Hospital. X-rays confirm Jenny's suspicions; he has a broken rib and a fractured ankle. He comes back with his abdomen tightly bound and a plaster cast on his foot, under strict orders to take it easy.

To placate Jenny by a show of good faith, Gus hobbles into Rees Lloyd and Partners, the law firm Bella works for, to discuss the options available in transferring title to Ncube. He speaks with Rees Lloyd himself, who views the whole idea somewhat sceptically, but suggests three possibilities: Gus could set up a company with Ncube as director. He could draw up a Joint-Venture Agreement, where technically Ncube has majority control. Or he could draw up a Suspensive Sale Agreement in which Ncube will have a set period to pay off the farm – Lloyd suggests ten years might be appropriate in this case. Unofficially it would be agreed that this would be a cosmetic transaction purely to disguise ownership – no payment will actually take place, rendering the agreement null and void after the ten-year period. While pointing out the risks (including the degree of trust Gus shows in Ncube, which Lloyd finds 'pretty extraordinary') Lloyd suggests the latter as potentially the most effective in buying time while Zimbabwe's political woes work themselves out, and in rendering Gus's profile least visible. But in a parting comment he wryly warns Gus about pinning his hopes on the law. 'At the end of the day, Mugabe just does as he pleases, anyway,' he says. 'If he wants your farm he'll take it. Simple as that.'

While in Shangani Gus spoke with Reverend Dlomo who offered to marry Bella and me on Thursday. But Bella is against being married in Shangani. Too many unhappy memories – a magistrate's court will be fine for her, she says. How we get married is neither here nor there with me, so I make the necessary enquiries at the Office of the Clerk of the Civil Court in Fort Street. There I'm informed that delays in civil marriages are huge; the court is booked up for the next six months. Likewise, we discover there are no churches in Bulawayo available at such short notice. So Bella finally agrees to Shangani.

Gus offers the Burnside house as a venue for an informal reception. Bella is happy with this arrangement but Oom Jasper seems keen to fritter away his dwindling financial resources on a more formal reception at the Bulawayo Club. But the Club has functions booked the entire week, so the father of the bride eventually concedes to the Burnside venue, on condition that he 'buys the grog'. In the meantime Bella goes about getting her affairs in order. As she predicted, the legal firm she works for is sympathetic towards her decision and agrees to let her go with immediate effect. As it turns out, two of the partners confide in her that they are also leaving for 'Oz' and that the future of the firm is uncertain anyway. We purchase rings at a Swiss jeweller in Jason Moyo Street. Simple gold bands, nothing fancy. I phone the Australian High Commission in Harare to confirm the emigration procedures for Bella. I manage to book her on the same flights as mine – Bulawayo to Johannesburg, connecting to Sydney – and pay her fare. Oom Jasper greets this sudden, momentous activity with tears of joy and sadness. Mopping his eyes with a handkerchief, he presents Bella with all of his wife's jewellery as a wedding gift. He gives the Victoria Falls excursion his blessing, insisting we get away on our own to 'cement our vows'.

We are married at St Pauls in Shangani on Thursday. The small service is attended only by family, Ncube, and Joseph and Anna. Gus fills in as best man, Jessica and Lauren are Bella's bridesmaids; Oom Jasper is there to give his daughter away. Forced to make do with what Bulawayo Bridal Boutique was able to knock together in two days, Bella wears a simple white satin dress without frills. And since his formal gear was stolen at the roadblock last Sunday, Gus wears an absurd ensemble consisting of a hired suit jacket and tie and a pair of khaki shorts (he couldn't fit his plaster cast through the suit's long trousers). Reverend Dlomo performs the ceremony in his solemn manner, making much symbolic reference to the rain. The old organ player in the frayed navy blue jacket and pre-Borg tennis shoes has not managed to shed that distinct hint of the psychedelic era from his repertoire. We say our vows, exchange rings, kiss, sign papers and leave the church to a musical accompaniment curiously reminiscent of the warped, lilting strains of the Beatles' *Fool on the Hill.*

We return to Bulawayo for the reception in Burnside. The rain has spared us another of my brother's braais; instead, Jenny and Gladys have managed a marvellous cold buffet of roast beef, pork and chicken. I don't know most of the people who turn up: Bella's friends and work acquaintances, Gus and Jenny's diminishing social circle. Ncube arrives with Reverend Dlomo and Joseph and Anna – the old couple immediately seek refuge with Gladys in the kitchen. Coincidentally, Big Bull Durnford drops in on his way back to South Africa. He is shocked by Gus's appearance and voluble in his anger – Big Bull was always a noisy beast. I notice, too, that he spends much time chatting up Angela, pulling in his gut as he talks. Since school he's had a crush on her and in all these years never twigged that she is gay.

Gus cuts a dashing figure as an orator with his bandaged head, black eye, khaki shorts and plaster cast. Tanked up with Lion Lager, he delivers a ribald, below-the-belt speech in which he likens me to some geriatric American millionaire who recently married a *Playboy* centrefold. Gales of laughter suggest his lavatory humour has struck a chord in all but Reverend Dlomo (who frowns dutifully) – even Angela, I notice, wipes tears from her eyes. Disappointingly, too, my tipsy wife laughs like a drain – the loudest, in fact. Consequently my own speech

243

that follows, sensitive and carefully crafted though it undoubtedly is, is rendered completely ineffectual – the rabble have ears attuned only to clowns.

In the end I'm forced to do as the Romans do. Led into debauchery, I am lucky not to injure myself after falling on my back doing the limbo under the dining room table, cigarette in mouth, drink in hand, while the mob clap and chant.

How low can you go ...

We spend our first married night in the Churchill Hotel. We both pass out fully dressed on the bed before cementing any vows.

*

It's a four-hour drive down to Victoria Falls. We take Bella's car, loaded up with spare cans of petrol (courtesy of Gus), since fuel supplies along the way can't be guaranteed. We manage a reasonably early start, all things considered. After climbing the Kalahari Sand Escarpment beyond Nyamandhlovu, the skies begin to clear and it becomes hot and humid as we descend into the Gwaai River Valley. The car's air-conditioner decides to give up the ghost and we sweat even with the windows wound down.

We stop for an egg-and-bacon brunch at the Gwaai River Hotel. The petrol pumps at Hwange are open for business and there's no queue. As we top up Bella carries on like we hit the jackpot – such are the small joys in Zimbabwe. We enter baobab territory. Glimpses of game among mopane trees: impala, kudu, warthog. Goats nibbling at the new growth in the Jotsholo Communal Lands. Thin herd boys in dirty rags wave and make begging gestures as we go by. I think of Gus and Ncube and the terrible things that took place during the war in this hot and inhospitable wilderness, unspeakable events that somehow forged the basis of a friendship beyond my understanding.

After travelling through seemingly endless Rhodesian teak and mukwa forests, we see, far off, like a distant veld fire, a wispy cloud of spray. I remember the many family trips we made to the Falls, how as kids we'd call out 'David Livingstone!' to claim first sight of the spray.

We reach the small resort town of Victoria Falls around two o'clock. Once a Mecca for travellers, the place now appears run down and empty of visitors, though choked with desperate-looking locals loitering around denuded shops. The town has been seriously hit by the collapse in tourism and we've been warned to watch out for thieves who prey on visitors. An Australian tourist was murdered for his wallet just weeks ago.

We book in for two nights at the Victoria Falls Hotel. In its colonial heyday, this grand old Edwardian building, with its archways and columns, hosted prime ministers and royalty, and it still carries an air of quiet stateliness. We follow the porter up to our air-conditioned room which has a good view of the railway bridge over the gorge. In the distance there is the roar of water. After unpacking our suitcases we go downstairs to the brick terrace out front and order cold beers. We have sweated out the bulk of last night's excesses, so the beers go down like nectar. From the terrace we can hear the screams of some nutcases bungy-jumping off the bridge. After the beers we amble down to the gorge, the sun bearing down hot and heavy on our shoulders.

The receptionist at the hotel says we are lucky: the Falls was just a trickle a week ago; now with the rains the Zambezi is in full flow. We walk through the rain forest along the edge of the gorge to a vantage point where we watch the mighty river, more than a mile wide, plunge a hundred metres down onto the black rocks below. Gigantic, fearsome – for me, it's a sight that has lost none of its gut-lurching magnificence. We sit there in the spray above the eerie black gorge, mesmerised, silenced. My father always said it's good to be humbled by nature, and that the Falls could cow the heart of the bravest man. When the old romantic poets and painters tried to evoke the sublime terror of nature, they might have killed for a spectacle like this. The colossal plunge into that dark, whirling cauldron below, the roar and the billowing spray ... Mosi-oa-tunya is its African name. The Smoke that Thunders. Why would David Livingstone have called it anything else?

On the way back to the hotel we stop near the Devil's Cataract to take photographs of each other beneath Livingstone's statue. The bronze figure stands atop a base inscribed with the words, *Explorer, Missionary, Saviour*. He gazes into the chasm. In his shadow, I try to imagine what it must have been like for him, the first white man to lay eyes on this wonder, with nothing to prepare him for it. A single line – his words – I learned off by heart at school comes back to me: ... *scenes so lovely they must have been gazed upon by angels in flight.*

Back at the hotel we cool off in the pool and in the evening we relax in wicker chairs outside on the terrace. The waiters cater energetically to those who, like us, have suffered the ravages of heat and after a few drinks a comfortable glow sets in. The world – *this* world – seems marvellous with its wild date

246

palms and baobabs against the sky and the chatter of monkeys and birds in the mahobohobo trees. And, of course, Bella's presence. She sits close to me, holding my hand, a little subdued. We talk about life in Australia. I assure her I will resume my job at the university. Yes, I will get my act together. She giggles, amused by any suggestions of professional ineptitude on my part – impossible, by her reckoning. At the far end of the terrace a marimba band begins to play. A Scandinavian couple are trying to get into the groove, shaking their backsides to the amusement of the hotel staff. Sentimental as it may be, I feel a heartbreaking love for the myth that Africa sometimes pretends to be.

In our room we can hear the plunging water: a deep eternal roar from the open mouth of Africa. We can feel the weight and fury of the water as it shakes the land. It makes us feel scared and insignificant, yet in the darkness it gives us some of itself. I see Bella's face turned to the window, drawn by the power. She gazes at the cloud of spray rising from the gorge, at the thin lunar rainbow. She pushes back her long hair and shrugs, overwhelmed. Then she looks at me, her eyes bright and intense. I see her and know her truly for the first time. Knowing I will rip her like a plant from its soil, a sorrow overwhelms me. Now she moans softly as I kiss her breasts. Her fingers smooth the lines on my forehead. With the power of the river I hold her, I breathe in her scent and taste the salt of her flesh. She grips me and bites my skin gently. In the humid air we sweat as I press into her, and she utters sounds that are meaningless without the roar and smell of a river falling to the centre of the earth.

*

Sunday. We take an early-morning cruise up the Zambezi. It's another hot and humid day. We are relaxed and carefree – for a precious moment we have shaken off that invisible burden of tension that everyone seems to carry in Zimbabwe. Bella snaps away at the sights with her old Pentax camera. We see lots of hippo, one crocodile and a herd of elephants along the shore. Bella gets the Scandinavian couple, the African dance specialists who've joined us on the cruise, to take pictures of us hamming it up at the back of the river launch. I'm uncharacteristically playful and animated.

We return to the hotel. While Bella goes upstairs to freshen up before lunch, I sit in the lounge reading an old publication called *The Victoria Falls Illustrated* from the hotel's book collection. It has an account of Livingstone's first observation of the Falls in 1855. I am surprised by his words. I'd always envisaged Livingstone as a romantic – a view based, no doubt, on that single line (gazed upon by angels, etcetera) I learned at school. Despite dramatic moments, the intrepid Victorian's objective style makes for curiously dry reading.

Having got small and very light canoes further down we went in the care of persons well acquainted with the rapids and sailed swiftly down to an island situated at the middle end on the Northern verge of the precipice over which the water roars. At one time we seemed to be going right to the gulph but though I felt a little tremor I said nothing, believing I could face a difficulty as well as my guides. The falls are singularly formed. They are simply the whole mass of the Zambesi waters rushing into a fissure or rent made right across the bed of the river. In other falls we usually have a great change of level both in the bed of the river and adjacent country and after the leap the river is not much different from what it was above the falls. But here the river flowing rapidly among the numerous islands and from 800 to 1,000 yards wide meets a rent in the bed at least 100 feet deep and at right angles with its course, or nearly due east and west, leaps into it …

That Livingstone could miscalculate the height of the Falls by over two hundred feet astonishes me. Clearly, he was not cast from the same mould as the romantic poets or painters of a generation slightly older – imagine the exaggerations that might have stemmed from the hands of Byron or Turner! Still, there's something compelling in this matter-of-fact account; Livingstone's Spartan grip on emotion dissolves my long-cherished conviction that had I been born in an earlier time I might have been an explorer – explorers, it seems, were not the type to be overwhelmed by feelings of awe. They were also not bereft of faith. On the contrary, it was faith – in God and Empire – that dispelled fear of the unknown.

My reading is interrupted when a waiter calls me to the phone at Reception.

It's Angela.

'I've been trying to get hold of you all morning,' she says. 'You'd better get back. There's been trouble at the farm. Saxon phoned this morning. He said the vets attacked the workers at the compound last night. He didn't give much detail but I gather it's pretty bad – he's had to take some of them to hospital in Gweru. The headman, Witness, is missing.'

The world seems to drain of its colour.

'And Joseph and Anna?' I ask.

'I don't know. I've been trying Saxon's cell but can't get through. I'm worried, Vaughn. Gus went straight off back to Shangani when he heard. I've rung the house. No answer there either.'

I sigh. 'Bloody Gus! Damn pigheaded fool ...'

'No point in getting uptight, Vaughn. Just get back as soon as you can, okay?'

I go upstairs to the room. Bella's face clouds over when I explain what has happened. When I tell her we will have to return to Bulawayo she just nods resignedly.

We pack our bags and make the long journey back to Bulawayo. We don't talk much on the way. Too many imponderables lie ahead. Bella caresses the back of my neck as I drive. I push her poor car to its limit and we make it to Burnside by mid-afternoon. Jenny and Angela are waiting for us in the house. Bella hugs and kisses them. We sit around the dining room table, near the phone. Jenny is red-eyed and distraught.

'Have you heard anything?' I ask.

Jenny shakes her head. 'Not a word. Something's wrong. I can feel it.'

'Where're the girls?' Bella asks.

'I dropped them off at a friend's place,' Jenny replies. 'It's best they don't know.'

'I tried the police in Shangani and Fort Rixon,' Angela says. 'At first they just played dumb. When I pressed the issue they got stroppy and gave me the usual crap about not interfering in political issues. Bastards!'

'Have you tried the police here in Bulawayo?' I ask. 'Someone more senior?'

Angela nods. 'Same story. Not interested.'

'What about the hospital in Gweru? You said Saxon had taken the injured workers there – surely they know something?'

'All the hospital could tell us was that Saxon left seven

injured people there, and then left. Three were women who'd been gang-raped. One of the injured men has since died.'

Jenny starts crying. Bella sits with her on the couch, holding her hand. A feeble inner voice tells me that duty calls. But I just sit there, frightened, helpless. Angela makes up my mind for me.

'I'm going back,' she announces. 'I want to know what the hell's going on – I want to see if Joseph and Anna are safe.'

'Ange ...'

'No, Vaughn. I'm going. That's all there is to it.'

'That's crazy, Ange! Let's wait to hear from Gus.'

'We've been waiting all day.'

'You know I can't let you go on your own.'

'I'm not expecting anything. You can come with me or stay. It's up to you.'

'I'll go with you,' Jenny says.

Angela shakes her head. 'I told you no. You've got two girls to look after.'

'You're bloody mad, Angela!' Bella exclaims angrily. 'You see what these people have done already. Now you want to endanger yourself and Vaughn as well!' She turns to me. 'Vaughn, don't go. Don't be stupid.'

I sigh. This is beyond me.

Angela and Jenny are looking at me. There is no choice in the matter. Against every instinct, I say, 'Let me go then, Ange. You stay here. There's no point in both of us going.'

Angela smiles and shakes her head. 'Oh no, brother. It's my idea.'

Bella turns on Angela. 'This is madness! I'll never forgive you if something happens!'

Angela just gives her a hard, resolute look.

*

And so we climb into Jenny's station wagon and head off to God knows what. Angela drives with the accelerator flat all the way. Past the cement factory the overturned truck has been removed, finally. One disaster making way for another, I fear. Angela talks persistently, as is her wont under duress. At one point her voice falters and I turn to see tears streaming down her face. When I reach across and put my arm around her shoulders, she shakes her head angrily and grips the steering wheel, her knuckles white.

'The thing I hate most is the helplessness,' she says. 'The worst is that there's absolutely no one to turn to. For the first time I understand – truly understand – how life must be in this place for people who just happen to be on the wrong side of the political fence. For the Ndebeles who were massacred back in the eighties, for all the people Mugabe has terrorised since – and to think that bastard's still regarded as a hero!'

'Hero?' I say. 'Who other than his party thugs and cronies could possibly see him as a hero?'

'Don't you worry, brother, he has his admirers. Not so much in Zimbabwe but elsewhere in Africa. Because he hates whites and vilifies Britain and America, he's seen as a noble fighter for the African cause – as some kind of latter-day Shaka Zulu.'

'Anyone who admires Mugabe can have absolutely no under-standing of what he's doing here.'

Angela shrugs. 'Oh, they understand. They just don't care. For them, the politics of revenge overrides all else.' She laughs bitterly. 'What a bloody mess he's made of this place. When he took power in 1980, people were dancing around the streets singing about freedom. Little did they know what lay in store for them. The poor suckers would never have

dreamt of the unspeakable freedoms that Mugabe would be-
stow on himself.'

I stare at the passing countryside, wishing the car had wings
to fly us far away from this cursed place. If only this were a
nightmare from which I could wake. But, no, I am caught in a
chaotic reality where sanity is in short supply. Now I begin to
see as Zimbabweans see. Through a fog of fear.

We reach Shangani and go directly to Ncube's house behind
the post office, but the place is locked and deserted. For a few
minutes we debate whether going to the police station is an
option, on the off chance there might just be a decent law-abid-
ing cop on duty willing to assist in the cause of justice. But
such a notion seems almost surreal and we push on to the farm.

To avoid driving past the veterans' camp on the Gerbers'
farm we take the more circular route to Hopelands's eastern
entrance via the Nalatale Ruins Road. I tell Angela to slow
down after she nearly hits a stray donkey in the road. We cross
the cattle grid onto the farm. I notice the newly-fixed boundary
fence has been torn down again and the wire pilfered. The sun
is going down behind Long Cross Hill as we wind our way
down to the river, stopping to open and close several gates.
Angela comments absently on the new growth on the land and
the reborn streams that trickle down to meet the river. We
splash across the weir, now a foot under water. As we begin to
climb the hill to the house the workers' compound down near
the Fort Rixon Road comes into view. Just charred shells remain of the buildings.

The security gate to the house is unlocked. The Cressida is
parked in front of the house, the driver's door hanging open.
As Angela pulls up and we get out, the dogs come bounding

down the veranda steps and mill around us, whining. I shush Frik when he begins another senseless tirade. We inspect the Cressida. The keys are still in the ignition; a sports bag of Gus's clothes are in the boot. I check under the driver's seat and find the revolver and a torch hidden under an old towel. I remove the revolver and stick it in the back of my waistband.

The house is unlocked. Angela goes inside while I look around the sheds. Aside from the missing Cruiser, nothing seems out of place. The tractor and trailer are parked in the open barn, the tools and implements stacked or hung neatly against the walls of the toolshed. One of the dogs unearths a stray chicken from behind the old Dodge truck. I just about shit myself with its sudden flapping and squawking.

I meet Angela back on the veranda. 'Nothing?' she asks.

I shake my head. 'The Cruiser's gone. Anything in the house?'

'The gun safe's empty.'

Frik and Tiny push up against my leg, whining.

'They haven't been fed,' I say.

We look out at the darkening bush.

'Where the hell is he?' Angela says.

We go inside. While Angela tries to phone Ncube I rummage around in the pantry for some dog food, without success. I look in the fridge and find a few left-over lamb chops. These along with some stale maize bread and a bucket of water I leave outside the kitchen door. I whistle for the dogs. They coming running around the house and immediately begin bolting down the food.

Angela can't get through to Ncube and hangs up. She slaps her hands on her thighs in frustration. There is a hint of resignation in her voice when she says, 'Let's see if the old people are okay.'

We go outside to the Cressida where I retrieve the torch from under the driver's seat. Then, closing the security gates behind us, we walk quickly down the hill towards Joseph and Anna's kraal. I carry the torch for when it gets dark, though now it's still light enough for us to follow the path through the trees. The revolver in my waistband is uncomfortable so I remove it and place it in my trouser pocket.

Angela glances at me. 'What do you intend doing with that?'

'I haven't the faintest idea,' I reply.

A gentle headwind brings the rancid smell of smoke to us. We stop in the gloom and listen. Nothing but the sound of crickets and roosting birds.

'Oh God, please,' Angela whispers.

But as we come within sight of the kraal we know there is to be no divine reprieve. Still-smouldering black heaps of earth and timber are all that remain of the huts. The cement block abode Joseph and Anna used as a storeroom is a burnt-out shell, the corrugated iron roofing collapsed and twisted. A section of the roofing makes a screeching noise as it lifts and falls beneath a sudden gust of wind. A lone rooster daintily picks its way across the ash-covered ground, around the corpse of the thin dog that lies among smashed clay pots and strewn belongings.

We make our way through the razed kraal, shining the torch through the debris. The donkey lies hacked to death, bloated and foul-smelling, still tethered to its tree. The goat enclosure is empty. We look around at the dark bush and call out for the old people – hoping, praying that they got away and are perhaps hiding nearby.

255

But a sudden rank whiff from beneath the rubble of Joseph's hut tells us there are to be no such mercies. From the residue lying around it appears that timber had been stacked up against the hut to intensify the blaze. In my mind are the horror stories from the war where whole families were burned alive in their huts – such were the methods of liberation.

We find them amid the rubble, barely distinguishable from the smouldering coals and blackened earth. Lying fixed in a frantic, twisted embrace, encrusted together. Limbs roasted to stumps. Scorched skulls bursting through shrivelled faces. A terrible thing happens when I attempt to prise away some rubble with a pole. The bodies snap apart, bits of one remaining attached to the other. Withered intestines slither from a ruptured abdomen into the hot ash, making a hissing sound. Angela turns away, gasping. She goes down on her haunches. For a moment I think she is going to faint. I reach out to catch her but she steadies herself and waves me away, her hand shaking.

'Cover them, please,' she says in a voice I can barely hear. 'So animals don't get to them.'

Animals have already got to them, I think as I comply, levering the debris back over the charred corpses with the pole. I can hardly breathe. Nausea overwhelms me. I break out in a sweat.

'Come on,' I say, grabbing Angela by the arm and pulling her to her feet. 'Let's get out of here. There's nothing we can do. Let's get the hell off this farm.'

'I'm not going anywhere until I find out what's happened to Gus,' Angela replies.

'There's nothing we can do about Gus. Come on, Ange!'

'You can do what you like, Vaughn. I'm staying till I find out.'
Irrational, resolute, Angela stares at me through the gloom.
'Come on,' I say, taking her hand. 'At least let's get away
from here.'

We make our way back to the house by torchlight. We are
silent in the enormity of what we have seen. I shake uncontrol-
lably, as though I'm freezing.

Back at the house I phone Jenny. My voice trembles as I tell
her what has happened. She still hasn't heard from Gus. As I
speak I notice Ncube's cell number on a piece of paper stuck
to the wall next to the phone. I finish talking to Jenny, then
Bella comes on the line.

'Get away from there,' she pleads. 'Please, Vaughn. Don't
fool around with these people. I phoned my boss. He knows a
magistrate ...'

Outside the dogs start barking at the faint sound of an
approaching vehicle. Angela calls out to me from the veranda.
I put the phone down, cutting Bella off, and on impulse dial
Ncube's number. Angela calls again, more urgently, 'Come on,
Vaughn!' Ncube doesn't answer. Instead, an infuriatingly
pleasant recorded voice informs me that he is unavailable and
invites me to leave a message. Now the dogs are going berserk.
I hear Angela trying to restrain them.

In a hoarse voice, I say, 'Saxon, Angela and I are on the
farm. I think we have uninvited guests ...'

I put the phone down, unable to think of anything else to say.
Before I go outside I take the revolver out of my pocket, flick
the safety catch off and stick it in the back of my waistband
once more, pulling out my shirt to cover it.

Out on the veranda I can just make out a battered white

Datsun pickup outside the fence and a group of men standing at the gate watching as Angela struggles to control the dogs. As I hurry down I feel a surge of panic. My sense of helplessness is not alleviated by the knowledge that the gate is unlocked. I shout at the dogs, the way Gus does; to my surprise they quieten down.

'Go back to the house,' I say to Angela. 'I'll see what they want.'

Angela shakes her head. 'Try not to look so nervous, Vaughn.'

The glow from the veranda lights is enough for me to recognise Mtunzi, Yengwa and the man who held a gun to my head at the roadblock. Mtunzi is wearing Joseph's new sports jacket. The handle of an automatic pistol protrudes from the side pocket. Yengwa has a badly swollen top lip, no doubt from when Gus punched him. He carries a panga and a sjambok. The man from the roadblock stands with the barrel of his FN resting on his foot. There are four others, all armed with axes and knobkerries. They all appear doped up or drunk.

'Litshonile,' I greet. 'Ufunani? Can I help you?'

Yengwa mutters something in Mtunzi's ear. Mtunzi nods. He beholds me with an amused, spaced-out expression and doesn't bother with any pleasantries. He speaks in English. 'Where is your brother, Mr Bourke?'

'Ungubani ibizo lakho?' I ask.

Mtunzi laughs. 'Don't try to impress me, Mr Bourke. You are not African, so don't make a fool of yourself trying to be one.' He gestures at Angela. 'Who is this?'

'My sister, Angela Bourke.'

'Your sister is pretty, despite her age.'

'What is your business here?' Angela demands. 'Tell us what you want.'

Mtunzi raises his eyebrows and smiles. 'Oh yes, madam. I will do anything you say, missus. I will dance to your tune.'

The other men laugh. Mtunzi turns back to me. 'You have been told not to come back here, but still you come back. Why? Do you feel homesick?'

'In a civilised world a man can return to what is his without fear.'

Mtunzi affects surprise. 'A civilised world? Then you are in the wrong place. This is not a civilised world, Mr Bourke. This is a world belonging to barbarians, to terrorists.' He gestures at his comrades. 'We are terrorists, all of us. We are in charge of this country.'

There is a long silence. I'm unnerved by Mtunzi's lazy drawl and his stare. The dogs begin growling. Angela grabs their collars.

'I must ask you to leave,' I say. 'There is nothing for you here.'

'Where's your brother, Mr Bourke? We have been looking for him.'

'I don't know. We are looking for him ourselves. That's why we are here.'

'Oh? Then we have a mutual interest, not so? Why are you shaking, Mr Bourke? Are you cold?'

The phone begins ringing up at the house. It seems a million miles away.

'Go and answer,' I say to Angela.

Angela hesitates, then hurries back to the house. Mtunzi calls after her, 'If it's your brother, tell him the barbarians are at the gate!'

As Angela reaches the veranda the ringing stops. She turns to me and holds her hands out. 'Just wait!' I call out to her. 'Maybe they'll ring again!'

Mtunzi begins fiddling with the gate. 'We are hungry terrorists, Mr Bourke. Perhaps your sister can cook some food for us, hey?'

'No, I will not allow you inside.'

Mtunzi laughs. 'You will not allow it? This is not your property anymore, Mr Bourke. And, besides, your sister looks the type who likes to entertain hungry men. You cannot go against your sister's will – if she wishes to entertain us, then you must bend to her will.'

My body seethes with adrenalin. Now, I say to myself. Pull the damn gun. This is your last chance to take control. But I don't. My hands seem paralysed by fear. I know the instant I draw the revolver we will have reached a point of no return. There will be no going back. The dreadful finality of it terrifies me. Stupidly, I think there must still be a way to resolve this peacefully.

But Mtunzi has seen the gate is unlocked. He slides the bolt and begins to push it open. My hands find life and I slam it shut. The sudden movement sets the dogs off. They leap at the fence, snarling and barking. Mtunzi and his men take a step backwards.

'Move away!' I warn.

The man with the FN begins to raise it. And now, finally, blind instinct takes over. I wrench the revolver from under my shirt and aim it through the fence at Mtunzi's face. The men shrink back, one of them exclaiming, 'Ah! Ah! Ah!'

'Tell him to put that rifle down, Mtunzi. Go on, tell him or I swear to God I'll blow your bloody head off!'

Mtunzi looks at me. A veil has lifted from his eyes, revealing a naked, crazy anger. My hand shakes as I hold the revolver less than a foot from his face.

'You are making a big mistake, Bourke.'

'Fucking do it, you mad bastard! Tell him to put that rifle down.'

Mtunzi turns to the man with the half-raised FN and gestures to him to lower it. The man complies. The dogs are in a frenzy, biting and snapping at the fence.

I have to shout to be heard. 'Now take this fucking scum of yours and get off my property! Now!'

Mtunzi has regained his composure. He barks an order at his men and they retreat towards the pickup. He sashays slowly, mockingly, as he backs away. His men laugh. 'You have signed your own death warrant, Bourke,' he says, smiling. 'I will finish you. All of you Bourkes!'

'Just fuck off, you swine. Hamba!'

I keep the revolver pointed in their direction as the men climb on the back of the pickup. Mtunzi and Yengwa get in the front. Mtunzi starts the vehicle. He does a sharp wheelspin, showering me with dust and grit, as he takes off down the hill, the headlights disappearing eventually into the bush.

Angela has witnessed the scene from the veranda. She watches as I climb the steps, the revolver still in my hand. The dogs continue to bark down at the gate. My thoughts tumble over each other in a frantic effort to work out what to do next. One thing is certain: Mtunzi and his men will be back. In my mind I see Tienus Gerber trapped in his farmhouse, alone, surrounded. Beyond help.

'I don't want to hear any more crap from you, Ange,' I say. 'Get into the fucking car. We're going.'

'What about Gus? We can't ...'

'To hell with Gus! Get in the car, or I'll bloody well throw you in!'

Angela moves to go inside. I grab her arm. 'Did you hear what I said, Ange?'

She shakes herself free. 'Please, Vaughn. Give me one minute, okay?'

She runs inside and returns clasping the family photographs from the dining room wall. 'All right, let's go,' she says.

We jump into Jenny's station wagon and tear off down to the security gate. I wait, revving the engine while Angela opens it. A wave of exhaustion overwhelms me suddenly. Angela seems almost wraithlike in the headlights. I shake my head. This has been the longest day of my life. Frik and Tiny come running up to the car, our two shabby knights of the realm, looking mighty pleased with themselves. Frik gives an oafish bark at my window. I get out and open the station wagon's tail gate. 'Come on, get in!' I command. But they just stand there panting, mouths agape, looking at me.

'Get in, you bloody stupid mutts!' I yell.

But they won't obey. Forlornly, I realise they will not leave their posts; trouble is afoot and they will heed only the call of duty. Cursing the world for such peculiar, untimely problems, I attempt to lift Frik into the back. His entire body reverberates with a ferocious growling, and I desist. We leave the gate open so at least the dogs can get out if, by a miracle, they can develop a prompt sense of self-preservation.

We hurtle down the hill. I lean forward over the steering wheel, straining my eyes as the headlights barrel through the darkness. The road has deep corrugations and the vehicle shudders over them. Twice I nearly lose control. I had placed the revolver on the seat between my legs, a stupid decision as it has now fallen onto the floor and is rolling around my feet. Angela sits nervously, watching the road, holding the family pictures on her lap. It's about a kilometre from the house to where the road splits in two directions: one heading towards the Fort Rixon Road, the other towards the eastern boundary – the way we'd come in. I figure we'll be safe if we can make the eastern boundary road.

My stomach lurches as the road dips down to a culvert that crosses a small stream bed at the base of the hill. As we roar across the culvert and rise over the opposite embankment there is a sudden terrific hammering against the car. Holes burst through the windscreen. The car jolts and lurches violently. As it rams up against the side of the embankment the windscreen disintegrates. Angela cries out and clutches at my shoulder as we are showered with glass. A sharp metallic staccato against her side of the car. One of the headlights bursts and goes out. Angela starts to scream, then makes a choking sound. It has all happened so fast that only now do I realise we are being ambushed. Frantically I grip the steering wheel, trying to steer through the killing ground. A tyre bursts; I lose control and career off into a sandy ditch alongside the road.

The station wagon is lying on its side. The radiator has ruptured, sending steam hissing up from under the crumpled bonnet. The single headlight shines upwards through the long grass, illuminating a long shaft of thick, swirling dust. I am lying pinned against the door with Angela on top of me. Her body jerks spasmodically. I am drenched in blood.

I lift my hand to her face. 'Ange ... Ange, are you all right?'

Her hands clutch weakly at me. An awful laboured gurgling emanates from her throat. Then she goes limp.

'Ange ... come on, please!'

But she is just a dead, bleeding weight. I feel the gaping hole in her neck.

Voices, shouts. Two more shots slam through the side of the car.

'Stop!' I scream. 'Don't shoot! Please don't shoot!'

More voices. Footsteps. Grunts of effort as the vehicle rocks, this way and that, and then is righted. Angela rolls off me back to her seat. I reach over and try to stem the flow of blood from her neck with my fingers.

Faces lit dimly by the headlight appear at the broken windows. Mtunzi stands at my door, pistol in hand.

'Help us, for God's sake!' I plead.

Mtunzi tries to open my smashed door, but can't. He says something to his men and the passenger door opens. They pull Angela out of the vehicle.

'She's hurt. Be careful with her,' I say.

Mtunzi goes round to where they have laid Angela on the ground. Voices mutter and curse.

'Don't just stand there!' I yell. 'Please, she needs help!'

Yengwa reaches in through the passenger doorway and drags me by the scruff of my neck across the seats and out of the car. He throws me to the ground next to Angela. Mtunzi kicks me hard in the ribs. 'Where is your gun, Bourke?' he demands.

'I don't know. In the car somewhere. On the floor.'

With a jerk of his head, Mtunzi orders one of his men to search for the gun. While the man rummages around in the vehicle, Mtunzi kicks me again at least a dozen times. I try to protect my face with my hands.

'This is what happens when you don't listen, Bourke!' he grunts. 'Who are the swine and the scum now? Not so brave with your words now, hey?'

Panting heavily, Mtunzi turns his attention to Angela. He lifts her face to the light with the toe of his boot. He shakes his head. 'Now your pretty sister is unavailable to entertain us. A pity. That is your fault too.'

'Please, help her,' I say.

Mtunzi laughs. 'Help her? Not even God Almighty can help her.'

He shoves her head roughly with his foot. Her face sinks back to the ground. She seems serene, aloof. I reach across to hold her. Mtunzi kicks my hand away.

The man in the car has found the revolver. He emerges and hands it to Mtunzi who inspects it in the gleam of the headlight. It is apparently no better than his own, so he hands it to Yengwa. He turns back to me.

'Now it's time to find your brother,' he says.

I'm hauled to my feet and frogmarched to the Datsun pickup which is lying concealed behind some trees alongside the road. When I resist – more from a searing pain in my side than any show of pluck – I don't see the blow that fells me. Just a white flash in my head and I collapse, floundering to the ground. More blows rain down on me. I'm picked up and thrown bodily onto the back of the pickup. I lie face down on the ridged steel floor as the men climb on. The pickup reverses onto the road, turns and heads back up the hill.

As we bump along, the thought of Angela lying alone in the

darkness eclipses my fear and pain. I am filled with guilt and sorrow. My decision to make a run for it must have been so predictable for Mtunzi. All he had to do was set the trap and wait. I lie there stunned, resigned. The thought that this day will be my last seems inconsequential.

I hear the dogs barking as we drive through the gate and up to the house. The vehicle stops. The dogs circle, snarling and barking. The men on the back trample on me as they scramble to avoid them. Two shots. A terrible yelping ensues. I am hauled off the pickup and dumped on the ground. I have lost my glasses. Blood is running down my forehead into my eyes. Vaguely I see Frik sprawled dead on the ground, and Tiny, gut-shot, spinning around in circles. Mtunzi watches Tiny, pistol in hand, amused by the sight.

I am pulled to my feet by my hair and marched up to the house. Through a film of blood I see Mtunzi and Yengwa up on the lighted veranda, laughing at the way my legs are buckling. I must look a sight, covered in Angela's blood, the front of my shirt ripped open, staggering like a drunkard. There is a roaring, electric buzzing in my ears. Distantly, I hear Tiny's throat-torn yelping.

I am dragged up the stairs to the veranda. They tie me with bits of rope and wire to the chair with wide armrests that Gus made at school. I sit passively, watching as they go about binding my arms and legs. Yengwa removes my watch and puts it in his pocket. Mtunzi takes a knobkerrie from one of his men and commences proceedings with a heavy blow to the side of my face. A warm gush of blood fills my mouth. I spit out a tooth.

'Where is your brother, Bourke?' Mtunzi asks. 'Your brother and Ncube – where are they?'

I shake my head, stunned. Mtunzi nods at Yengwe. Yengwa
steps forward and casually lashes me with his sjambok, a cigarette dangling from his lips. He stands to one side, taking wide
swipes, the tip of the sjambok cutting into my chest and shoulders. I screw my eyes up tight when he hits my face, terrified
that I might be blinded. I scream when he hits my groin.
Mtunzi asks the same question, again and again: Where is your
brother and Ncube? I cannot even think of a lie to tell him.
Yengwa goes on and on. My body seems on fire. I writhe and
scream. Mtunzi instructs two of the men to hold the chair still.
Mtunzi stops asking about Gus and Ncube – he knows I have
no possible answer to give. Instead, he mocks me: Swine and
scum, hey? Not so brave now, hey? And the flogging goes on.
The other men stand there watching. They laugh at my frantic
motions. I am simply an object upon which they can vent their
hatred. No, I am less than that – I am nothing but entertain-
ment, a figure of fun. Mtunzi takes the sjambok from Yengwa
and weighs into me with a wild ferocity. I cry and wail. I beg
for mercy. I urinate.

When I pass out they revive me by burning my arms with
cigarettes. It goes on. I'm revived again and again. Finally, they
have had enough. Sweating and exhausted, Mtunzi kicks me
over backwards in my chair. The back of my head hits the floor.
I lie there, dazed, upside down, while the men go inside the
house. My nose is bleeding; the blood runs into my mouth and
I swallow to keep from choking. I am too weak to struggle
against my bonds. Sounds of upheaval. Furniture breaking,
glass breaking. Laughter and frivolity as they find the beer in
the fridge. Far off, Tiny's yelping has changed to a low whine.

I struggle to remain conscious. Looking up at the blurred

rafters of the veranda, I can just make out my mother's old wire hooks for her hanging plants, still draped over the beams. There is the flash of memory of hot days long ago when I'd lie on my back on the cool stone veranda floor, looking up at Nan's suspended petunias, fuchsias and geraniums, bright and vivid against the thatched roof. It always struck me as marvellous, her relentless quest to soften this world.

A shadow appears at the lighted doorway. One of the men stands there, inverted, a bottle of beer in his hand. His face is in shadow as he watches me. I stare back at the blurred sockets of his eyes. What does the sight of me offer? A salve for old wounds? Moisture for a violent thirst? Perhaps he is just innocently curious; it's not every day that he gets to see an upside-down white man. I feel his eyes boring into mine, probing. He goes back inside. The all-pervading pain becomes a glow.

Dark waves lap at me.

I sink into a merciful black sea, warm and soft. Silent. A wonderful relief overwhelms me as I descend into the blackness. If this is death, so be it.

*

Only one memory accompanies me. Angela as a girl on the back of my father's truck. Like Boadicea riding a chariot, her face lifted to the wind.

Whatever will be will be ...

*

My ears ring with the concussion of gunfire. I shrink from the noise; I try to sink deeper into the blackness. But the blackness will no longer have me. It convulses suddenly, and I am washed back up into the light. My eyes open to a blurred upside-down world.

The man with the FN rifle is lying near the steps, his eyes and mouth open in a stupid, dazed expression, a pool of blood spreading around his head. A plaster cast thumps past my head. Gus says, 'Don't you fucking bleed on my floor.'

For a second I think he's talking to me. But then he grips the man by his belt and collar and throws him bodily off the veranda. I hear the thud of his body on the ground below.

Gus disappears from view. There is the sound of another body being dragged off the veranda. Yengwa. His limp head bumps down the stairs. Then the chair is righted. Ncube kneels next to me and undoes my bonds. Over at one end of the veranda I can vaguely make out Mtunzi and the rest of his men lying face down on the floor. Witness is tying their hands behind their backs. There are other men with guns watching Witness. Mtunzi's glasses are broken. He is drunkenly protesting, bargaining, begging. He receives a kick in the face for his troubles. When Ncube finishes untying my hands and feet I try to get up but can't. Ncube reaches over and gently touches my face. He shakes his head. I can feel what his fingers feel, the swollen softness of my concave cheek, the broken nose, the weals and lacerations.

Gus comes over. He looks at me. 'Jesus,' he says.

I try to speak. 'Angela ...'

My voice is barely a croak.

Gus nods. 'I know ... we found her, boet.'

269

He turns away quickly and clasps his eyes. A deep, animal sob bursts from his chest. His shoulders shake as he weeps.

Ncube puts a hand on his shoulder. 'Come, umngane wami. You must get this one to hospital. Leave the rest to us.'

Gus composes himself. He turns back, his face angry and streaked with tears. 'I want no trace of them, okay? Get the men to wash this blood off the floor.'

'Don't worry, umngane. It will be like they never existed.'

Hearing this, Mtunzi begins his jabbering again. Gus goes over and rams a pistol in his mouth. Mtunzi's eyes behind his shattered glasses are wide with terror.

'Leave him,' Ncube says. 'I'll personally take care of that one.'

'Don't do it,' I hear myself say. It's as though the words have come from another mouth. From a stranger that I wish would be silent.

Ncube and Gus turn to me.

'Don't do it,' I say again. 'Don't become like them.'

Ncube shakes his head. 'It has gone too far. There is no other choice.'

PART IV

WAITING FOR BIRDS

Witness was the chosen one. After they attacked the compound he said they took him with them to Joseph and Anna's kraal. They made him and the old people lie on the ground, face down, while they bludgeoned the yapping dog and had sport hacking at the donkey with axes and pangas. They stole the chickens, bundling them up in sacks. They tied the goats together and herded them off. They ransacked the huts, stealing anything of value. Then they beat the three of them with staves as they lay on the ground. For at least an hour this went on, Witness said. Their cries for mercy went unheeded. Then, when the beating was over, Mtunzi delivered a long sermon. He said they had come to punish them for being the white man's dogs. They, Witness and the other workers, Joseph and Anna, were collaborators; they were the ones who protected the white man's interests. We will teach you to turn against your brothers, Mtunzi said. Joseph begged for Anna's life. I am the one you want – I am the white man's dog. He was clubbed across the mouth to silence him. Then Mtunzi turned to Witness. You are lucky, he said. You are the chosen one. Witness must witness. Yes, you must carry the message to others who may choose to betray their African brothers. So Witness was ordered to collect wood. Piles of wood. Mtunzi and his men sat and waited while he dragged branches and logs from the bush. The old people were pushed inside Joseph's hut. Then Witness was told to stack the wood around the hut. The hut became a pyre. When he was finished, Witness was given a box of matches. A gift which he could keep, Mtunzi said. They made him set fire to the hut. Mtunzi waved his arms like an orchestra conductor as they listened to the old people shrieking. Then Mtunzi and his men set about burning the rest of the kraal.

Then they left him.

Gus and Ncube found him wandering aimlessly along the road, a blaze burning in his soul.

*

Such is the random lot of humanity. That heartless men wield power. That others must suffer that power. No doubt in times to come this obscure bit of history will be looked upon as nothing more than the ebb and flow of human affairs, nothing more than the domination of one group by another. Cause and effect. Cruelty begets cruelty. For did this cruelty not have its origins in the colonial past? When white men tamed the tribes, first with trickery, then with force. When Lobengula's warriors were scythed down like weeds with Maxim guns. Or when rebels were exterminated like rats after the Chimurenga uprising. Or even before the colonial past, when Ndebeles terrorised the Shonas, massacring the men and stealing their women. Slaughter and subjugation – the sacred imperative of power in Africa.

Cause and effect. There is always cause, some will argue. But how easily does cruelty born of injustice turn into cruelty born of itself. And how inevitable is the day when effect becomes cause.

When new hatreds will need expression ...

*

274

A journalist posing as a family friend arrives one day at the hospital. He pulls out a camera from his bag and takes a picture of me in my bed. The same journalist has already been to the farm and photographed the razed compound and the wrecked car. He has clandestinely interviewed the injured workers in Gweru hospital. For a short while the story of the attack on the farm becomes news to the world. That one picture of my battered face, along with those of Angela, the 'wildlife heroine', plundered from British art magazines and old newspaper reviews, become synonymous with Zimbabwe's violence. Such was Angela's popularity as an artist in Britain that her death is mourned as a national tragedy. Prime Minister Blair describes the incident as 'an act of unspeakable barbarity'.

There are no photographs of Joseph and Anna, or any of the injured workers. Their lives slip beneath the shadow of Angela and me, the white Africans. Ordinary people, remembered only by those who one day may seek to settle old scores.

So it goes with Africa.

*

I am stabilised at the Mater Dei Hospital in Bulawayo. More than once, I thank God for those noble souls in my university administration – the grey bureaucrats whom I deride so easily – who took out travel insurance on my behalf. My injuries are various. I have a broken nose, a badly depressed cheekbone, lost teeth, broken ribs, a broken right hand, a fractured patella, sizeable haematomas in my lower abdomen, and countless lacerations, weals, burns and bruisings. My face is black and blue, swollen beyond recognition – an appearance not enhanced by the temporary use of an extra pair of Angela's fancy spectacles which Jenny found among her things.

Bella comes to see me every day. She sits by my bed and tries to be bright and cheerful. She teases me about the grey stubble on my chin which she says makes me look like Clint Eastwood in *Hang 'em High*. In a sarcastic tone, she reads the articles from the local state-controlled newspapers which infer that Angela and I were asking for trouble by meddling in Zimbabwe's land rights issues. She quotes: 'If foreigners wish to abuse the privilege of visiting Zimbabwe, if they wish to trespass on land which does not belong to them, then they must suffer the consequences.' Ja, she says, wagging her finger at me, that's what you get for being a bloody trespasser. But her cheerfulness is paper thin. There are moments when her eyes grow angry and tearful and she is forced to take a 'smoke break' outside.

I have other visitors. Gus and Jenny. Ncube and Reverend Dlomo. Jenny apologises for not bringing the girls, but feels the sight of me will be too disturbing for them. She tells me that an anxious Beth called to say she was booked on the first plane to Zimbabwe – Jenny persuaded her to cancel her ticket since I'd be returning to Australia in a matter of days. Oom Jasper, coughing and cursing for not being allowed to smoke in hospitals, as they used to in the good old days. An official from the Australian High Commission in Harare travels down to Bulawayo to check my condition and to pass on wishes from the Foreign Affairs Minister for a speedy recovery and safe return to Australia.

Gus tells me he will be packing up and leaving for Britain, just as soon as he has finalised the sale agreement with Ncube. A bit late, I think. Though I mouth words of encouragement,

I can't help the anger I feel towards him. I blame Gus for Angela's death as much as I blame Mugabe's thugs. It is an anger I will harbour for a long time.

On four occasions I am interviewed by the police and the CIO. Lengthy grillings about what exactly happened. They take statements. They tell me Mtunzi and some of his men have disappeared. In hiding, they surmise, no doubt because of the publicity surrounding Angela's murder. I repeat myself endlessly. I tell them the truth, up to a point. I keep it simple, as Gus and Ncube instructed. Angela and I went back to the farm. We discovered the bodies of Joseph and Anna in their razed kraal. There was a confrontation at the security gate between us and Mtunzi and his men. Mtunzi threatened us and went away. We were ambushed while trying to flee the farm. Angela was killed, I was beaten unconscious. That is how my brother and Ncube found us.

One of the policemen, Detective Superintendent Masuku from the CID Law and Order Section, doesn't buy my story entirely. 'And where were your brother and Ncube while all this murder and mayhem was going on?' he asks.

'Ask them,' I say. 'As far as I know they were in Gweru seeing to their injured workers.'

A fat man in an expensive suit, Masuku eyes me sceptically. 'There are things that just don't add up, Mr Bourke. Why would Mtunzi leave you alive? You and not your sister?'

'I don't know. I was unconscious. I was covered in blood. Maybe he thought I was dead.'

Masuku purses his lips and shrugs. 'Mmm, maybe. But it still seems strange to me that Mtunzi would run away. From what I know of him, it is not in his character to run.'

'Who would know what a murderer thinks?' I say.

Masuku eyes the weals on my face. He raises an eyebrow and nods.

In the last interview I have with them Masuku informs me that I have been declared an undesirable alien. Apparently, I am considered a threat to national security. My visitor's visa has been revoked and I must leave the country as soon as I am discharged from hospital. Failure to comply will result in imprisonment pending deportation. He hands me official papers citing clauses from the Immigration Act to this effect. No reasons are given.

'Why?' I ask. 'Have I done something wrong?'

He shrugs. 'You are just trouble. You and your dead sister.'

'I've told you everything I know. You know I'm leaving Zimbabwe as soon as I'm well enough to travel. These are trumped-up charges. Why go to these lengths?'

Masuku shrugs again, smiling. 'It's in no one's interest that you return to Zimbabwe, Mr Bourke.'

'This is my place of birth. If this was a free country it would accord me the right to return.'

'You are lucky this is not your place of death, Mr Bourke. You should count your blessings.'

Every night I wake to a relentless, throbbing pain in my head. I listen to the night-shift nurses going about their duties and the snores and groans of other patients. And I think of Angela and mourn for her. I think of Joseph and Anna and weep bitter tears. The pain in my head becomes a welcome distraction when the thoughts get too much.

*

While I'm in hospital Angela is buried in St Paul's cemetery in Shangani. Bella describes it for me. How Gus broke down while delivering the eulogy. Reverend Dlomo's impassioned sermon for an end to senseless violence. For peace in the land.

Words like dust.

Bella also tells me that a new phase of violence is sweeping the country. Mugabe has ordered the clearing of Harare's slums and market places. Having destroyed the MDC's support base among workers on white commercial farms, he is now intent on finishing the job by persecuting Zimbabwe's urban poor – the core constituency of the MDC. The police have begun to bulldoze and burn. They are under orders to remove the homeless to transit camps, pending relocation to the country. Ncube's prophesy has come to pass. The nation teeters towards Year Zero.

*

Gus, Jenny and Oom Jasper see us off at the airport. Detective Superintendent Masuku is also there, but he keeps his distance as we part company to go through customs. Oom Jasper weeps copiously as he hugs and kisses Bella.

Bella cries too. 'Kom, Papa,' she says. 'It's just for a short while. It's not forever. Kom nou, Papa!'

There is a clumsy moment when Oom Jasper reaches out to shake hands with me. I hold out my hand, before remembering it is in a plaster cast. We hesitate, then shake with our left hands. I promise to look after his daughter. If my battered appearance makes such a pledge seem ludicrous, Oom Jasper gives no indication of it. He just nods, wiping away tears. I kiss

Jenny, apologising for taking such bad care of her car. My flippancy makes her laugh, then cry.

Gus hovers in the background, ill at ease with all this emotion. He affects a show of hale-heartiness. 'Who knows? We may even come and give Australia a look-see,' he says. Then his chin puckers and his voice falters. 'Keep in touch, boet.'

For the first time in his life he embraces me. I cry out in pain. Over his shoulder Robert Mugabe stares at us from his picture on the wall.

Bella helps me shuffle on my single crutch through customs. Masuku appears and does the explaining when they can't recognise me from my passport photo. The array of customs officials seem more concerned about whether we are smuggling local currency out of the country. They confiscate even our small change.

After we pass through the metal detector, Masuku turns and leaves, saying over his shoulder, 'Have a safe journey back to Australia, Mr Bourke.'

*

I spend a while undergoing reconstructive surgery at the John Hunter Hospital in Newcastle. They put a plate in my face to repair my sunken cheekbone. My nose is straightened. My hand will never be the same again. At least now I have an excuse for artistic incompetence, I tell the dean of my faculty when she pops in for a short visit. Perhaps now, afflicted with a clumsy hand, I can finally make the grade as a contemporary artist, I jest. She dismisses my facetiousness and gives me a pep talk on how to get my academic life back on track.

Bella visits twice a day in between getting to know the lie of the land in Newcastle. I'm so doped up with painkillers I think I'm dreaming when Beth and Michael appear one morning. Michael is looking tall and fit; he has filled out since I last saw him. He is shaken by my appearance – my face is still a disaster zone, made worse by the fact that I'm still wearing Angela's glasses. Beth, too, is looking as though the Brisbane climate agrees with her. She has blond streaks in her hair and looks trim and attractive in her jeans and T-shirt. She kisses me and tries to hide her own shock by saying, 'Nice specs, Vaughn.'

I introduce them to Bella. Beth and Bella hug and kiss. Michael hesitates before kissing Bella. When Bella hugs him he pats her back awkwardly, embarrassed. He turns to me. We shake with our left hands.

'How're you doing, Dad?' he asks.

'Okay,' I reply. 'How're you, Mikey?'

'Good.'

'How's the surfing? I hear you've scored a hell chick.'

Michael gives a lopsided grin, amused by my phoney hip talk.

'Yeh, she's all right. We were worried sick about you, Dad.'

'I'm sorry, Mikey.'

A long silence follows. Beth tries to keep things cheery. 'You're a real couple of conversationalists, aren't you!' she laughs. 'It looks like I'll have to do the talking.'

And she does, as only Beth can. As she waffles on about the flight down from Brisbane and the cost of taxi fares from the airport at Williamtown, her eyes scan my face, sizing up my injuries. The professional carer. Dear Beth. Forever looking after others.

281

They stay with Bella until I'm discharged. They visit each day. I am truly blessed.

*

And my dear sister blesses me too. Angela's estate has been left to Gus and me. She leaves wealth beyond my wildest expectations, all the product of a life devoted to a painting genre I maligned and ridiculed. Her elephants and baobabs secure my freedom. I can now walk away from the frustrations of academe and paint full time, crippled hand notwithstanding – the ironies of my life are endless. I vow to retrace the journey she and I made to Alice Springs, so long ago, where we found so little to inspire us. This time I will find something. I will devote myself to empty landscapes.

*

A month after I'm discharged Gus and Ncube are arrested on suspicion of murder. Mtunzi's pickup was found in a remote forested wilderness in the Mateke Hills near the South African border. The remains of a number of people were discovered in the burnt-out vehicle. Gus had been in the process of vacating the Burnside house prior to moving to Britain when they were arrested. Jenny and the girls had already left the country and were staying in Angela's house in Hampshire.

It was Jenny who phoned to tell us the news. She has hired a team of lawyers to represent them. She will be flying back to be with him. Jenny believes the prosecution has no case. Nothing can be tied to Gus or Ncube, she said. Even so, Gus and Ncube have been refused bail and are currently locked up in Khami Maximum Security Prison outside Bulawayo.

The story of Gus and Ncube's arrest is portrayed as a grotesque sequel to Angela's murder by the international media. Two innocents caught up in the nightmare of Zimbabwe's violence. One night they appear on television – a brief glimpse in an SBS News clip. Brothers, the two of them. In their prison greens, handcuffed together, barefoot, hobbling along in leg irons. Detective Superintendent Masuku leads them through the street to the court. A crowd watches. They pass by close to the camera. It is apparent both have been beaten – Gus's arm is bandaged, there are bruises on his face; Ncube limps and one eye is swollen shut. Neither displays any emotion.

I expect a clamour from the crowd but the people are silent as they watch them hobble along. Is what Gus and Ncube represents to them more ominous than pathetic? If the authorities wish to make an example of them by this public humiliation, it appears not to be working. My heart in my mouth, I scan the faces in the crowd and see pity and anger in the eyes of many. And I hear, barely audible, a woman in the crowd call out in SiNdebele, 'Shame! Shame on their nation!'

I feel a rush of gratitude so deep and overwhelming that I struggle to breathe.

*

And so I wait in this limbo between places. It seems that belonging will always elude me. It is a painful realisation. I know there were moments when Africa seemed to accept me back. To offer me a place again. When those Ndebele women began singing at the funeral, when the great Zambezi poured some of itself into my soul, Africa reached out and embraced me, its lost son. But then it cast me out again.

Now there is just the residue. Jenny's optimism is not something I share – for someone who has lived in Zimbabwe, her faith in the due process of law astounds me. What do justice and law mean when all that counts is tooth and claw? The Mugabe regime has the whiff of revolt in its nostrils; it will not be easily deterred from ferreting out its enemies. The future holds grave dangers for Gus and Ncube – I'm sure they are under no illusions about their predicament. They know the score. Burned in my memory are their impassive faces as they were led to court. Expressions of stone that have only one interpretation: They understand and accept the consequence of their actions. They accept the consequence of choice. The rule of tooth and claw ...

In the place of unspeakable freedoms, who knows what lies ahead? Each day there are fresh reports of violence in Zimbabwe. Operation Murambatsvina, Mugabe's campaign to rid Zimbabwe's cities and towns of slum-dwellers – the nation's 'trash', as he describes it – has gathered momentum. Children have been crushed by bulldozers. Over a million people are homeless. Who knows how much more of this lies in store for Zimbabweans? Only one thing is certain: death and dispossession will be the defining legacy of Mugabe. Of that there is no doubt. The choices for the persecuted are few. Soon there will come a time when just one choice, one path, remains.

As it did for those in power when liberation was just a dream.

But now I must let go of this. It's time to emerge – part of my healing will be to emerge. That's easier said than done. I struggle with it. While I live in Australia, my thoughts and dreams remain trapped behind in my place of birth. I'm plagued by the effects of post-traumatic shock. Beset by fears and insecurities, I undergo weekly therapy. I fall into black holes of pathetic depression in which I grieve for my sister. I harbour an impotent fury against my brother. At the same time I fear for him. That Bella sticks by me through it is remarkable, but then she would understand it better than most.

I have acquired a new habit of waking before daybreak. Still troubled by dreams of Africa, I lie in the darkness next to Bella, disoriented, frightened, waiting for Australia's bird-calls to disperse my fears. Waiting for birds to bring me home.